TSIL CAFÉ

INGREDIENTS OF THE

NEW WORLD COOKED

NEW MEXICO STYLE

THE *TSIL* KACHINA IS THE ONE
WHO STUFFS RED PEPPER IN
THE MOUTHS OF RUNNERS
OVERTAKEN IN A RACE.

THE CREED OF THE COOK
AND RESTAURANT OWNER

I believe people should learn their foodstuffs—preparation and cooking—and that they should learn to please themselves by becoming cooks. I dislike the pretentious word *chef* and all its connotations. I am an experienced cook of the foods I choose to work with. I please myself, and hope to please you, but I welcome you to eat elsewhere: Many of you are cooks, too, and if you can do better than I have, stay home. That said, there are also many good reasons to eat at a restaurant, and that is why I opened the Tsil Café.

First, some ingredients are exotic or rare or difficult to work with: You need a cook of experience to truly bring out the potential in buffalo tongue, or nopal tamal, for example.

Next, there are recipes too time-consuming to prepare as often as you might want to eat them. I make my living with food, to satisfy that desire for the difficult or time-consuming. Try the Sage-Smoked Chile-Infused Turkey, or any of the dishes made with my specialty honeys or vinegars.

Next, a cook of experience should push you to your limits of taste, spice, or boldness in eating. Try the Sweet Habanero Salsa, or Shrimp in Pepper Marinade.

Finally, the cook of experience sets a standard for how a food should taste, if brought to its potential. Good cooks like to eat away from their kitchens to test their own sense of possibility, taste, and choice against other cooks. I serve only choice buffalo meat, the finest New World grains, and the most savory sage and allspice found in the world.

I hope I can combine rare ingredients, experience, painstaking care, and high standards to prepare for you an enjoyable meal, an experience of fine dining at the Tsil Café.

—*Robert Hingler*

A GUIDE TO HEAT

☙ contains chiles, but mostly as an aftertaste

☙☙ chiles compete with other ingredients for dominant flavor

☙☙☙ chiles dominate flavor, but are mild to hot chiles

☙☙☙☙ hot chiles dominate; mouth is hot; stomach is hot

☙☙☙☙☙ be prepared to weep, and beg for salvation

APPETIZERS

☙ **BLACK BEAN AND GOOSEBERRY ENCHILADAS**
A mild enchilada with a sweetly spicy filling and a hearty sauce.

☙ **ANCHOVY PALTA CON TORTILLAS FRITAS**
Take the salty anchovy sea and add it to the earthy avocado in this lightly spicy dip for the Tsil's homemade corn tortilla chips.

☙☙☙☙ **SHRIMP DE INFIERNO**
Six shrimp flown in from the Gulf are "cooked" by marinading in peppers so hot you'd swear they were cooked over flame and all we served was the flame.

☙☙ **NOPAL TAMAL**
A small tamal filled with strips of prickly pear cactus cooked with tomato, corn, and a touch of smoky chipotle pepper. Served with your choice of salsas.

☙☙☙☙☙ **TORTILLAS FRITAS WITH SWEET HABANERO SALSA**
Only for those who truly like it hot! Our homemade corn tortilla chips are the vessel for as much or as little of the hottest sauce you'll ever taste: Look for roasted pumpkin and pumpkin seed, tomato, and the thin orange strips of the world's hottest little pepper.

SOUPS

BLACK BEAN
A thick and hearty version of this traditional soup, drizzled with a tomatillo and green chile salsa.

TURKEY AND POSOLE
A satisfying stew full of nuts, beans, chiles, and meat.

POTATO AND GREEN CHILE
A soup for lovers. Turkey broth is the base for *sopa* of thinly sliced turkey liver, New Mexico green chile, and finely grated golden potato.

PLEASE NOTE: Any appetizer can be turned into a main dish—ask for quantity and appropriate side dishes.

SIDES AND VEGETABLES

WATERCRESS SALAD WITH ROASTED SUNFLOWER DRESSING
Crunchy watercress harvested from mountain streams is enhanced by a dressing of mild New Mexico chile powder, roasted tomatoes, and lightly browned sunflower seeds.

SMOKY POLENTA
Don't ever call it cornmeal mush. Our polenta is cooked with sunflower meal, chile-dried tomatoes, and chipotle peppers and served in thin strips.

PAPAS, PAPAS, Y MÁS PAPAS
From more than two hundred kinds of potatoes, we select the best red, white, blue, yellow, and black, and serve them with

your choice of salsas: habanero, chipotle barbecue, or roasted
sunflower. Specify fried, boiled, mashed, or steamed.

RICE OF THE AMERICAS
A Minnesota grass yields "wild" rice, not a true rice, but
crunchier, with a strong flavor of tea. Ours is cooked with
ancho peppers and an assortment of seeds and nuts.

QUINOA
This fine, complete grain has a vegetable taste, a texture
like rice, and a burst of energy that tells you it surpasses
all others in protein and mineral content. We combine it
with a touch of jalepeño, pecans, and corn for maximum
flavor.

TORTILLAS DE MAÍZ
We mill corn into fine meal to make the thinnest, tastiest
tortillas in Kansas City. For chips, we cut them into strips
and deep-fry them in sunflower oil. Ask for them warm or
fried.

GREEN BEANS IN SWEET JALEPEÑO SAUCE
The ordinary green bean, a little sweeter, with a tang.

PUMPKIN FRITTERS
Roasted pumpkin, puréed, then breaded and fried.

CHILE SUN-DRIED TOMATOES
Tomatoes, with their flavor distilled, served juicy with a
mild dusting of allspice and mild New Mexico chile powder.

SQUASH
Winter squashes, baked, then rebaked with maple syrup,
ancho chiles, vanilla, and pecans.

SWEET POTATOES IN CASHEW-PINEAPPLE SAUCE

Your choice of steamed, baked in the skin, or fried, with a hearty sauce of pineapple, jalapeño, and roasted cashews.

NOTE: Sides and vegetables can be served separately or with main dishes.

MAIN DISHES

TO SAGE-SMOKED TURKEY INFUSED WITH CHILES

Turkey infused with your choice of chile: ancho, New Mexico green or red, jalapeño, chipotle, or habanero.

VANILLA BUFFALO WITH CRANBERRY-CHILE PESTO

Prime bison steaks in a vanilla-sage marinade, grilled and served with a pesto of tomato, ancho chile, pine nuts, and cranberries.

BLACKENED TURKEY BREAST

Turkey breast dusted with three chile powders and broiled.

SHRIMP WITH NUTS

A savory stir-fry with shrimp, mild and hot peppers, zucchini, and an assortment of New World nuts, from hickory to peanut.

TAMALES: SHRIMP, BUFFALO, TURKEY, OR DOG (WHEN AVAILABLE)

Corn husk–wrapped masa filled with the spicy meat of your choice. A traditional item, but guaranteed moist, light, and savory.

BUFFALO TONGUE WITH CHIPOTLE BAR-BECUE SAUCE

Native Americans, trappers, and European explorers all considered bison tongue a rare treat. Ours is boiled, then roasted, and served with a smoky, sweet tomato sauce hotter and finer than any in Kansas City.

DESSERTS

PALTA PUDDING WITH RASPBERRY COCOA SAUCE

Avocado and gooseberry blended with vanilla and honey, then topped with chocolate and raspberries.

PINEAPPLE TAMAL

A small, delicately sweet tamal filled with pineapple and smothered in marigold honey.

PASTALES

A traditional dessert from Mexico—light and refreshing.

ICES

Take any of the New World fruits, from cranberry to strawberry, and we have our sorbet. Ask your waiter for availability.

BEVERAGES

HOT CHOCOLATE

No milk, just chocolate, the way it was first drunk and first brought to Europe. Flavored with allspice, vanilla, and even chiles, upon request.

FRUIT JUICES

Your choice of juice from any of the New World berries or fruits: cranberry, mango, strawberry, guava, blackberry, papaya, blueberry, pineapple, chokecherry, juneberry, or dewberry, or any combination. Subject to seasonal limitations.

ALCOHOL

Although those in the New World did not make an art and science of brewing, fermenting, and distilling, certain alcoholic drinks were invented here. We serve one of those, *Pulque* (a wine punch made from the agave), when available. We also have a range of wines and distilled drinks whose primary ingredients are foodstuffs of the New World—everything from Pineapple Liqueur to Mescal (also from the agave cactus) to Tequila. Visit our bar or ask your server.

SECRETS
OF THE
TSIL CAFÉ

THOMAS
FOX
AVERILL

BLUEHEN BOOKS

A MEMBER OF PENGUIN PUTNAM INC.

NEW YORK

2001

SECRETS
OF THE
TSIL CAFÉ

A NOVEL WITH RECIPES

F I C

This is a work of fiction. Names, characters, places, and incidents either are the product of the author's imagination or are used fictitiously, and any resemblance to actual persons, living or dead, business establishments, events, or locales is entirely coincidental.

The recipes in this book are to be followed exactly as written. Neither the publisher nor the author is responsible for your specific health or allergy needs that may require medical supervision, or for any adverse reactions to the recipes in this book.

BlueHen Books
a member of
Penguin Putnam Inc.
375 Hudson Street
New York, NY 10014

Library of Congress Cataloging-in-Publication Data

Averill, Thomas Fox, date.
Secrets of the Tsil Café : a novel with recipes /
Thomas Fox Averill.
p.   cm.
ISBN 0-399-14755-1
I. Kansas City (Mo.)—Fiction.   2. Caterers and catering—
Fiction.   3. Restaurants—Fiction.   4. Cookery—
Fiction.   5. Boys—Fiction.   6. Cookery, American—
New Mexico.   7. Cookery, Italian.

PS3551.V375 S43   2001   00-066710
              813'.54—dc21

Printed in the United States of America

1   3   5   7   9   10   8   6   4   2

This book is printed on acid-free paper. ∞

Book design by Marysarah Quinn

FOR
JEFFREY ANN GOUDIE
AS ALWAYS

I.

AT THE TABLE, IN THE KITCHEN

Achiote (seed of the tropical American annatto tree): *This tiny seed is used mostly for its deep yellow and orange coloring, enhancing sauces and enriching flavor.*

My father, Robert Hingler, ground the small seeds and heated them in corn oil, until their pungency and color burst, and the pan turned yellow, then orange. The hearty smell of achiote, sharp, crisp, filled his kitchen. It was a sunrise, a sunset. The world, always turning, is a seed; its many colors light our days. I, Weston Tito Hingler, started the world as a seed, too, in the kitchens of my parents.

My mother, Maria Tito Hingler, made her kitchen both the family kitchen and the center of Buen AppeTito, her catering business. She had few recipes. When she took a job, she sat down with whoever hired her. "After twenty minutes," she always said, "I know exactly what will please some-one. I adapt my cooking to them—spicy, bland, exotic, ordinary, sweet, salty. It's their party."

Though she began her catering with the Italian food of her girlhood, she could cook anything: from a huge, cheesy lasagna to caviar-stuffed ravioli; from spaghetti and meatballs to shrimp-paste pasta with capered cream sauce; from chocolate cake to her famous torte-tart, a pastry with the lightest filling imaginable. She didn't care which she made: She pleased her customers, not herself; their pleasure was hers.

My father? He had his recipes, and he stuck to them, and the customer was expected to adapt to his ingredients, to his cooking style, to his menu. The same with me. He made me into a son of the Tsil Café: Ingredients of the New World Cooked New Mexico Style.

And what is *tsil*? In their rituals, the Hopi Indians of the Southwest dress as their mythical ancestors. With the proper headdress, mask, and body paint, they become the elements, or sacred foods, or animals, or another gift from their gods. In some rituals they dance, in others they run. The *tsil* is their name for that sacred food, the chile pepper, come to life with a red pepper headdress and a cylindrical mask the color of corn. My father always pronounced it like the first syllable of chile, but with a hissing *t* at the beginning. When a Hopi represents the *tsil*, he carries a yucca stick in one hand, red chiles in the other, and challenges all to a foot race. Any runner the *tsil* overtakes in a race has his mouth quickly stuffed with hot peppers. Besides costuming for ritual, the Hopi also represent their ancestors and their gods' gifts through the carving of dolls, called kachinas. A *tsil* kachina—complete with headdress and chile pepper in hand—stood guard over my father's kitchen: the perfect totem for my father, who loved spice and heat, and gladly stuffed peppers into the mouths of son, wife, family, and customer.

So, I grew up with the Old World foods of my mother, the New World foods of my father. I was fed by one parent, stuffed by another. I was marked by both, nurtured by both.

BLACK AND BLUE:
THE DIFFERENT CHILD

*M*y crib, and then my bed, were in my mother's kitchen, where she spent most of her time. Sunshine streamed into her southern windows and onto her plants, pots, pans, bottles, and jars. And on her cookbooks, shelves of them. The bottom shelf, though, was mine. By the time I was three, I had learned that my mother would stop almost anything if I asked her to read me a book. I would run to that bottom shelf and pull out *Winnie-the-Pooh,* and we would read the adventures of Christopher Robin, Pooh, Piglet, and the rest. My mother was a tall woman and I loved jumping into her lap, being engulfed by her arms, looking at the pictures, and the words. Her long braid was often curled around her shoulder, and I sometimes held it, pretending it was Eeyore's tail.

One day, when we were reading *Pooh,* my mother pointed to the word *honey.* "This is a word, Wes," she said. "It says *honey.*" She stood up, leaving me to sit on the kitchen chair. "But it isn't honey. It's only a word. You know what honey really is, don't you?" She took down her honey jar and brought two spoons. "Let's taste this word," she said. She dipped a spoon in the honey and brought it out, twirling it in the sunlight. The honey glowed. She put it in my mouth, where it was warm and golden and sweet, where it coated my tongue and melted into my throat.

"Mothers make milk for their babies," said my mother. "I made milk for you." She twirled another spoonful of honey in the air and put it in her mouth. "And bees make honey for their babies, Wes. Those are the only two natural foods, made only to be eaten. They're not anything else—not seeds, not flowers, not fruits, not leaves, not roots. They're food, and food alone."

"I want some milk," I said. And we drank.

"Milk and honey," she said. "When you're a baby, you live in the land of milk and honey."

"Can we taste other words?" I asked.

From then on, when we read, we tasted words. With *Mother Goose* we had a "little nutmeg" and a "golden pear." We ate Peter Piper's "pickled peppers" from my mother's jars of pepperoncinis and cherry peppers. Once, we were "pumpkin eaters" like Peter, Peter. Like Jack Horner, we put "plums on our thumbs" and said I was a "good boy." We even ate lamb, though my mother insisted it was not Mary's "little lamb." We stopped short of "four and twenty blackbirds."

In my mother's and then my father's kitchen, I learned my letters. My blocks were brightly painted with the letters of the alphabet. Next to *C* my father placed a cayenne. The *Y* was not for yellow, but for yucca cactus. I learned my colors from the orange of pumpkins, the blue of native corn. And my shapes? Tortillas were round, raviolis square, cob corn cylindrical. In my kitchen primer, I learned a catechism from Anchovy to Zucchini, tasting all the way through.

My parents' stories were about food. When I was five, in my afternoon bath—that's when my parents could supervise me before they busied themselves in their kitchens—my father showed me how Kansas City water drains in a counter-clockwise funnel. He described living on a Navy cruiser, not hard to imagine because he was fond of khaki pants and T-shirts, his kitchen uniform. His thick hair was still cut in a military crew. His arms were long and lean, but muscled, as though he did push-ups as part of his training.

"*Below* the equator, water drains clockwise." Once, he told me, cooking for the ship, he pulled the plug of a sink. The water whirled counterclockwise. Suddenly, the funnel slowed, then stopped. When the water drained again, it slowly twirled clockwise. "Imagine your bathwater doing that right now," he said. "You're cooking, and you're crossing the equa-tor." After my bath, my father dried me, dressed me, and took me to his kitchen.

I watched him make tamales. The masa dough had been resting in the refrigerator, and he brought it to the counter where he'd sat me down. Corn husks soaked in a huge pot. The filling—cactus strips and kernels of corn in a chile-tomato sauce—had been ready since morning. He took a husk from the water, threw a small ball of dough onto it, pressed it down with another husk until it made a thin square, spooned on some filling, rolled the husk so the dough enclosed the filling, and wrapped until the whole thing was a thin tube. Last, he folded down the top of the husk to seal the tamal.

While he worked, he talked. About the time he'd bought

an old car and traveled the back roads, looking for the unusual: the *taqueria* with beef tongue tacos, the honey-piñon candies, the Indian reservations where they still ate dogs. "The mouth can talk," he said, "but tasting is first. Talk is just the translation." He put some cactus filling in my mouth.

"It's spicy," I said.

"Don't talk, taste," he said.

I let the chile heat subside, and tasted the other flavors and textures, the hearty tomato, the sweet corn, the crunch of prickly pear cactus. "It's *not* spicy," I said.

"That's my boy," he said. "When you taste, things just are what they are."

"What's the name of the hot?" I asked.

"Chipotle," he said. He went to a jar in his kitchen and brought me a dark, shriveled pepper the size of my little finger. "Smell it," he said.

"Smoke," I said.

"That's right. It's a smoked, dried, red jalapeño. Chipotle."

"Chipotle," I said. "It tastes good."

By the time I went to school, I was my parents' child in my food tastes. The first year of grade school, they brought me home for lunch. By second grade, I wanted to stay at school. Other kids ate in the lunchroom, food they'd brought from home, and then they had more time to swing and slide and play four-square and tetherball.

My father sent me with two cactus tamales for lunch, and some black and blue berries with chocolate sauce in a little cup with a lid. I sat in the lunchroom, unwrapping corn husks to the stares of my classmates. Everyone around me had unwrapped white bread with peanut butter and jelly or bologna inside. They had carrots, or apple slices. I picked some masa dough off one of the corn husks.

"What is that?" a kid asked me.

"A tamal," I said.

"You don't eat that paper stuff?" he asked.

"It's a corn husk," I said. "Like what covers corn on the cob."

"I like corn on the cob," the boy said.

"Me, too," I said.

"But I don't like *that*," he said. "I hate that." He held his nose in horror.

On the playground, after lunch, a group of older boys surrounded me. "Hot tamale, hot tamale," they chanted. "Mexican Wes, Mexican Wes."

"Tamales are good," I said. I hadn't spent enough time with other children to fear a group of them.

"They're made with dog food," said a boy.

"Dog food, dog food," the boys chanted. One of them poked me in the chest, and down I went.

I managed to stand up. "It's not dog food," I yelled. "It's dog."

The boys began to close in.

"My dad makes tamales out of dogs," I yelled. "He'll catch yours someday, and I'll eat it."

The boys punched, kicked, and scratched until I curled into a lifeless ball. When a teacher blew her whistle, the boys scattered. I slowly uncurled and stood up. Bits of gravel stuck to my knees.

The school nurse was Miss McGwinn. Her office smelled of bleach. The kids joked that the smell was embalming fluid, and once you went in, you never came out. Miss McGwinn had a pug nose, and the boys all called her Miss McGwinnie Pig. I showed her my scraped knees, the small cuts on my lip and above my eye.

"Let's wash you up," she said. Miss McGwinn stuck my head into a plugged sink and turned on frigid water. The cold, she said, would help stop the bleeding. My blood dripped and dispersed, a little cloud, like when a drop of buffalo blood hit water in the kitchen sink of my father's Tsil Café.

"They're mean old bullies," I said as Miss McGwinn put a towel to my head.

"What did they do?"

"They called my tamal dog food," I said.

"And you?"

"I told them it was made from dog. My father ate a dog tamal once."

"You must mean tamale," said Miss McGwinn. "It's called a tamale."

"It's a tamal," I said, though suddenly I wasn't certain.

"Tamale," said Miss McGwinn. She pulled the plug of the sink.

I watched the water form its little funnel. "My father says water drains the opposite way on the other side of the equator. He saw it," I said, "when he was cooking in the Navy. The funnel goes like this." I spun my finger clockwise.

Miss McGwinn snuffed, then sighed. She went to the cabinet for a bandage. "I don't care what your father eats," she said, "or what he tells you about water. You should just get along. You don't need to make up stories about your food. You don't need to impress anyone. That's the quick way to trouble."

"I'm not making up stories," I said.

"Fine," said Miss McGwinn. "I'll call your parents. Do you want to talk to the principal, and report the boys who hit you?"

"No." I was that smart, at least.

"You're not much hurt anyway," said Miss McGwinn.

When I returned home, my parents rushed to examine my face and knees. "The nurse called," said my mother.

"They really let you have it, didn't they?" asked my father.

I began to cry.

"What is it?" asked my mother.

"Miss McGwinn said it was tamale, not tamal," I sputtered between sobs. "We call her McGwinnie Pig." I laughed, even though I'd never called her that.

"Don't use names," said my father.

"The boys called me names," I said. "Mexican Wes."

"They're stupid," he said.

"Let's not call names." My mother held me and I began to cry all over again.

That night, after dinner in my mother's kitchen, I went to the kitchen of the Tsil Café to say good night to my father. "I'm sorry you had a tough day," he said. "Tomorrow will be better."

Pablito, my father's greeter and bartender, admired my battle wounds. He took my fingers in his hands and traced three small ridges in his light brown skin, two along his eyebrows and one above his lip. *"Mis heridas,"* he said. "They used to hit, and hit, and hit me."

Our waitress, Cocoa, came over to touch my bandages. "My little man," she said.

When I went to bed, I didn't feel brave. I felt tired, and sore, and lonely. I knew the other kids hated me because I was different. And the reason I was different? My parents, of course.

The next day, my father handed me a sack lunch. Inside was a turkey steak, some leftover quinoa, pineapple slices baked the night before in a cashew coating, and more black and blue berries.* I burst some of the berries against my face, rubbing them into my sores to make what looked like impressive bruises. I dumped the lunch into the alley Dumpster. Being hungry would be better than being teased.

Miss McGwinn was the proctor in the lunchroom that day. She asked why I wasn't eating. "We ran out of dog," I told her.

She bent down to examine my sore spots. She touched my bruises. I didn't wince soon enough. "What's this stain?" she asked. When I told her, she vowed to call my parents again.

The next day, my mother gave me a peanut butter and

---

*Black and Blue Berry** (New World, North American fruit): *A New Jersey botanist, Frederick Covine, developed a fat, nearly seedless blueberry in 1910. Before that, blueberries were about as popular as chokecherries and other native berries—more coveted by birds than humans. Blackberries, on brambly bushes, have been actively cultivated from the early 1800s and are used most often in pies, puddings, jellies, syrups, and brandy. Both mix well with other New World flavors—vanilla, chocolate, mild chiles, and other berries. The two are those rare colors for foods: deep black and true blue.*

jelly sandwich, a small bag of potato chips, and two Twinkies. I sat in the lunchroom and tried to eat the unfamiliar food. The sandwich tasted like a sweet sponge, the potato chips like salt, the Twinkies like sugar. Everything had the same texture: no texture at all. Nothing was rich, complicated. But nobody teased me on the playground.

When I came home, I asked my father for a cactus tamal. "When I was a boy, all the *gringos* loved tamales," he said. "But they thought when you ate just one it would be a tamale. They didn't know that Spanish makes a plural with -*es*. So it's tamal."

"Just like I said?" I asked. I picked at the masa stuck to the corn husk.

"I didn't know that when I was your age," he said.

I wolfed down the tamal, hungry even for what had brought me ridicule. The cactus strips, spiced with chipotle, brought the warm, smoky heat into my mouth and nostrils.

NOPAL TAMAL

TAMALES

Corn husks

1 teaspoon baking powder

½ teaspoon salt

1 teaspoon Chimayo chile powder

2 cups masa

Just under 2 cups warm water (or turkey broth)

⅓, or less, cup corn oil

Bring corn husks to boil in large pan, then put in refrigerator to soak for two hours.

Put baking powder, salt, and chile powder in masa and mix. Add lukewarm water (or turkey broth) and work with hands into a paste. Slowly add oil and work with fingers or a mixer until dough is spongy. Chill for at least an hour. Make a square of dough, about four inches, on a corn husk (sometimes two), fill with cactus, and roll tightly.

Steam tamales for 2 to 2½ hours—until dough separates easily from corn husk. Serve with salsa, or with leftover filling.

FILLING

6 prickly pear* pads, needles removed, cut into strips
3 ears corn, kernels cut off cob
1 can tomato paste
2 chipotle, cut into bits
2 capfuls mescal
Water for consistency

Boil cactus strips until they lose some of their viscosity and shrivel slightly. Drain, add other ingredients, and cook down to a paste.

*Napoles (prickly pear pad, also called beavertail): *Prickly pear cactus, native to the western deserts of America and Mexico, grows clumpy pads, one sprouting from another. The pads produce waxy flowers (two or more) from their tops, and red, edible fruits. The young pads,* *three inches or so in diameter, are often harvested, the thin thorns scraped off and then boiled. The pads have a very thick, mucilaginous juice (like okra) because the plant thickens its water intake against periods of drought.*

From my playground beating on, I either went home for lunch or disguised my Tsil or Buen AppeTito food. Wonder bread could cover a piece of buffalo meat marinated in vanilla and sage. My mother could stuff caramelized onions into a hard roll, and nobody would be the wiser. She gave me mints for garlic on my breath, and my father sometimes blended tamales so they looked like pudding. I lived a double life: Midwestern boy by day; by night the son of my father's eccentric Tsil Café and my mother's exotic Buen AppeTito.

Bill was my first childhood friend. I kept him away from the Tsil Café until we were both ten. Finally, I took him into the kitchen of the restaurant to meet my father, who liked to have people watch him cook. My father shook Bill's hand and made the joke he always made with Bills. "I suppose you want to be paid." He handed each of us a menu. "Choose anything you want. I'll have Cocoa bring it out."

We sat in a booth. Bill studied the menu I knew by heart, smell, taste, touch. "*Palta?*" he asked. "*Chipotle? Nopal? Habanero? Posole? Tomatillo?*"

When I interpreted, he'd say, "Do I want that?"

I couldn't tell him what he'd like. Even in the semidarkness of the Tsil dining room, Bill looked pale.

"What do you usually eat?"

"Hot dogs," he said. "Onion rings. Macaroni."

"Let's go upstairs," I said. I waved Cocoa away.

Bill followed me through our private door up into my mother's kitchen. She had a catering job, a late-night reception at one of the country clubs. "What're you making?" I asked.

"Stuffed mushrooms."

"What else?"

"Pâté, my curried eggplant, olive salad, roasted garlic."

"What's that?" I pointed to what looked safest, little pillows of pasta, ready to boil.

"Gingered duck ravioli." My mother smiled. "You guys hungry? There's always eggs. Or there's leftover pasta in the fridge. You could do a quick *puttanesca*."

"What's that?" asked Bill.

"Make some, Wes," said my mother.

I grabbed onion, tomatoes, garlic, a few capers and olives. I put a pan on the stove and poured in olive oil. When my mother left the room, I whispered to Bill, "This is what the whores in Italy eat."

"What's a whore?" he asked.

"Women who stay up late. To do things they're not supposed to do." I smiled at Bill. He didn't seem to understand. "With men," I added.

Bill looked blank as a napkin.

"Anyway, they throw together food for a midnight snack. Whatever's close by, they cook it up and mix it with leftover pasta." I went to the refrigerator for the penne pasta and some mozzarella.

"That's not spaghetti," said Bill.

I said nothing, my tongue eager for the browning onion, the acid salt of a caper, the musky clove of garlic. I finished cooking and ate eagerly. Bill got some down once we smothered it with catsup.

MARIA TITO'S PASTA
PUTTANESCA

Tomato, fresh or sun-dried
Garlic, the more the better
Olive oil
"The rest," as my mother always said, "is up to you." This might
    include anchovies,* black or green olives, capers, red or
    white or pencil onions, sausage, artichoke hearts, etc.
Any leftover pasta
Mozzarella, grated

Sauté anything that needs it in the olive oil, add "the rest" of your chosen ingredients, then mix in the pasta. Put grated mozzarella on top and broil until cheese is slightly brown and bubbled.

***Anchovy** (Engradulidae—small, herringlike marine fish): *American anchovies, around four inches long, live in warm seas and are mostly used as fishmeal for animal feed. Mediterranean anchovies, often used as pizza topping, are cured by fermentation and salt. After being introduced to the latter, Thomas Jefferson, having returned from Paris, wrote back to the continent for Parmesan cheese, mustard, Vinaigre d'Estragon, and anchovies.*

"I'm glad I'm not one of those whores," Bill said after we'd eaten. He left the next morning before breakfast.

"I'm not normal," I told my parents at the breakfast table.

Neither had much sympathy. My father dumped more green chile sauce on his eggs. "Normal is for wimps," he said.

"When you're an adult, the world will catch up to you," said my mother. She offered me another of her gingered duck raviolis, left over from the night before. I ate it eagerly, but not without sadness. No one else my age in Kansas City is eating this for breakfast, I thought.

By the time I was fourteen, I tried to replace sadness with adventure. Surely someone could admire my exotic tastes. Someone like Marci Harding. She was eager to find out about my family. Hers, she said, was exhaustingly normal. They went to church on Wednesday nights and Sunday mornings. They ate the same menu every week. "MASTIC-eight," she called it, her acronym for Macaroni and Cheese on Monday, American (hamburgers and french fries) on Tuesday, Steak on Wednesday, TV dinners on Thursday, Italian (spaghetti or pizza) on Friday, Chicken on Saturday, and out to eat at eight o'clock every Sunday.

Marci's family went to the movies every Friday. They lived in a house with a front porch, a dog, and a cat named Tabby. Their furniture was covered with sheets and their carpet with plastic, so nothing would stain or wear out. "I'm the one who is worn out," Marci told me on our first date.

Soon, I took a risk and invited Marci to visit our building on 39th Street, the home of the Tsil Café and Buen AppeTito. She loved it: the chaos, the mess, the darkness, the spills, the permanent stains, the food everywhere, the raised voices belting out orders and demands, the people coming and going, the odd smells. After we'd hung out there a couple of afternoons, after I'd taken her to a couple of movies, after we'd taken walks that ended in long sessions of "making out," I invited her to dinner at the Tsil.

"You order," she said.

I relied on Pablito's knack for divining people's tastes. "Order an appetizer," I said. "Just anything that looks good."

"Everything *looks* good," said Marci. "Even *you* look good."

Her boldness shocked me. Nobody but Cocoa had ever flirted with me, and that was only in fun. "Just choose," I said. "Everything here tastes really good."

Marci raised her eyebrows, two lines, plucked thin. Her coy smile made me wish we were alone, upstairs, cooking some Pasta *Puttanesca* and "borrowing" some red wine from my mother's closet.

She chose the Black Bean and Gooseberry Enchiladas.

Pablito took it from there. "I'll have what she's having," I told him.

"But you're ordering for me," Marci said.

"Pablito knows what you want. I want it, too."

"You two must be careful," said Pablito. "All this wanting."

Marci laughed. She maintained her good humor through the appetizer. My father cooked black beans with ancho peppers, and they were sweet and rich, like an Oriental bean paste. Gooseberries gave them the citrus bite people like in their Mexican food. By the time the bean mixture was wrapped in a blue corn tortilla and covered with a tangy red sauce, my father had a light, rich appetizer—two thin ones to a plate—that left any diner with room for more. "That was interesting," Marci said.

My father always hated that word, especially when used to describe his food.

"Your next course," said Pablito, "will be the soup for the lovers."

"Lovers? What's in it?" asked Marci.

Pablito quickly left the table. Not everyone, he knew, liked liver. Especially people my age. So I answered for him. "Turkey and potato, mostly. Don't worry, I've been eating it since I was in kindergarten."

"Were you a lover back then?" Marci asked.

"I loved my mother," I said. "And liver. I was a liver lover back then."

"Wes," said Marci, "you're not only different, you're sickening."

The soup came. Marci's first spoon held mostly turkey broth and golden potato. Then she spooned some thinly sliced turkey liver. Her throat constricted. Pablito hovered nearby, where Marci couldn't see him. He hurried over. "Wrong soup," he said. "I told the cook to leave out the liver."

My father never left out any of his ingredients, no matter what a customer demanded. But Pablito returned with a fresh bowl, one with only a small amount of potato and green chile swimming in clear broth. Pablito had strained the soup himself. Marci tried a couple more spoonfuls. "I can still taste that liver." She swallowed dramatically.

Through the rest of dinner, she tried to be brave. We talked less and less, like people who are tired and still have to finish a climb up a mountain path. She liked the watercress salad, but not the dressing for it. She ate her sweet potatoes, but not the cashew sauce. She didn't touch her meat— Pablito had made her a sampler of Vanilla Buffalo, Smoked Chile-Stuffed Turkey, and Buffalo Tongue. Her response: "I do *not* want to know what it's like to be French-kissed by a woolly old buffalo."

She ate the pineapple filling from her dessert tamal, along with some strawberry ice. Finally, Cocoa cleared our plates. "I'm sorry you didn't like it better," I said.

"I liked it fine," she said. "It's better than what I get at home."

"You want to go out somewhere? For a walk?"

We walked a long ways. She told me about her family. Her normal dad, who worked in a bank. Her normal mom, who stayed home, who volunteered at church, who brought cookies to school for birthdays. My mom brought butter croissants stuffed with honey and black walnuts. "Sometimes," I told Marci, "I wish I had your normal family, with its normal food—the same thing every day, every week."

"No, you don't," she said.

We ended our long walk in Loose Park, where we sat under the rose arbor, kissing. Then we meandered to Marci's house. She was hungry, she said, and her mother ushered us into an avocado kitchen—the color, not the plants, as in my mother's kitchen. "There's always peanut butter," Marci's mother said cheerfully.

Marci spread huge dollops of crunchy peanut butter onto Wonder bread, poured sugar over it, put margarine and strawberry jelly on another piece of bread and brought them together.

"Aren't you hungry?" asked Marci.

"I ate a lot at the Café."

She hadn't. "There's something about a plain old peanut butter and jelly sandwich." Marci stuffed half the sandwich into her mouth.

The mouth I'd just kissed. I looked around the kitchen, all spic-and-span, the blender and toaster and mixer all covered with laminated, daisy-print cloth, everything gleaming and matching, all the food hidden in cupboards and bread boxes and canisters.

Marci wolfed down the rest of the sandwich. "I better get going," I said. We walked past her parents, who sat stiff as robots on the couch watching television. Marci saw me out the door.

My mother had the nerve to ask about my date. I told her it was fine until we got back to Marci's house. "Then," I said, "she ate this huge peanut butter sandwich. She hated our food."

"Your father's food," said my mother.

My father clomped up the last stair, into my mother's kitchen. "I heard that," he said.

"Nobody's ever going to like me," I said. "Not once they see what we eat."

"The right ones will like you," said my father.

"There's worse things than being betrayed by a peanut butter sandwich, Wes," said my mother.

By then, of course, I knew that. Why else would I long to be normal?

ANCHOVY: KITCHENS

*T*hey say the nose has the longest memory of any of the senses. To this day I cannot cut garlic and onion, or smell the sudden sharpness of melting cheese, without remembering my mother's kitchen.

My mother remodeled her kitchen in the upstairs living quarters above the Tsil Café. Buen AppeTito—named for her Italian roots and her name—was very successful. Her kitchen was as big as my father's. "I told your father I must have space, and windows. Light," she said, "is the key to good cooking." Doing most of the work herself, she tore out a wall and took the space I later learned might have been my bedroom. She knocked out bricks on the exterior wall and fashioned a long bank of south-facing windows. For money, she used her savings so she could dictate what her kitchen might look like, and what it might have in it: every pan, bowl, dish, skewer, grater, and utensil imaginable, every appliance available, as soon as it was available.

She hung her kitchen in plants: hanging baskets that sprouted parsley, oregano, basil, fennel, dill, sage, mints, chives, each with its own distinctive shape shining in sunlight, or, on a moonlit night, shadowed against the windows as though memory knew only silhouette and smell. Against one wall a constant series of avocado seeds were always splitting, thrusting up tendrils my mother hoped to grow into trunks. A bay tree grew in the corner.

I slept in that kitchen the first three years of my life. I watched my mother from my crib as she blended pesto in a food processor the size of a small barrel. She seemed giant. "When I made this kitchen," she told me later, "a short man came to install my countertop. *I'm not a standard woman*, I told him. Still, he had to go to his truck for extra shims."

I imagine her building that kitchen, my first room: She pounded in Sheetrock; did the mud work herself ("As simple as frosting a cake"); painted the walls; laid squares of black-and-white linoleum; hammered in the baseboard (which she'd already varnished); and installed a ceiling fan to keep us cool through long summers of her cooking.

As I grew, I would wake in the middle of a moonlit night and watch shapes take form. I was in a forest, among the dappled shadows of plants. Or in a factory, with all the hulking machinery of production surrounding me. Or in a shop, everything neatly placed to attract the eye of a customer.

When I was almost three years old, I spent hours playing in my mother's cabinets, pulling out pots and pans, banging on them, stacking them around me like some children build forts or sand castles. At the back of one cabinet, in the upper corner, I found a little handle on a chain. When I pulled it, the back board gave way to darkness, and I crawled into the space I'd found. The kitchen gave me just enough light to see that I was in a closet-sized room, with a chair and a small table and a pole lamp. On the table, like in my *Goodnight Moon* book, was "a comb and a brush." Also a package of cigarettes and an ashtray.

I sat on the floor, enjoying the secret place, the semidarkness. Until I heard my mother. "Wes?" she called into the empty kitchen. "Wes?" and she clattered pots from in front of the cabinet. And then a shout. "Wes!" She crawled in to pull me out. "You are never to be in there. Never!" She swatted my bottom.

The next day, when she left the kitchen, I ran to the cabinet door and reached for the little handle that would pop out the thin back board so I could crawl into the secret place. The handle was gone. The back of the cabinet had no give when I pounded it. The secret place had disappeared, was, seemingly, nothing but a figment of my imagination. When my mother came back into the kitchen and saw the pots and pans from that cabinet littering the floor, she said, simply, "It went bye-bye." Soon after the confusing discovery and disappearance of the secret place, my mother and father decided I should no longer sleep in a crib. They bought me what they called a "big boy bed," and I reached my "big boy" growth in it, first in a narrow room that had been half-storeroom, half-closet ("It's only for sleeping, Wes," they said), and then in the basement of the Tsil Café. By then I knew my father's kitchen, too.

I had to earn that right. My father was a small-batch cook who spent hours tasting, correcting, perfecting his recipes. He did not want me in the Tsil kitchen until I understood his intensity about food, until I would respect any command he gave me, until I had proven myself.

At about the same time I lost the memory of the taste of my mother's milk, I remember the sharp taste of the anchovy paste my father squeezed onto his finger and stuck into my mouth. When I spat it out, he shook his head. "He's not ready," my father said, and retreated between the double doors of his kitchen. He repeated the ritual several times.

By the time I was nearly four, I pestered my mother. "What is it on Daddy's finger?"

"Anchovy. A salted fish."

"Why does it taste so bad?"

"To your father, and to me, it tastes like the sea."

"What sea?"

"For me, the Mediterranean. For your father, the Gulf of Mexico. At least that's what he pretends."

"Pretends?"

"He cooks only with foods from the New World."

"The New World?"

"The Americas, North and South."

"Americas?"

Such was my catechism, repeated, with variation, according to whatever food my parents spoke of. Or tempered by the challenge of what I might eat next: my mother's fingers smeared with avocado; the artichoke petals she dipped in garlic and olive oil and put in my mouth, telling me to leave tooth marks; my father's twice-baked squash, full of pecans and maple sugar, spooned into my open mouth; or a roasted red bell pepper, slimy and sweet, and shaped like the anchovy I refused.

TWICE-BAKED
WINTER SQUASH

4 acorn squash, cut in half and seeded

½ cup pecans

4 tablespoons vanilla

4 tablespoons maple* sugar, or syrup

2 or more ancho chiles, reconstituted in water
    and cut into tiny pieces

Put squash into baking sheet with sides, and bake in 375°F oven in a quarter inch of water for 15–20 minutes, or until just soft.

Blend remaining ingredients in a food processor until smooth. With a spoon, dig squash out of skin, and combine in a bowl with other ingredients, in amounts, or to taste. Spoon combined ingredients back into squash skins and return to oven for 10–15 minutes, or until hot. Sweeten even more for a young person, or for a dessert.

*Maple (*Aceraceae saccharum* and *A. nigrum*): The sweet, flavorful sap of the sugar maple of eastern North America rises during the late-winter, early-spring days of below-freezing nights and above-freezing days. The sap might have first been tasted as "sapsicles" that leaked from broken twigs on the trees. Native Americans (as do producers today) collected the sap and boiled it into cakes for later use—to flavor food, to sweeten food, or to make into drinks. First used almost exclusively as sugar (it has the same chemical composition as cane sugar), maple sap now becomes maple syrup because cane sugar is inexpensive and ubiquitous in all foods.

"When can I go in Daddy's kitchen?" I asked again and again.

"Eat the anchovy," my mother would say.

"Can I pretend to?"

"There's no make-believe with food. When he puts his finger in your mouth, there it is, Wes."

"When you are ready, son," said my father.

Curiosity overwhelmed distaste on my fourth birthday. I said, simply, "I'm ready."

My father served me an anchovy on an appetizer dish from his restaurant. The salt, the oil, the almost rotten smell of the fish made me shudder. Now, I can only describe that first anchovy by invoking other smells and tastes: salty popcorn, the biting smell of the insides of old tennis shoes, sardines, and sweetened capers. I thought of only one thing: entering my father's kitchen.

I swallowed. And tried to smile. "Better than birthday cake!" I said. My father swooped me up and carried me into the heart of the Tsil, his kitchen, into a new world of smells and tastes.

He set me to work. Four years old, and my first job was chopping avocados with a butter knife to mix with anchovies for his unique guacamole. After my father peeled them, I cut them into odd shapes and sizes. I never asked him why I had to chop, since he blended them later, anyway. Now I understand he was teaching me to work. I was an eager student.

ANTI-APPETITE:
FAMILY LEGENDS

*M*y parents came from a long line of neglect. My father was that only child who seemed an oddity to his parents. My mother's mother, I was told, died giving birth to her, and my mother was raised equally in the home of her father and grandmother. Both shared her name: Her father was Mario Tito, and her grandmother was Maria Tito. Great-grandmother Maria Tito, my mother told me, spent her days in her kitchen. When she could, she sold the extra of whatever she prepared to the restaurants, groceries, or markets on The Hill, an Italian neighborhood in St. Louis, where she lived. Mario Tito worked by day in a specialty store that sold capers by the quart, homemade pastas and breads, crocks full of kalamata olives. His nights were spent hoping that just one more glass of wine would help him with the grief of having lost his wife. "I was the reminder of his great love lost," my mother told me. "I wish he could have loved me greatly instead."

When my parents found each other, they were looking for what had been missing in their childhoods: intense focus. They were certainly intense: about each other, about food, about me. They set up a family business, in the family home, so I would never feel neglected. But, of course, customers had to come first; even pasta, boiling on the stove, had to be drained and rinsed before my needs might be met. When I woke up early, my parents were sleeping, and when I was tired, they had to squeeze my bedtime into demanding work schedules.

On the other hand, a restaurant like the Tsil Café could be a magical place, highly entertaining to a boy growing up. I never knew who might walk in my front door—it was, after all, a public entrance. And I was surrounded by people like Pablito and Cocoa.

The Tsil Café was located in a two-story brick building on 39th Street in Kansas City, Missouri. My parents bought into the rundown neighborhood because it was inexpensive, but within twenty years 39th Street had become a popular place for small shops and fine restaurants. Next door to their brick building they bought a vacant lot for a garden and playground. They already knew I was splitting cells in my mother's womb.

The birth and growth of the Tsil matches my own birth and growth. I've been told the story by my parents, and by Maria Tito, who was there. When my parents moved in, their building needed windows, doors, repointed bricks, a new tarred roof. The vacant lot was littered with rocks, bottles, bricks, hubcaps, mattresses. Any exposed ground sprouted sunflowers, pigweed, ragweed, jimsonweed, dock, and crabgrass. My father cleared the lot, making sure to eat the sunflower root, pigweed, dock, and anything else he could forage. Then he tilled and fertilized.

He fenced the lot and brought in another native of the New World: a dog, from the pound, a mutt, part terrier, part pug, whose bark actually sounded like "bark." The dog would warn my father should anyone come into his garden. My mother objected—she was overwhelmed by the prospect of having me to care for. My father joked that if they tired of the mutt, they'd eat him. He named him When Available, anticipating an inside joke—on his Tsil menu the item Tamales gave the customer a choice of Shrimp, Turkey, Buffalo, or Dog (When Available). I didn't get that joke until a couple of years after I started reading.

But I haven't described my birth. "One July morning," my father told me, "just as the sun rose pink in the eastern sky, Weston Tito Hingler was born at Saint Luke's Hospital." My father was not allowed much visiting time, and he went home to work in his garden. Grandmother Tito would arrive by rail in the afternoon.

My father's garden, twenty by forty feet, sprouted rare potatoes, green beans, a variety of chiles, rows of corn, dozens of tomato plants. He'd just seen one harvest in the hospital—me. As red as a tomato, as noisy as When Available keeping squirrels away, as full of potential fertilizer, and as needy of attention as any garden. Great-grandmother Tito came to help.

He recognized Maria Tito as she trembled in the door of the train car above the portable steps, her hair in a white bun on the very top of her head, her hand on a railing. In a moment of joy, he ran to her, lifted her into his arms, and swept her onto the platform. "Save your strength for the child you will carry home," she told him. But she laughed and swiped away tears.

Once I was home from the hospital, and they inspected me more closely, they found purple birthmarks, three of them, at the base of my spine. Great-grandmother Tito looked at my mother's fingers and saw three smashed black and blue nails from the kitchen remodeling. She crossed herself. "This is how we mark our children," she said.

She tried for several days to lighten my birthmarks with a solution of salt and lemon juice, though my mother kept insisting that a birthmark was not a stain.

My father thought the birthmarks, exactly the size, shape, and color of the blue corn so prized by the Hopi, must be a good sign: "A true New World boy," he said. "He will grow up with New World food, in a New World restaurant."

The Tsil building was still in progress. My great-grandmother Tito shrugged her way through the mess, the plans, the dust, and the frustration. My parents were building my father's business, and moving my mother's. "You might as well have had triplets," said my great-grandmother.

Maria Tito took care of me, and helped in the kitchen. "I could tell where your mother learned to cook," said my father. "That woman could chop, peel, cut, mince, stuff, score, braise, boil, clean, bake, and . . . what have I left out?"

"Eat," said my mother.

"God, yes. Could she eat."

"Like you," my mother said to me. "Nothing but appetite."

Both of us ate with ravenous gusto, with smacking of lips and coos of appreciation. Both of us ate something at least once an hour, but remained thin and wiry. Both of us had productive bowels. I grew out of that, but my great-grandmother never did. When I was a boy, I remember Maria Tito's visits. She would take her humor magazines into the bathroom and spend hours reading and what she called "constituting."

My great-grandmother was strong. When she wasn't cooking, or taking care of me, she lifted Sheetrock into place and held it while my father secured it. She carried half-sheets of plywood into the basement where he was building storage shelves. She sawed lumber, hammered nails, drilled holes, planed two-by-fours. After, she would bum a Lucky Strike from my father. Every night she went out for a single bottle of Chianti. She poured a glass for my father, then finished the rest herself. She didn't allow my mother to drink, since she was nursing me.

"She said I'd have plenty of time for wine when I was her age," my mother said.

"Plenty of time, and more money," my father said.

"Back then we didn't have either," my mother said.

The Tsil building, and the potential restaurant in it, had to meet all the specifications, all the codes, all the licensing requirements for food service, liquor service, and business zoning. My father wanted to cook, but that was only one part of the restaurant business.

"Money's the most important," he lamented. "We had to borrow money, and we weren't sure what bank might invest in the Tsil. I got tired of explaining the name, of explaining the menu."

"You wouldn't change it," said my mother.

"You know me better than that," he said.

He thought his grandmother-in-law had money. My mother insisted she didn't. One night, after a couple of beers, then the Chianti with Maria Tito, my father cleared his throat. "You see what we're doing here," he said to her. "The family, the restaurant, the menu. We need money to start. We're short."

She took his Lucky Strike from the ashtray and inhaled deeply. She blew a perfect smoke ring and watched it spill out of its circle and disappear. "You'll be fine," she said, and hobbled off to bed. He didn't say another word about money.

After she returned to St. Louis, she sent a thank-you card for the hospitality. Inside was a money order for a thousand dollars.

My father called his parents, too. "They hated *tsil* cooking," he told me, "and they doubted the success of a restaurant with only New World food. My father was an investor, but in silver mines, not food."

At times during that first year after I was born, my father wanted to give up the idea of the restaurant and help my mother with the already successful Buen AppeTito. She knew where that would lead: He'd meddle in her dishes, her business, her contacts; he'd feel unproductive. He wouldn't win converts. He wouldn't affect the food tastes of Kansas City and the larger world.

My parents spent nine months preparing for me, then another nine months preparing for the opening of the Tsil Café. My father couldn't have done the restaurant except by compromising, but not on food, or cookware, or menu. I knew where the compromises had been, because when I was a child, and my father made money, improvements undid the compromised beginning. When I was three, he laid down the patio tiles of his New Mexico over the painted plywood floor. When I was four, he replaced the inexpensive light fixtures with ceiling fans and soft hanging lamps that looked like inverted mushrooms. Every day when I returned home from kindergarten, I spent hours watching an artist paint the beige walls in murals: the hunting of buffalo; the planting, harvesting, and grinding of corn; the fields of red peppers; the bunches of cactus flowers; the stalks of amaranth, and the cocked heads of sunflowers; the baskets of fruits and vegetables from the New World. The jerry-built tables were replaced by pedestal tables with marble tops, and the chairs, bought at a school closing, became the ones with woven webbing my father and I found when we visited Old Town in Albuquerque when I was seven.

The Tsil Café opened when I was one year old, on my birthday. I have a picture of guests and patrons blowing out single birthday candles stuck into dessert tamales instead of cake. At the end of the evening, my mother says, my father came upstairs, into her kitchen, and handed me to her. "What have I gotten myself into?" he asked.

She wasn't sure if he meant marriage, child, or restaurant—or all three, those triplets my great-grandmother had named. "Sometimes, the *tsil* kachina will overtake you," she said.

"I'll have to get in shape," he told her.

He did. He opened, he hired help, he made improvements, and within a few years he was breaking even. He had regulars, and enough curious eaters to call himself established. He called my Hingler grandparents and invited them to see what he was doing in Kansas City.

I don't remember their visit, but I've seen photographs, and been told about it by my parents and by Pablito, who had the choicest details.

Pablito seated and pleased my father's customers. He had some trouble with English, but he was a happy man, observant, and observable: People liked to watch him. His back was slightly humped, his neck formed so he seemed always to be looking askance, like a bird does. As a small man he was comfortable in the restaurant business, where people spent most of their time seated. He loved children, too, because he didn't have to look up to them. When he was behind the bar of the Tsil Café, he stood on a six-inch stool, mounted on wheels, and he scooted up and down like a mechanical man.

"*Tus abuelos*," he told me, "when they see me, they must think, Oh no, more Mexicans."

My father thought of my Hingler grandparents as *conquistadores*. My grandfather Hingler, a mining engineer, had migrated to New Mexico to find, exploit, and grow rich from natural resources. Grandmother Hingler lived in a social circle of transplanted women with professional husbands. She hired Juan and Conseca Saenz, Mexican immigrants, husband and wife, to grocery shop, cook, and work with the people who came to the house for repair, plumbing, and delivery. Juan gardened and took care of the house and lawn. Conseca learned to cook for parties in the style of the urban east. They had a son, Domingo, close in age to my father.

When Pablito sensed my grandparents' dismay at seeing him, perhaps he also sensed their dismay that their child, my father, had left New Mexico only to drag the culture and people to Kansas City. The Tsil Café, my father was proud of pointing out, was just blocks from Westport, where so many wagon trains had outfitted for the Santa Fe Trail. Their destination was the very place he'd come from. "With the Tsil Café," he'd say, "you can have New Mexican food coming or going."

My grandparents came for Thanksgiving, that meal where New World food—turkey, potato, cranberry, green bean, pumpkin, pecan—is cooked Old World style, and both are celebrated.

"Your mother," Pablito told me, "Maria, would be cook. But *tus abuelos*, they look at me, they look at the Tsil, and Roberto, your father, comes from the kitchen. He sees the look. And oh, oh, oh. I knew he would be cooking, too."

My father hugged his mother until she broke the embrace, then shook his father's hand. He showed them the bed he'd made for them in the basement. He offered to help them bring in their bags and repark their car off the street. And then he called me and my mother down from the upstairs kitchen. My parents thought I would soften my grand-parents' hearts.

I came down, found myself in the dining room with my father and Pablito and two strangers, and I ran to the bar and picked up menus as Pablito had taught me to do. "*Bienvenido,*" I shouted, and handed them menus. They stared at me. My parents were both silent. Pablito stared at the floor. I threw the menus at my grandparents and ran crying up the stairs.

My grandparents stayed at a hotel and returned in the evening for their first Tsil Café meal, which they asked my father to prepare without much spice. They picked at their food. They were quiet. I ate my favorite, turkey tamales and quinoa, and my mother tried to impress her in-laws with my vocabulary: *anchovy, yucca, artichoke, quinoa, amaranth.* I spilled half of what I drank and mushed half of what I ate into my face or onto my lap. Too soon, my grandparents folded their napkins and asked what time they should return the next day for the Thanksgiving meal.

"I'm cooking traditional," said my mother.

"I'm cooking traditional to the New World," my father interjected. "Something to stretch you a little."

My mother gave him a look. "Come at five o'clock," she told my grandparents.

My mother spent her day cooking. So did my father. She fixed old-fashioned turkey with dressing, mashed potatoes with brown gravy, corn and green beans, pumpkin and pecan pies with whipped cream, and strong coffee. She'd fixed those things many times during her years as Buen AppeTito.

My father challenged his parents: chile-smoked turkey over a sage fire; fire-roasted potatoes with a cranberry-ancho chile glaze; sweet potatoes in chipotle barbecue sauce; roasted green and red bell peppers marinated in cayenne corn oil; pineapple and squash pudding with jalapeño syrup for dessert.

SWEET POTATO FRIES WITH CHIPOTLE BARBECUE SAUCE

FRIES

Sweet potatoes, peeled and sliced thin
Corn oil
Salt to taste

Put cut potatoes into a plastic bag, and add enough corn oil to lightly coat all surfaces. Put on a baking sheet in a 400°F oven for about 20 minutes, until potatoes just begin to blacken on the edges or bottoms. Turn onto paper towels to cool. Salt to taste and serve immediately with Chipotle Barbecue Sauce.

BARBECUE SAUCE

2 small cans tomato paste
½ cup water or cranberry juice
2–3 chipotle* peppers, chopped fine
2 ancho peppers, chopped fine
¼ cup dried cranberries

¼–½ *cup sage vinegar (soak liberal amount of sage in vinegar*
      overnight)
Sugar to taste
Salt to taste
Water as needed

Put all ingredients in a saucepan and cook until
thickened. Adjust all ingredients according to taste.
This will be like a thick catsup/barbecue sauce, with
a spicy, smoky flavor.

*Chipotle (dried, ripened jalapeño, smoked): *The chipotle pep-*
per gives its smoky flavor to any dish: soup, salsa, meat. Those who know
chiles so well they remark on them like wine aficionados, note its to-
bacco/chocolate tones and its Brazil-nut finish. Those who don't know
chiles as well simply know the chipotle's smooth, deep heat.

Instead of arguing about which meal should be served,
my parents served both. Besides my grandparents, and my
parents and me, Carson Flinn, the restaurant reviewer in
town, came to that dinner, as did Pablito and Cocoa. My
mother had invited her grandmother and her father, but
Mario Tito said he couldn't travel.

My parents could have invited many families and still had
plenty of food. The only one who truly appreciated the
abundance was reviewer Carson Flinn, who was used to eating prodigiously, a little of a lot. My father refused to eat any
of my mother's food, and she, to make her in-laws comfortable, ate only her own cooking, as they did. As for me, I did

something uncharacteristic. I'd had a big lunch, and I refused to eat anything for dinner at all. My little plate was full of bits of everything—I might have been a miniature Carson Flinn—but, according to my mother, I picked up food with my fork, or spoon, or sometimes with my fingers, and then rearranged my plate as though I were playing in a sand pile.

"Tension kills appetite," my mother told me. "Nobody ate well, not even Pablito or Cocoa. Oh, Carson Flinn ate, but nothing stops him. I had to slap his hand to keep him from taking notes—his unconscious habit at the table. He tried conversation, naming restaurants where he'd eaten in Santa Fe. Or answering questions about Kansas City restaurants where your father's parents had been told to eat—the Golden Ox and the Savoy Grill. But there was no thanks giving or thanks getting."

My mother, who never forgot anything, did not remember that staple of the American Thanksgiving table: cranberry sauce. Her mother-in-law turned to her, tried a smile, and asked, "Don't you have just one can of it? Somewhere in the building, dear?"

"We don't buy things in cans," said my father. "Cans are for those who don't care about food."

"About *your* food?" said his mother.

"I should have remembered," said my mother.

The meal limped along, infamous in the larder of family legends. By dessert, my father had turned surly.

"You could at least try *some*thing," my father said to his parents. "I *am* a cook, you know."

"And so is your wife, Robert," said his mother. "An excellent one, I might add."

"So you've forgiven the lack of cranberry sauce?" said my father.

Grandfather Hingler tried some of my father's dessert, the pineapple-squash pudding with the jalapeño syrup. He left half his pudding on his plate.

"You don't like it?" asked my father.

"I'm full," said his father, though he reached for a piece of pecan pie.

"Careful," said my father. "Pecans are a New World food."

"People don't cook pecan pies with peppers," said his father.

"People cook boring food because they're unadventurous."

"Some people prefer comfort to adventure," said his father.

"Your wife cooks a traditional pie, and cooks it well," said Grandmother Hingler. "There's something to be said for tradition."

"You seem to have only one tradition," said my father. "Convention."

"That's not fair," said his mother.

"You've never learned New Mexico traditions," said my father. "You simply exploit the place for money." He turned to his father. "Have you mined all the minerals from around Santa Fe yet? When you retire, will you retire in the Southwest? No. You just take what's valuable and leave."

"I haven't left," said his father. "*You* have. And you've taken all the knowledge of the food with you. How are you different from me? Better than me? *You* exploit the culture for money, too. And you do it much more"—he looked around the restaurant—"inauthentically than I do. At least I don't have gimmicks."

My father stood up, angry, but said nothing. He left the table, tapping a Lucky Strike on the bar and lighting up. His father and mother soon left. As for me, I finally declared that I'd had it, too. I vomited what little I had in my stomach onto the table, and sent the rest of the diners away. I went to bed with a fever that lasted two days. By the time I was well, my grandparents—after trying recommended restaurants and seeing a few Kansas City sights—had returned home.

I wouldn't see them again for several years. My father, who had to have the last word back then, sent his mother a case of A & P cranberry sauce, with a note: "May you never run out of tradition again."

The real tradition in my father's family was conflict. I knew that by the time I was three years old. My mother's family tradition was tolerance and avoidance. Her grandmother was tolerance: a curious combination of hard work, discipline, understanding, and acceptance. Her father was avoidance, helped along by alcohol. I didn't meet him until I was six years old.

On the morning my grandfather and great-grandmother Tito were to arrive, my father's most regular customer, Ronald, called the Tsil. He thought he'd left his dental plate on his dinner plate, and had we found it. We had not, and the last best hope was the trash, which Pablito had taken to the Dumpster in the alley before he'd closed the Tsil the night before. My father and mother and I went out and stared at the huge metal box. "I guess I'll get a chair, climb on in," my father sighed.

I was small and wiry, the one my father sent scrabbling up mountain rocks along the stream where he'd spotted the best New Mexico watercress. The one my mother sent into crevices and behind furniture when something was lost. The one pushed through the kitchen window of the Tsil Café when my parents forgot a key.

"Boost me up," I said eagerly. "I can do it."

"It's not going to be pretty in there," my father warned, but he already had me by the waist.

"Robert," my mother said.

"I'll find it real fast," I insisted.

My father lifted me until I grabbed the top lip and threw my leg over. Four feet down was the pile of trash. "Maybe in a napkin," said my father. "Wrapped up. That's probably why we missed it."

In kitchens, I'd grown accustomed to potent smells. Every day of my life my father's turkeys simmered for broth, his buffalo tongues boiled to tenderness. My mother's kitchen smelled of wine-soaked olives, garlic and onions, of savory sausage, of bay and oregano.

But what whets the appetite when fresh or cooking can drown the appetite on the other end of consumption: a Dumpster full of the leavings of my father's restaurant and my mother's catering business. From the Tsil: corn husks, turkey skin and bones, potato skins, puddings, melted sorbets, beans, dressings, chile pestos, quinoa, cranberries, and guacamole. From the Buen AppeTito: olive pits, tomato and white sauces, chicken skin and bones, onion and garlic skin, wilted lettuce, mushy eggplant, basil pesto, cheese curds and whey. In that Dumpster, the New World met the Old, and they both stank. I stood on a two-foot pile of garbage and couldn't begin.

"Are you looking?" my father yelled.

I gagged, then took a deep breath.

"You want me to come in with you?" my father asked.

"No," I insisted. My parents had raised me to be a helper: an avocado chopper, a plate clearer, a menu carrier, a hand with the garden hoe. I kicked some of the garbage into a corner, making as much of a bare spot as I could. That way, when I finished combing through garbage, I could move it to the bare side, and I wouldn't have to sort through it again.

I certainly learned more about texture that day than I ever had before: the grit of coffee grounds, the rough rinds of oranges and grapefruit, the paste of refried beans, the half-set glue of cooked cheese, the slime of cooked squash, the sharpness of bones, the mucus of raw poultry skin. I took deep, gulping breaths. Whenever my father called my name, I shouted, "Not yet! Not yet!" I was trying to convince myself I was making progress, that there would be a *yet*, when I'd rise, triumphant, Ronald's dental plate in hand.

Then I heard more voices outside the Dumpster. "Wes?" my mother called. "They're here, Wes!" She meant her father and her grandmother, Mario and Maria Tito.

"I'm finding it soon," I said. But I wasn't so sure. What six-year-old would be, four feet down in a barely lit Dumpster, surrounded by the nightmare of anti-appetite? I squeezed garbage through my hands, hoping to feel something solid that was not a bone.

I must have been in there for half an hour. My T-shirt and shorts were covered with garbage. My shoes squished. I heard a voice I knew must be Grandfather Tito's. "Please," it implored, "get the boy out of there. I'll buy this customer another dental plate."

"For three hundred dollars?" asked my father.

"I won't buy one then," said Mario Tito's voice. "But I want to meet my grandson."

As though at his command, I pinched the dental plate, more solid than bone, between my fingers. "I've got it. I think."

"Reach it out, Wes," said my father. He fished for my hand. "That's a dental plate," he said. "Can you grab hold of me?"

I tried, but my fingers and hands were too slimy. I panicked. "I can't get out!"

My father appeared over the lip of the Dumpster. "I'm going in," my father said, and he vaulted into the Dumpster, squishing garbage himself. I was glad to see him.

"Whew," he said.

"I'm handing him out," my father yelled. He picked me up. "He's slippery!"

The next thing I knew, I was perched on the edge of the Dumpster, looking for arms to grab me. My mother reached up and I fell into her arms. A small man, shorter than my mother, thinner than my great-grandmother, started toward us from the shade of the building. That's when I slipped from my mother's arms, landing hard on the alley bricks. I hit my head and was overcome by a dizzying blackness.

"My son never had a stomach for this world," Great-grandmother Tito told me. My mother says she stood over me, a trail of putrescent slime on her clothing. Blood seeped from my forehead, and I was covered in the offal of the Dumpster. Grandfather Tito, who had come to welcome me back to sunlight, fainted instead onto the alley bricks next to me.

"You looked like a newborn," said my mother. "Not appetizing, I'll admit, but we were glad to see you, anyway. And my father? He looked like any father—a little lost, a little overwhelmed. He woke up soon."

I woke up, too, and they cleaned my head and took off my clothes. I was as naked as the day I was born, and as healthy—except for a bruise on my noggin. They praised my persistence, my triumph in the Dumpster, until I became embarrassed and ran upstairs with my mother for a quick shower and clothes. When we came down, everyone was in the dining room of the Tsil Café, my father in a new pair of pants and shoes.

"Praise God," said Grandfather Tito. "I looked at you and all I could think of was your mother. The day she was born. But wait," he said. "Turn around." He lifted my shirt and pulled down my pants far enough to reveal my birthmarks. "I saw your little stains, like wine on a linen napkin. They have been there since birth?"

"I told you that," said his mother.

"Let's have a glass of wine," said Grandfather Tito.

My father opened a bottle of wine and called Ronald to come for his dental plate. When Ronald showed up, he gave me a five-dollar bill and stuck his tongue comically through the hole made by the lack of three front teeth.

"You don't have to give him anything," said my father.

I was disappointed. Even at that age I knew five dollars was a lot of money.

"Keep the money," Ronald said to me. Again he flicked the tip of his tongue through his missing teeth. "Consider it a tip," he joked, "for a fine boy and a fine job."

Mario Tito was drunk. "This boy," he muttered, "was born today. In birth, is death. You don't know what he's been through. You don't know what I've been through."

Maria Tito finally took him to the bed in the basement of the Tsil and told him to go to sleep. "I never could grow that man up," she said. "I'm sorry, Maria."

My mother, tears in her eyes, simply looked at me. "We'll grow this one up instead," she said.

That first visit with Mario Tito was spent listening to him recall my fall from my mother's arms, and his fall from the happiness of love into grief.

"Remember," my mother told me later. "When you fall, you don't have to lie there. You *can* get up."

CHILE DE ÁRBOL!:
KITCHEN SCARS

efore I was old enough to object, my father put me to real work in his kitchen. "Builds character," he'd say. For a long time, though I was building it, I had no idea what character was. From the way my father talked, character was like a muscle, becoming stronger the more I used it. I lifted supplies, scrubbed and rinsed vegetables, ran up and down the basement stairs to the big freezer, or up and down to Mother's kitchen if there was an emergency at the Tsil and my father needed anything from another knife to another hand. My father praised my effort, calling me *big* even though I was small and skinny. He admired my energy. "That's *my* boy," he said frequently. I was the son of the Tsil Café.

Though I begged him, my father didn't trust me with more than a dull knife until I was almost ten years old. For my birthday, he gave me a little paring knife. "Don't want you cutting off anything bigger than your finger," he told me. He instructed me on my first precise job: I was to take the fresh cayenne* peppers he harvested by the basketful from

---

****Cayenne** (Ginnie pepper; *chile de árbol* and *guajillo* peppers are in the same family): *A bright red pepper, thin, anywhere from two to four inches long. Can be eaten fresh, but most often cayennes are dried and made into powder that can be pure fire.*

his garden, hold them by the stem and top, and cut them to the point, making as many thin strips as possible.

I spread the strips into a whip—as though I were making a miniature cat-o'-nine-tails. My father took each cayenne and stuck its stem into the cob of a two-inch piece of corn. The cayenne became a headdress, the stub of corn a mask, with achiote seeds for eyes. The whole thing created the head of the *tsil* kachina, totem of my father's restaurant.

My father served this edible mask with each main dish, though few customers ate one. I was happy to help. I tried hard to make as many little strips as possible. "You're going to make a cook," my father said to me each day.

I cut, separated the strips, and twirled the peppers. Seeds sprinkled the counter, and soon the cutting board and my hands were stained bright red with chile oil. "Don't touch your eyes," my father warned. "Or pick your nose. When you're finished, we'll soak your hands."

One day, when I was cutting cayenne, my father, in a foul mood, muttered that maybe we were both wasting our time. "Most of these end up in the trash." Usually when he muttered to himself, I ignored him. But I was ten, and working hard on the corn kachina masks.

"How about putting just one on each table?"

"Some people eat theirs," said my father.

"Most people don't," I said.

"You're not getting out of work that easily," he said.

I cut. Maybe it was pepper juice, but my eyes blurred with tears. Maybe I was tired of building character. Maybe I was hurt because he wouldn't consider my suggestion. Maybe I was angry because he thought I was lazy when I liked to work. I almost threw down my knife and ran out of the kitchen, but I couldn't. Instead, I made the excuse every kid makes to get away: "I have to go to the bathroom."

My father waved me away, distracted by his frustration.

I went to the private bathroom off the kitchen, unzipped my pants, and reached in through the hole in my underwear to pull out my penis. About halfway through my stream, though, I felt real pain. My cayenne-stained fingers held my penis, which burned as though someone had set a match to it. I pulled my hands away. My stream had stopped, and my scrotum had shriveled. I didn't know what to do. I couldn't touch myself again. I did a little dance, scooching down and bending my knees and hoping my penis would withdraw into my underpants. But it simply hung there, burning like a limp candle. I wept with the pain, and finally, I walked out into the kitchen, my red hands held up.

My father knew right away what had happened. "Damn it, Wes. I'm sorry." He knelt down beside me and returned my penis through the hole and back into my underwear. "How bad is it?" he asked.

Before I could answer, my body heat intensified the pepper heat. I felt the searing spread of chile oil onto my leg. I burst into tears.

My father stripped off my pants. "Pablito!" he yelled. Pablito came into the kitchen in time to see my father take off my underwear. "Chile burns," my father said.

Pablito eyed my penis in his sideways fashion, like a bird looks at a worm. "*Qué lástima*," he said. "No place for hot spice." He went to the shelf and pulled down the salt. Then he went to his refrigerator at the bar and brought back three limes. He ran hot water into a bowl.

My father knew what was going to happen, but I didn't. When he laughed, I was hurt even more and began sobbing again. Pablito cut the limes, squeezed them into the water, then poured in a stream of salt. "Margarita!" he shouted, and smiled at me. He carried the bowl to the center of the kitchen and placed it on the floor. He brought another bowl, a wooden salad bowl, and set it, upside down, next to the water bowl. "Sit." He patted the inverted bowl.

I sat on the edge of one bowl and dangled myself into the other. My penis floated in the warm salt water, surrounded by lime rind and pulp, and my father and Pablito laughed. When the pain began to soak away, I tried to laugh, too. Pablito brought another bowl for soaking my hands, and, after fifteen long minutes, the pain lessened.

"Stand," said Pablito. "The air says how you are."

I stood up and tried to dry off, but the pain came back. "More water," said Pablito. He added more warm water and told me to sit again.

I sat. All seemed well. Until, in spite of myself, my floating penis began to stiffen. I'd had involuntary erections before—a stiffening in my jeans that went away, as natural as a yawn and a stretch and then back to reading. But I was naked, in the middle of the kitchen. My father and Pablito didn't notice me, at least not until Cocoa showed up for work and, not finding Pablito at the bar, wandered into the kitchen.

I jumped up, tipping over the bowl of lime water. I tried to cover my penis, but it seemed extraordinarily large. All three adults saw my problem before I ran into the bathroom.

Nobody chastised me for spilling the salty lime water. Pablito, in fact, brought me another bowl. "A little longer," he said. "We won't pickle your pepper."

Cocoa knocked on the door. "Wes honey," she said. "I'm sorry I came in on you like that. I'm sorry you burned your little thing."

By then it *was* little, all shriveled in the water, and it hurt, and I cried by myself. Why did I have to hurt myself, and end up nothing but a joke?

My father came to the door to ask how I was doing. I didn't answer him. He heard me snap the lock. "Wes," he said. His knuckles hit the door.

"I hate your stupid kachinas," I said.

"Sometimes we have to do what we hate," he said. "You're building character." His voice softened. "And I think you're building a great one."

"It hurts," I said. But I unlocked the door.

"You know what?" he asked. He squatted on the floor next to me. "Suffering builds character, too."

"When am I going to have my character?" I asked.

"Soon," he said. "You're a good worker. You've got a lot of good character already."

Over dinner, he said, "Wes, every time you hurt it's because you tried—it's true in kitchens, in love, in life. Pain is a kind of courage."

Two years later, I learned more of pain and courage. I was

twelve years old, just starting to find a frog in my throat and pimples on my chin. My father and mother had finally let me grow my hair out from its childhood crew cut. As soon as he noticed the fuzz above my lip, my father shaved his mustache, and for months his upper lip looked naked.

The day he shaved, my mother shook her head at the breakfast table like she did when When Available slopped his water on her floor. "I liked your mustache."

"Too much gray in it," he said.

"Vanity," said my mother.

"I don't need to advertise my age," he said.

"It went nicely with your little potbelly," she said.

My father stood up, pulled in his stomach, and strutted toward the stairs, and his kitchen. He made a parting comment: "I won't be the potbelly calling the kettle drum fat."

"Our bodies thicken with age," she yelled after him. "You don't have to be thickheaded, too." She turned to me. "You're getting thicker, too," she said, and tousled my newly grown hair. "Just keep your mind limber."

That summer, my god-grandparents came for a visit. Juan and Conseca Saenz had practically raised my father, along with their own son, Domingo. Juan had taught my father and Domingo to garden, and the two boys had spent day after summer day growing, hoeing, watering, weeding, eating, and playing in their New Mexico lot.

As soon as he arrived in Kansas City, Juan turned his attention to me and to our garden; he and I spent most of our time together there.

I enjoyed being outside. Juan told me stories of corn.

Soon, the common cob of yellow kernels began to seem as bland as homogenized milk. Juan taught me that kernels had different colors: blue, purple, white, brown, black. And kernels had different shapes: from flour kernels, to pop, to sweet, to dent, to flint. Cobs came in all lengths, in all circumferences from fat to skinny, and in all deformities: He'd once harvested an ear long and thin at its top, dense and bulky at the bottom. When he'd husked it, he'd held in his hand a corn penis, complete with testicles.

In the evenings, Juan made corn bread. "The Indian way," he said. He and I ate that and nothing else.

PEPPER CORN BREAD

2 large red or yellow bell peppers
3 ears corn*
2 roasted New Mexico green chiles
½ cup masa flour
1 teaspoon baking powder
½ teaspoon baking soda

Wash peppers, core, and cut lengthwise into halves or thirds.

Remove kernels from corn, put in food processor with green chiles, and blend until very soupy—it will be bubbly. Add masa, baking powder, and baking soda, and spoon into pepper boats. Bake in 375°F oven for 40 minutes, then broil for an additional 5 minutes.

*Corn (zea mays): *America's grain, now king of grains all over the world. Corn on the cob is a fine vegetable; cornmeal, in various forms, is the basis of corn breads, polentas, masa for tamales; hominy, or posole, is corn kernels processed in lye to remove the hull and to alter the starch for a nutritional boost. Corn grows so quickly as to be miraculous, drinking water in great quantity, pushing up with such a rapid thrust that cultivators claim they can measure the growth each hour. Husks are saved by Native Americans to wrap tamales and vegetables and meats for cooking over a fire.*

Juan loved corn like a baby loves a parent. Some nights, he slept between the corn rows. "You can hear corn grow," he told me. "Come outside to sleep tonight."

He watered the young stalks twice that day, morning and evening, and talked to them in Spanish. When the sun went down, I brought out my sleeping bag and put it in the row next to the row where he lay on a pallet. He told a story of a god who was burned, and whose bones were ground like cornmeal, and who reinvented himself as a fish. Then the fish swam onto land and became a human figure, dancing and falling to the ground. He disappeared, but where he fell, corn grew, a gift to all people. He told me of Corn Mother, who killed herself, a sacrifice to her starving people, directing them to spread her flesh in the earth and return in one year's time. She sprouted as corn, and her people have been fed ever since.

When Juan finished his whispered stories, we listened to another whispering, the wind through the broad corn leaves. Then, as the moon entered the sky from the east, we heard the corn grow: a weak shiver like the sound a wet finger makes on a slick surface; a slight groan like a baby yawning in its sleep. I fell asleep to that adjustment of newly created plant cells, that stretching of the earth toward sky.

The next day, Juan and I checked the stake we'd driven into the earth to the same height as one of the cornstalks. Overnight, the stalk had outgrown the stake by two inches. I had grown, too, in my love of the garden, and Juan. I also understood my father's stubborn insistence that a corn-mask kachina be served with every dinner plate at his Tsil Café. Corn and peppers were gifts.

By that time, I was totally responsible for creating the *tsil* heads. On my twelfth birthday, my mother suggested I be paid if I was going to spend a couple of hours in the kitchen of the Tsil Café after school each day, and on the weekends. My father started me at a dollar an hour.

Once Juan came, I wanted to be with him, in the garden, watching his brown hands hoe, or pull weeds, or pinch toma-toes, or gently pull off the zucchini blossoms Conseca breaded and fried for his dinner. But I served my time in the kitchen, putting the largest pot to boil, husking corn, break-ing the cobs into small sections and throwing them into the water, cutting cayenne into headdresses, sorting achiote seeds to find the ones with points to stick between kernels for eyes.

The day before my god-grandparents were to leave, I

stayed up late, sleeping in the garden with Juan again. We talked, and listened to the wind and the corn after the traffic noises died in the city. The next day I was tired, and dragged myself into the kitchen at 3:30. By 5:30, I'd have a hundred *tsil* heads ready, and I could have my dinner. Juan and Conseca would eat with me, then pack their camper and drive back to New Mexico during the night, in the cool air. "When the sun comes up," said Juan, "we'll be seeing mountains."

I was sad they were leaving. I forced myself to work. Juan and Conseca were both in the kitchen, Conseca to help cut cayenne, Juan to husk and break corn, and we worked quickly, to give me extra time. I grabbed the tongs so I could recover some of the corn lengths from the boiling water. I was still short enough that I had to hook my arm over the pot, then fish out a piece of corn. When I accidentally dropped the tongs into the water, I reached for them without thinking. The pot teetered toward the edge of the stove and I grabbed it with my hands. Heat seared my palms and fingertips. When I pulled away, too late to prevent a terrible burn, some of my flesh stuck to the pot.

Conseca pulled me to the sink. My burned skin was bright red, and she stuck it under the cold tap, where the tips of my fingers wrinkled and turned white. I might have been holding wet paper. I fainted. When I woke up, on the kitchen floor, my hands were immersed in ice water. My father was telling Pablito how to finish cooking several specials for the evening. My mother was out front in the car, honking furiously.

On the way to the hospital, my father kept telling my mother to hurry. I whimpered. Conseca cooed in my ear like a mourning dove. Juan dug his fingers into my thigh, as though one kind of pain could distract me from another. "Go through," my father shouted when a light turned yellow.

My mother slowed to a stop. "You work him too hard," she said.

"He likes to work, and be glad he does," said my father.

"We'll talk about that," she said. The light turned green.

"Just go," said my father.

"I am," she said. "You can bet I am." Then I didn't hear them, because I fainted again.

Juan and Conseca didn't leave that night after all. I returned from the hospital with third-degree burns, my throbbing hands wrapped in gauze. Every day, Conseca took off the old gauze, covered my hands with cream, and rewrapped them. When Available stayed at my bedside. I taught him to carry my empty glass in his mouth to Conseca, to let her know I was thirsty. She was the perfect nurse. "Always available," we all joked.

My right hand was much worse than my left, and soon I could pick things up, eat, even try to write with my off hand. I enjoyed the time away from my father's kitchen. Nobody spoke of my returning there to make the *tsil* heads.

Juan encouraged me. "Your bandages are like husks," he said. After the first hand was shucked, he admired the new skin. "Every day your hands grow strong and healthy again, like corn. The left has ripened first."

Juan and Conseca stayed until my hands were healed. Juan tried to make me proud of my scars. My hand was smooth with the new skin that grew back, and it shone, slick, in a strange way. When I put it near heat, it throbbed. I never had fingerprints on my right hand again. "You are marked by Mother Corn," said Juan. "You have made a sacrifice, just as everything sacrifices itself so that we can eat. That is the way of the world."

My father looked at my hands every once in a while. "I'm so sorry," he'd say, still guilty that I'd come to harm in his kitchen.

My mother would look at my scars and sigh. "So young to be so marked. To learn the dangers of life."

"I'm okay," I'd tell both of them. Each seemed to be saying something into an ear other than mine. In fact, they weren't talking a lot to each other. Once, they'd always taken their breakfasts and lunches together; now they often ate in their own kitchens.

By the time I started junior high school, I was fully recovered. No one had mentioned anything about going back to work in the kitchen, and I was glad. One night, as we ate silently together, I said, "I don't want to make kachina heads anymore."

"You'll have homework now," said my mother. "And maybe some extracurricular activities?"

"Go ahead and say you don't want him working for me," my father said.

"It's me," I said. "I need some time off."

"Are you afraid?" he asked.

"No. I just need to be free to stay after school, to make some friends."

"I can hire it done," said my father. "But I won't find a better worker than you."

I looked at my scarred hand, at the shiny new skin. I remembered all the small knife cuts, the chile burns, the running up and down the stairs. My father looked a little sad, and I *almost* said, "Okay, I'll stay in the kitchen."

But my hand reminded me of how long I'd done what he asked of me, and of the pains I'd suffered in the kitchen. The glistening scar tissue seemed like a message, too: Wear a different skin. So I kept my mouth shut and risked his disapproval. He didn't beg, and I left the table relieved. I walked to my room, proud, as though I'd developed, for the first time, my own taste in things.

"SMOKED, HEARTY, SPICY, SHARP, EARTHY—": REVIEWS

*C*ooks rely on their own sense of taste, but they live and die by the tastes of others. For the first two months after my father opened his Tsil Café, he was glad for each customer, though one customer mattered most: the reviewer for the Kansas City paper.

At one time, Carson Flinn and my mother might have been lovers. I know they had a relationship before my mother traveled to the Southwest and met my father. I know they had the manner of old friends—she called him Car, making fun of both his name and his size; he simply called her Teet, her maiden name minus the O. I know my father always felt doubly reviewed when Carson was at the Tsil, whether for his work or family gatherings. To me, Flinn was an imposing man. He was almost entirely bald, with a huge appetite and finicky manners. He spoke flamboyantly, as though he were writing. Once, at a Thanksgiving meal my father prepared, he said, "New establishments need my good report; established establishments need my continued support; tired establishments need my comfort; morbid establishments need my words *de la mort.*"

My mother had met Carson Flinn at her first catering

job, a gallery opening. He loved her food. "He loved me," she said. "And I might have loved him back, except for his age. And he was too particular. Not just about food—you'd expect that—but about people, about his clothing, about all the cats he kept in his apartment back then."

The first time Carson visited the Tsil Café, he came disguised. My mother had anticipated this, so she gave Pablito, who had never met him, strict instructions to come for her if he noticed anyone with a small mole just above his lip, under his right nostril. Anyone with a suspicious hairpiece. Anyone who, before ordering, asked for an extra napkin. Anyone who studied the menu closely. Especially anyone who wrote anything down.

"Maybe tonight, Roberto," Pablito would say to my father each evening as they opened the doors at five. "*El Señor* Flinn, *El Coche*, could come tonight."

One night, Pablito pushed my father to the little window that allowed him to observe his patrons. Seated alone at a table near the bar, a large man with white hair, with a mole above his lip, with extra napkin and notebook, studied the menu. My father sent Pablito upstairs for my mother. "The back stairs. I don't want him to see her."

My mother sidled up to the window and nodded her head. "I don't know where he got the wig," she said. "And the sideburns look terrible. And he needs my advice on his clothing again. But it's him." She disappeared upstairs. She was preparing post-banquet snacks for a convention hospitality room at a downtown hotel. Before she left, she would put me to bed in her kitchen.

My father could hardly contain himself. "Pablito, steer him through the menu. Avoid the smoked turkey, it's dry tonight. Fresh black bean and gooseberry enchiladas. The tongue is very tender. Make sure his dishes have the full range of peppers and their heat . . ." He would have continued his anxious whisper, but Pablito was already back in the dining room.

Pablito bustled, my father bustled, and for the next two hours Carson Flinn, with his vanilla-white wig and curly sideburns, might have been the only customer in the Tsil. He was certainly the most important one. He stymied Pablito immediately by ordering both fruit juice and wine, and both the Shrimp de Infierno and the Nopal Tamal for appetizers. The man ate for hours, ordering two of nearly every course, eating slowly, taking notes, demanding more napkins, patting the sweat induced by his cheap wig and the hot peppers.

Finally, Carson finished his pineapple sorbet and downed his last sip of blackberry brandy, both on the house. "Such an eater, *qué apetito*," Pablito said to him. Carson Flinn seemed well pleased. He paid his bill and walked into the night. My father came out of the kitchen and flipped the sign on the door from OPEN to CLOSED. He was exhausted.

When the last customer left, Pablito and my father lit Lucky Strikes and toasted each other into the night, waiting for the thump of the Kansas City paper on the door. They waited for nothing.

The review did not appear for a nerve-racking week of slow business. Then my mother found it, in the Friday section, with a headline easy to celebrate. Years later, that yellowed review became, for me, like a sacred text a novitiate must memorize.

Tsil Café: Creative, Unique

Westphalia Road at 39th Street; Price $$$; Rating +++++; the Tsil is named for the hot pepper Hopi kachina who stuffs peppers in people's mouths; food is eclectic, ingredients from the New World only.

Maria Tito, now Hingler, is well known in this city as Buen AppeTito—that fine catering business. She told us some time ago of her plans to visit New Mexico, to bring a taste of Southwestern cuisine to her cooking. But we find she's brought something else to us as well: a husband, Robert Hingler, who has just opened the Tsil Café on 39th Street.

We visited recently, and intend to visit again. With a menu this unique, each dish must eventually be ordered, tasted, and savored. After all, Robert Hingler cooks only with the food known to the Americas *before* the arrival of Christopher Columbus.

Upon our arrival at the Tsil, we were greeted by Pablito, the bartender and manager. In a tropical shirt, with a smile as white as a just-opened coconut, Pablito sets the right tone: We know we are in a world slightly askew, slightly different, slightly exotic. We feel we are going to enjoy ourselves.

From a heavily spiced, varied menu, we tried to balance the hot and mild, the meat and vegetable, the sweet and the sour. We started with appetizers of fiery shrimp and earthy nopal (prickly pear cactus) tamal. We moved on to small cups of both the black bean and the potato and green chile soup. Shrimp and black beans are familiar. Cactus strips and turkey liver were not. But all was light, fresh, piquant. Even the potato soup, though generous in thin slices of turkey liver, had unique balance, with no single ingredient dominating.

Our watercress salad was dressed with a roasted tomato and sunflower dressing that tasted almost smoked.

Smoked, hearty, spicy, sharp, earthy—these are the words to describe the palette of food Robert Hingler offers. The vanilla buffalo steak with a cranberry-chile pesto offered as much flavor in a single dish as most restaurants offer in an entire menu. Our side dishes, smoky polenta and a generous portion of sweetly hot jalapeño green beans, suggested by Pablito, complemented the entrée perfectly.

If you don't have time for dinner, go in only for an appetizer and then browse the dessert menu. We had avocado pudding topped with a dark chocolate raspberry sauce and then finished our meal with a pineapple sorbet—perfectly fruity and not highly sweetened.

Certainly, Robert Hingler's unique cuisine is available nowhere else in the world. Hingler is trying to make the unknown, known; the common, extraordinary; the exotic, familiar. His attempts are, from our single experience, quite worthy. The future will tell if he can make his food familiar enough to attract regular customers to his restaurant.

On the same evening we ate our fine meal at the Tsil Café, we happened into a downtown hotel for our usual coffee, and found that Maria Tito Hingler had catered one of her usual feasts, disguised as finger and snack food. We are pleased to report that her food continues to be some of the best in Kansas City, and her company some of the finest, as well.

My parents stood over a table in the restaurant and read the review. My mother thought it was wonderful, until she read the last paragraph. "He shouldn't have put in that last part," she said.

"Makes me wonder what he *really* thought of the food," said my father.

"I knew you'd do what you're doing," my mother accused.

"I just wanted a clean review. Of the Tsil Café," he said.

"Don't worry. Carson likes me, but he loves his reputation more than he'll ever love any person."

"So that's why you didn't end up with him."

"I ended up with you," she said.

Pablito served them each a small glass of wine.

That evening, my father posted the review in the entryway, to be the first thing a customer would see upon opening the door. The next day, when Pablito came to work, he brought another, and they taped it in the window, hoping to catch the eyes of passersby. Both copies of the review, neatly cut from the newspaper, lacked the final paragraph.

Cutting the last paragraph was symbolic. A restaurateur never feels fully reviewed. Carson Flinn revisited the Tsil Café, in part because he liked the food, in part because he liked my mother. Often, he would write brief snippets in his weekly food column. Things like:

> Robert Hingler, whose garden lot next to the Tsil Café is testament to the freshness of his food, has recently added a new crop, not often seen in the area. Cactus. Prickly pear, to be exact. It grows in pads, one on top of the other. In late June, he says, it flowers, and the tiny pear will become a delicacy in his restaurant. Pads will be harvested, as needed, for his Nopal Tamal.

Or, when he first discovered the joke about Dog Tamal in my father's menu:

> We've always wondered something about Robert Hingler's menu at the Tsil Café. Under Tamales, he lists Shrimp, Buffalo, Turkey, or Dog (When Available). When pressed about the availability of dog as a meat in these famous tamales, the cook surprised me. "When Available!" he cried. Then he whistled. "When Available!" A dog came running down the stairs from the Hingler living quarters. The terrier with a bulldog face sniffed his way across the floor. "Meet When Available." Robert Hingler smiled.
>
> "He's not available, I take it?" we asked.
>
> "No, he's not Not Available, he's When Available."

Carson Flinn frequently mentioned my mother's cooking. Usually very short, like:

> Maria Tito Hingler, of Buen AppeTito Catering, continues to be one of the best chefs in the city. We attended a Hungarian wedding reception, and Buen AppeTito catered their request: goulash. Hers was no ordinary goulash, more like a thick minestrone smothered in cheese, with more tomato, and a dusky dusting of paprika. Do we rhapsodize? Call it Hungarian Rhapsody.

Or:

> Leave it to Buen AppeTito to appeal to all the senses, all the arts. Her newest dessert, served at a pri-

vate party on Ward Parkway, is titled Prufrock's Peaches. And we dared to eat it. Yes, coffee is also one of the ingredients, spooned on, of course. Some women may come and go, talking of Michelangelo, but everyone on Ward Parkway spoke of nothing but dessert.

Carson Flinn did another official review of the Tsil when my father, prompted by Pablito, began to serve lunch. Pablito was recently married, and he usually arrived at the Tsil around the same time I came home from school. We'd gather in the kitchen. I'd talk about my day at school, showing off papers and confessing to the homework I had to bring back the next day. Pablito talked about his new life with Teresita. My father wrote up a new special, maybe something to do with the buffalo testicles he'd been offered at a good price.

"Teresita and me, we're going to have a family someday," Pablito said one day. "We want a little *hombrecito*, like your Wes, *aquí.*" He reached over and pinched the skin behind my elbow, making a big show of it, though he knew that was one place where skin felt no pain. "Lunch. *Más dinero.* A good idea?"

My father talked to some of his customers. Most of them, primed by Pablito, told him they'd love lunch and would tell all their friends.

"I can't get enough of this stuff," said Ronald, the Tsil's most loyal customer, the one whose dental plate I'd recovered from the Dumpster when I was six. He worked for a janitorial service and wore a red-and-white-striped shirt with his name embroidered into a patch sewn over his left pocket. Ronald loved to bring friends into the Café, and best them at eating the spiciest dishes. "He must have no other social life," my father once told my mother. "I almost feel guilty— he spends so much money here."

"Customers have free will," said my mother. "He'll be your best lunch customer, too. You watch."

So, my father hired Pablito to manage from around eleven to around two. After much discussion with Pablito, my mother, and even Carson Flinn, my father created a menu that, to him, was full of compromises. Wheat buns for the buffalo and turkey burgers, catsup for those who needed it. Black pepper on the tables along with the little rockets of red pepper already there. "The first sandwich on my lunch menu was buffalo burger, because I was buffaloed into this," my father joked.

"*Compromise* is another word for business," said my mother.

My mother has told me many times how many hours my father spent designing his Tsil Café dinner menu, and how little time he spent on his lunch offering. He typed a quick series of offerings on white paper. At the top, he named his lunch business Tsil Buffalo. He posted the menu in the window. Pablito had a stack by the door, as well, and my father retyped whenever his customers smeared his originals with salsa from an overloaded chip, or catsup from an overdipped potato fry.

My father spent more time than he expected at the type-writer because business was good. He suspected people liked the compromised Tsil Buffalo food better than the pure Tsil on the dinner menu. "They're a different bunch," he said. "They want it fast, they wolf it down, they're thinking about work, about the parking meter. How can they taste?"

"They love it. It's *gusto*," said Pablito. "Some of them will be back, when it's dark."

"It's compromise to you," said my mother. "To them, it may be the first step toward thinking about what you're doing. Put a dinner menu on every table. Teach people."

Every once in a while a lunch customer would order from the Tsil Café instead of the Tsil Buffalo. If my father had the item, or could cook it quickly, he would oblige, even if he kept people waiting.

His most loyal lunch customer was Pablito's new wife, Teresita. During that first summer of the Tsil Buffalo, she sat near the window in a booth and insisted on eating with me. She was pregnant, and each day she moved the table a little farther from her swelling womb, a little closer to me, until the table poked me in the chest. "I want a New World boy," Teresita would say. "Like you. A boy who likes a little mouth of spice." I would smile. "And such good food to build a baby with." She'd smack her lips.

After lunch, Teresita retired to the basement of the Tsil, where Pablito had set up a cot against one wall, next to storage shelves where my father kept his wine. She didn't care about the lack of privacy, and sometimes, when she was asleep, I would sneak down the stairs and peek at her belly, round as the earth. Was there really, I wondered, a little boy in there, growing, getting ready to be born? Would it be like me, a New World boy? Would it look like Teresita, or Pablito?

I had one secret at the time, besides the fact that I spied on Teresita. I liked the lunch food from the Tsil Buffalo as well as the dinner food from the Tsil Café.

Tsil Buffalo: A Lunch Menu

Chips with Salsas—ask for blue, white, or yellow
corn chips with avocado, habanero, or tomato salsa

Nut-stuffed jalapeños—2 per order
=========================
Buffalo Burger

Turkey Burger

Smoked Turkey Sandwich

Chile Peanut Butter and Jalapeño Jelly Sandwich

Green Pepper Stuffed with Wild Rice

Note: Burgers and sandwiches (except the CPB & JJ)
are served with pestos, tomatoes, watercress, zucchini pickles, and Robert's own home-style catsup
and barbecue sauces.
=========================
Fries: both white and sweet potato
=========================
Black Bean Soup

Turkey Soup
=========================
Potato Salad—hot

Corn and Cactus Salad—mild

All-Bean Salad—medium

Quinoa Salad—mild
=========================
Sorbets for dessert—ask for fruits of the day

Inquire about prices, which vary from day to day
depending on availability and suppliers.

We knew Carson Flinn so well he couldn't wear a disguise when he came to review my father's lunch menu. He dissembled another way. He arrived on a hot summer Saturday with a question for my mother. Pablito asked me to take him upstairs. My father, cooking, didn't know Carson was there.

My mother was preparing portabello turnovers, cheese puffs, and miniature quiches for a Buen AppeTito job. As always, she began to feed Carson, and I started to leave. "Wait, Wes," he called me back. "Get me these things from the kitchen downstairs." He pulled a crinkled Tsil Buffalo menu from his jacket pocket. Half the items were circled. "Just samples," he said. "I'll eat it up here. Don't tell Pablito it's for me." Downstairs, I called it lunch, for my mother and me.

I brought Carson Flinn the nut-stuffed jalapeño for his appetizer. He dabbed his forehead with his handkerchief, all the time taking deep breaths and grinning at my mother.

I brought him the plate loaded with half a turkey burger, half a buffalo burger, and half a spicy peanut butter and jelly sandwich. Carson Flinn seemed to enjoy himself, though he scraped off some barbecue sauce and asked my mother if she really liked the zucchini pickles.

I brought him the potato fries—both sweet and russet potatoes. He used catsup from my mother's pantry. "It's still American food, even if it isn't laced with chiles," he insisted.

I brought him a sampler of salads. He spit out the potato salad. "I'll ruin my mouth later," he said. But he couldn't stop eating the quinoa salad, and the corn and cactus, too. "Beans," he said about the other, "I just can't eat them with any pleasure."

"You eat everything with pleasure," said my mother.

"With you, yes," said Carson Flinn. "Even the potato salad. See?" And he ate it.

PAPAS ESTILO DIABLO

*5 small purple/black potatoes**

5 small red potatoes

5 small white potatoes

10 roma tomatoes, dried

3–5 hot chiles (Hungarian wax, New Mexico red/green)

2 jalapeño chiles

1 habanero chile

1 cayenne chile

4 large tomatillos

¾ cup mango juice

½ cup sage vinegar

¼ cup pecans

½ cup peanuts

Salt to taste

Cut potatoes into small cubes and boil until just tender. Run cold water over them and set aside in a large bowl. Cut dried tomatoes in half and add to potatoes. Roast and peel the chiles, remove stems and seeds, cut into fine strips, and add to potatoes. Put the habanero, cayenne, tomatillos, mango juice, vinegar, pecans, and peanuts into a food processor and blend until very smooth. Add salt to taste. Pour this dressing over everything else and let sit for two hours. Eat and suffer.

Potato (*papa*): *Foodstuff of the Peruvian highlands, where the people processed it by alternately drying, freezing, and pounding it into* chuño. Chuño *flour could be made into bread. The Old World Irish were the first to take to the New World potato, cultivating it in such quantity that the average citizen there ate ten pounds of potatoes each day. Other cultures gave the potato ambivalent reviews, from the belief that potatoes caused leprosy to the belief that they aided lovemaking. Today, potatoes are everywhere, adapted to many climates, soils, and cuisines. But nowhere near the over two hundred potato varieties of the Incas can be found in most markets: the black potato, or the blue or purple; the nutty-tasting potato; the bitter ones that sweeten upon being frozen and dried* (chuño). *But potatoes remain a favorite—cheap, easy to grow, able to be fried, boiled, baked, mashed, whipped, steamed, or eaten raw, with salt.*

When he'd finished the potato salad, I started to leave. "Wes," my mother called after me. "Can you take the dishes?"

I did as I was told, but I didn't like it. I didn't like Carson Flinn, either. Not on that day.

Soon, my father didn't like him, either. The review shows why.

Tsil Buffalo

Westphalia Road at 39th Street; Price $$; Rating +++++; the Tsil Buffalo is Robert Hingler's lunch version of the Tsil Café. Most items for lunch are, as for dinner, from the New World only.

At the opening of the Tsil Café, we wondered how familiar Robert Hingler's pre-Columbian food might become to Kansas City. After five years, most diners have found themselves in the Tsil Café for either the food or the dining experience. Now, looking at a noon menu of more ordinary food—burgers, sandwiches (even the familiar peanut butter and jelly), fries, chips, soups, potato salad—the lunch bunch will at least see familiar items.

And they'll be satisfied with the well-prepared, interesting fare. But we would be less than honest if we didn't warn that they'll also find Robert Hingler's strong sense of taste and texture. Leave it to Robert Hingler to spice even the catsup with chile powder. Or to take that blandest, most comforting of American picnic foods—the potato salad—and turn it into a church-supper nightmare full of hot peppers, tomatillos, and peanuts. Made with red, white, and blue potatoes, this salad reminded us of the Fourth of July, only the fireworks were all exploding in our mouth.

The meats were prepared expertly, and anyone who hasn't had a buffalo burger or a turkey burger (raw dark meat is ground, spiced, and shaped into a patty) needs to experience what should not be a novelty but a lunch option in more places in our city. The salads, too, are newly concocted for the lunch menu and should also be imitated at other establishments, though perhaps with less chile heat.

As always, we were impressed by Robert Hingler's ability to make Kansas City try something new. The *tsil* kachina, his totem, is the one who stuffs peppers in the mouths of runners overtaken in a foot race. Kansas City is slow afoot, and therefore Robert Hingler has ample opportunity to stuff our mouths with his spicy fare. We will continue to swallow, and learn what we can from this missionary of New World foods.

My father read the review upstairs, at the table, while my mother ate her usual breakfast of fruit and raw oats. My father had fried one egg for me and another for him, and I'd made a sandwich with my egg—bread, a cheese slice, and plenty of chile-laced catsup. My father smothered his egg in cheese and green chile sauce, and ate beans on the side, as in *huevos rancheros*. Suddenly, he left the table and stomped down the stairs.

My mother read the review and followed him. When I heard their sharpened voices, I took a place on the stairs, just out of sight about halfway down. "No," my mother said. "You're wrong this time."

"He didn't even have the decency to talk to me," said my father.

"He can do his job however he wants."

"You don't have to help him. How did he get the food?"

I began to back up the stairs, but still I heard my name from my mother's mouth.

"That little . . . ," my father said.

I slumped on the step.

"He's just a boy," said my mother. "Blame me."

"I do," said my father. "You helped him cheat. Flinn sat up there in your kitchen, eating my food, smelling your food, wishing he could have you."

"That's not fair."

"He's a lost calf. He bawls your name in the newspaper like you're weaning him. He can't give me a review without wishing you were his."

"You're forgetting one thing, Robert. *I* don't wish I was his, or he was mine. I can't tell him what to say about you."

"Fucking lunch business, anyway," said my father.

"You're doing well. Who cares what Carson Flinn says. If you don't respect him, what does it matter?"

"Doing well doesn't matter. My reputation does."

"Carson can't hurt your reputation."

"The lunch thing can."

"So throw Pablito out in the cold when Teresita's expecting a baby. Throw the extra money down a hole. Everybody likes your lunch, except you. And maybe Carson Flinn. Why should that make you angry?"

"I don't like how he got his meal. Wes betrayed me."

"Leave Wes out of this," said my mother. "Let's finish breakfast. We can talk when we have more time."

I scooted back to the table. When my mother and father came up, he ripped the review out of the newspaper. "I'm not posting it," he said.

"Fine." My mother finished her fruit.

My father slowly ate his egg. "Can I have some of yours, Daddy?" I asked him.

"Sure," he said. He put a forkful of egg white, cheese, and green chile sauce on my plate.

"Beans, too?" I asked.

My mouth burned when I ate my father's food, but the heat of chiles, though it starts with pain, becomes a remembered pleasure. "I like your cooking, Daddy," I said.

"That's my boy," he said.

When Ronald came in that day, bringing a friend for lunch, he handed my father a copy of Carson Flinn's review, torn from the newspaper. "I thought you'd want to see this," he said.

"I've seen it."

"Look at it," said Ronald.

My father took it and saw what Ronald wanted him to see, the word "Bullshit" scrawled over the print. "You could double the heat in that potato salad," said Ronald. "I'll be here to eat it."

"Thanks," said my father. "Yours is on the house today."

"You don't need to," said Ronald.

"Be quiet," said my father.

Ronald was very quiet, because Carson Flinn had walked into the Tsil. He talked with Pablito, then saw me and Ronald and my father by the stairs. "How's my Wes?" he said.

I approached him. Before I could stop myself, I kicked him in the shin as hard as I could.

Carson Flinn yelped and grabbed his leg. He jumped up and down in pain. He looked like a bear on a pogo stick.

Pablito ran for a chair. My father apologized. Carson Flinn sat down. "He kicked me," said Carson Flinn to my father. "Hard." Flinn had tears in his eyes and I thought he would cry.

My father looked at me sternly. "We don't kick," he said.

Then he and Pablito and Ronald burst out laughing. My father turned to Carson Flinn. "His first review," he said. "Sometimes it hurts when you're on the receiving end."

Carson Flinn held his leg. "That's not fair," he said.

"That's what I said," my father told him, "about your re-view. Give the man a glass of wine," he told Pablito. "And anything he wants from the Tsil. Except my wife." He turned to leave, but shouted over his shoulder, "Ronald eats free to-day." Then he went back to his kitchen.

I ran upstairs. "Carson Flinn's here," I told my mother.

"Good," she said. "He and your father can work things out."

HABANERO: HOT TRICKS

*M*y mother cooked alone, hiring help only for delivery or for serving large parties. She cooked in large quantities, but preferred solving problems of scale by herself. "Better," she said, "than solving personnel problems."

The Tsil Café required constant help. The same person cannot greet customers, tend bar, wait tables, cook, and wash dishes. When my father started, Pablito–his manager and bartender—brought Cocoa to the Tsil. "We worked a Mexican restaurant," he said, "but all they want is customers—not quality, not attention. They want the money." And then, laughing, he said, "Just like Americans, with the boof-ette." He never could pronounce *buffet*, and the way my father cooked, he would never have to. Cocoa was the only wait staff at first, which meant hard work but exclusive tips. Pablito and Cocoa made up for the losers my father hired to help in the kitchen: the "cutters" and the "dishers," as he called them. Those in the first category cut work as often as they showed up. Those in the second category dished him nothing but trouble. There was an Al, with only one eye. My father fired him because he couldn't judge size and shape well enough. Pete smoked so much his ashes ended up in the food, dusting a tamal or peppering the surface of a pudding. Stroop almost got my father's kitchen closed because he refused to wear a hair net or shoes. Sheila had a tattoo of a bug on her leg, and slapped at it as though it were real. So many came and went that I stopped trying to befriend them.

Pablito and Cocoa, though, were family. Pablito showed me particular interest after his marriage, during Teresita's pregnancy. In those days, as my father started the Tsil Buffalo, Pablito made up poems and songs, and I would catch him muttering. Now I think he was speaking to the son he wanted. One day, between lunch and dinner at the Tsil, he sat me down. *"Escúchame,"* he said, and he read a poem he'd scribbled on the back of a napkin:

¡QUÉ!
El perro gruñe al hombre de andrajos
¡Qué dientes!
El gato duerme en las rodillas de la reina
¡Qué seda!
El cerdo del bosque come todas las trufas
¡Qué rico!
El ratón pierde su rabo en la trampa
¡Qué cuerdecita!
El sol da un traspié y se cae
¡Qué noche!
¡Qué noche!

"What does it mean?" I asked.

"For the baby," Pablito said.

"It means *for the baby?*"

"No. Babies don't care for meaning."

"I'm not a baby." I was seven.

Pablito translated: "The dog growls at the man in his rags. What teeth on the dog. And the cat, he sleeps on the queen, her knees, her silk. The pig eats the truffles in the forest. That's rich. And the mouse loses his little tail in a trap. What a little string. The sun trips and falls. What night, what night!"

"What does it mean?" I asked again.

"Words," said Pablito, "for the baby."

I didn't ask again because he would say the same thing. My father rarely argued with him. Most of the time, Pablito was right. Like about the lunch business. And he'd convinced my father to feed Teresita every day. With his slight deformity, Pablito was smaller than most men. Teresita was big-boned, much taller than Pablito. Carrying their child huge in front of her, she looked twice Pablito's size, but the bigger she became, the prouder he was. He once took my hand and put it on Teresita's womb. "Look what I have done," he said.

Since we were like family, I was the older sibling, jealous of the pending arrival. Sometimes I wished Teresita was not there, that Pablito hadn't married.

"Will you be my little one's friend?" Pablito would ask me.

"I guess so," I'd say.

"I will bring him each day, so you will know him well."

"I don't like Teresita," I said to my mother one night.

"Did she say something? Or do something you didn't like?"

"Pablito's acting strange," I said.

"Don't blame Teresita. People don't stay the same. Pablito's happy. Be happy for him."

I tried, but with his poems, with the songs he sang under his breath, with the new confidence in his stride, and, worst, the intensity of his interest in me, I often failed. One day, in what must have been her ninth month, Teresita came into the Tsil and asked me to sit with her. She scooted the table so I had only a tiny crack of space to sit down. She stood over me. Pablito hummed at the bar. "All morning, he kicks me," said Teresita. "You want to put your fingers there?"

"No," I said.

She grabbed my hand and tried to press it to her womb. I struggled away, afraid. I ran upstairs to my mother's kitchen.

"I want to eat with you," I said.

"You want to be with your mother," she said.

I stopped eating lunch with Teresita.

Then one day, at the end of that long summer of Teresita's pregnancy, I was at my mother's table. My father knocked at the stairway wall. "Maria," he whispered hoarsely. "We need you."

His urgency frightened me. My mother came back upstairs, crying. She moaned, wiped her eyes, shook her head. Twice, she said my name and hugged me until I could hardly breathe. I cried, too.

Finally, she pushed me away and held my shoulders. "Look at me," she said. Her eyes were swollen and dripping with tears. "Teresita's lost her baby," she said. "It was stillborn at the hospital this morning. We don't know why."

I didn't understand. *Still born* and *lost* were the words, but her grief said much more. Then she said words I understood. "Their little baby is dead."

I began to wail. I couldn't stop crying. Eventually, when Pablito held me, I stopped. For him.

I don't remember a funeral. I remember Pablito, slumped at the bar. "Recovering," my mother called it.

"Drinking," my father called it.

Pablito wrote one more poem and, with a sad smile, said part of it over and over one afternoon. "*Palitas abren la tierra, y estas sonrisas tragan semillas en una noche sin luna, sin estrellas.*"

"What's he saying?" I asked my father.

"Something about a shovel opening the earth and swallowing seeds. About a night without moon or stars." My father admired Pablito's songs and verses. But he was worried. "He's going a little crazy," my father told me.

"What does going crazy mean?" I asked Cocoa.

"Be glad you don't know," she said. She rolled her eyes. "When you find out, it's going to be too late."

"Daddy says Pablito is going crazy," I said to my mother.

"He's trying to understand why he has no son," she said.

"Are you still sad?" I asked her.

"Very," she said.

I knew I should be sad, too, but Pablito's grief was as present as his pride had been. Teresita disappeared along with the baby she never had.

After several months of grieving, during the Thanksgiving holiday, Pablito pulled up to the Tsil early one morning in a truck loaded with a chair, a mattress, a lamp, and a writing desk. My mother looked out our front room window. My father went to talk to Pablito. I followed.

"*El Señor* Hingler," said Pablito, and he took off his hat. "My Teresita and me, we cannot stop the fighting. I need to be out. To think."

"Where did you have in mind?" asked my father. Even I knew what Pablito wanted.

"*El sótano, por favor.*"

"*Un mes, sólo.*"

"*Gracias,*" said Pablito. He ran to unload his things into our basement before my father could change his mind. He moved two storage shelves, then hung a sheet on a line strung between them. The middle of the sheet opened like a pup-tent flap but without strings to tie it closed.

My father's one month, *sólo*, turned to two, then three, then nine months. Pablito became quieter, and thinner. Sometimes, my father sent me to the basement on an errand. Sometimes the errand was to wake Pablito from his siesta so that he might greet diners arriving for a drink before the kitchen opened. "And tell him to shower," my father sometimes yelled down the stairs after me, loud enough for Pablito to hear.

The little man lay on his mattress, his arms covering his eyes. He was the opposite of Teresita. I'd sneaked down to look at her fullness, at the huge ballooning of her womb. Pablito was a burst balloon, rumpled, wrinkled, thin as a string. When I touched his arm, he would gently move both

arms to his sides and fix my eyes in a gaze that terrified me:
He was grief and sadness; the portrait of the miserable; the
heartached, the pool-eyed, the sallow-skinned, the frozen-
faced. He was a wretched man.

"What can we do?" my father asked my mother.

"He was expecting his son for nine months. Let him
grieve for that long. He'll pull out of it, poor man."

The nine months became a year and a half. "Enough time
to gestate an elephant," said my father.

By the time I was nine, my father began to complain seri-
ously. On Monday, the day neither of my parents cooked,
they had what they called "meetings."

"He's drinking more and more."

"You could consider the wine as a raise."

"If I want to give him a raise, I'll give him a raise. Two
bottles of wine every day isn't a raise, it's a problem."

"You could threaten him," said my mother. "But you'd
have to follow up on it."

"Cocoa says if he goes, she goes," my father said.

"So?" said my mother.

"I need Cocoa."

"Then keep them."

Pablito continued to live in the basement. My father continued to threaten him with eviction. Cocoa went somewhere
else to sleep, but from ten-thirty in the morning to eleven at
night, Tuesday through Sunday, she was at the Tsil. Every
time my father threatened Pablito, Cocoa cornered him.
"You see how far you get without him. Without me," she'd

say. Or, "I see where loyalty gets you around here." Or, "Be glad you got no problems, 'cause we'll remember how you treated us when we got 'em."

One Saturday afternoon, when I was eleven, I heard Pablito and Cocoa's voices in the basement during Pablito's siesta time. I didn't hesitate to walk down.

I shouldn't have stopped on the stairs to watch them for as long as I did. Through the split in the sheet Pablito had hung, I saw them, naked. She lay on his mattress. He was on his knees between her legs, facing me, but with his eyes closed. I was mesmerized: by Cocoa's creamy brown breasts, and by the way Pablito gently touched them; by her muscular arms thrown back behind her head; by the blackness of her tuft of pubic hair and by the way Pablito's stiff penis, purple as an ear of ornamental corn, bobbed above her legs. Pablito muttered in Spanish, and Cocoa spoke such a stream of words I couldn't understand her. They seemed to want to fill the space between them with sound. I stood rooted to the stair until Pablito moved into Cocoa, and I felt a stiffness of my own. I ran away.

My father saw me breathless at the top of the stairs. "Quick," I said. "Mom wants you. I've been looking for you."

"In the basement? With the help? They're not help when they're resting." He followed me upstairs. "Help?" he shouted in mock seriousness. "Help!"

My mother sat in her kitchen chair, reading. "We came to move the bay tree," I lied. "I heard you say it needed sun on the other side."

"That's sweet, Wes. But Pablito and I moved it yesterday."

"So you don't need help in the kitchen," said my father.

"Pablito seems a little better, doesn't he?"

"Thank God," said my father. "His face was getting longer than When Available's tongue on a hot day."

Over the next several months, whenever I was home, I edged toward the basement stairs. If Pablito and Cocoa suspected my snooping, neither said anything. They never pulled the sheet together, as if unafraid of who might see what. I felt awkward around them, for in seeing them I had found my own persistent penis.

By the time I turned twelve, I had learned something of self-stimulation, and though I tried not to watch them, I couldn't help myself. I didn't know what would make them, or me, stop.

Then one day, I sat on the stair just out of their sight, waiting to hear their voices. I knew the lower, breathier, supplicating tone of desire: Just hearing it made me tremble. I realized I wasn't really anticipating them. I was waiting for myself, for my own fantasy.

I was lost in that thought when Cocoa screamed and rushed up the stairs in her slip. I couldn't have run or hidden. She slapped my face. Then she turned to shout down the stairs: "Never again. You hear me?"

She stared into my eyes. "Never again," she said quietly.

I couldn't look at her. My face stung, and my eyes were full of tears. She went downstairs, put on her dress, and brushed by me on the stairs. I worried that my father or mother would hear the commotion and ask me what was happening, so I hurried outside and leashed When Available for a walk.

Cocoa was right to be angry with me. She'd been angry with Pablito for something, maybe taking advantage of her on his mattress behind the sheet in the basement. But I'd taken advantage of her, too. I'd told myself not to, but I'd done it anyway.

"I need a bedroom of my own," I said to my parents that night.

"You have your bed," said my mother.

"It's not a bedroom, it's a bed closet." I stood up. "I'm getting bigger."

"He's not going to be a boy forever," my father said.

"I could fix up the basement," I said. "If Pablito wasn't there."

"So we just tell him to leave?" asked my mother.

"It's the excuse we need," said my father.

"He counts on us," said my mother.

"You care more about him than you do about me, don't you?" I accused my mother.

"He drinks our booze," said my father. "He's scaring away more customers than he's attracting. Ronald took me aside the other day and said so."

"He's been with Cocoa in the basement, on the mattress. I saw it," I blurted.

"Saw what?" said my mother.

"You watched them?" asked my father. "They shouldn't be down there doing that."

"What were they doing?" asked my mother.

I couldn't describe it. The only names for it I knew were naughty words.

"Wes?" asked my mother.

"They were doing *it*," I said.

"Don't make him tell the details," said my father. "He's told us enough. Pablito needs shaking up more than sympathy."

"We'll lose him," said my mother.

"We've already lost him," said my father. "And I don't want him taking any of us with him."

"I think you're wrong," said my mother.

I was hoping my father would win this argument. "I'm getting bigger," I repeated, "and I need a bedroom."

"We'll build you one," said my father. "No sheet hung between the shelves for you."

"Please?" I begged my mother.

"For you," she said.

Pablito was gone in a week. In another, my father—always ambivalent about the menu and impatient crowd—quit serving lunch. One noon my mother came down to an empty dining room, the morning paper in her hand. My father had stopped serving lunch two days before. Carson Flinn had written about it before my father told her. "I knew you'd figure it out soon. If you were paying attention," my father said.

> **Note:** If you've eaten at the Tsil Buffalo, the lunch menu of Robert Hingler's Tsil Café, then you'll miss

Kansas City's only buffalo and turkey burgers. Hingler stopped serving lunch this week. Evening dining is still available, from the familiar Tsil menu, from 5:00 P.M.–9:00 P.M.

"Don't count on my money if you lose income."

"With Pablito gone, I'll save money. Cocoa's agreed to manage. I've given her a raise. She's not exactly happy, but she'll get used to things."

"She's not seeing Pablito?" my mother asked.

"She said she just couldn't stand to see him so miserable," my father reported. "*So hungry,* she said. You've got to admit he was misery in a nutshell."

"Some of us are sympathetic." My mother spoke with an edge, as though she were commenting on two things at once. She was angry with my father, but I didn't know why.

I was the only happy one. Soon, I wasn't thinking about the stairs, wasn't planning my afternoon so I'd end up there, peeking into the basement. I would have my own space.

With two-by-fours and plywood sheets my parents and I built walls. I covered them with posters and with pictures from the food magazines my mother subscribed to. We bought a carpet remnant for the floor. We shopped for used furniture and I chose a bed, a dresser, a table for a desk, and two chairs. We hung a rod across one corner for my clothes. Both my parents loved work. They were good builders, movers, arrangers. We had fun together. The last thing to go on was the door. My father let me have a lock, but with one rule: He'd tear the door out if I ever locked myself in. "I did that once," he said. "Drove my parents crazy. I was so proud of my ornery self."

"You still are," said my mother.

My parents came down for an inspection once I finally moved. "Nice," my mother said. "I'll miss you, but you're growing so big, and I'm proud of you." I was twelve, but not big. I was thin and gangly. "Knobs and strings," my father said. "Like me when I was your age."

My parents had always had spats. They were both stubborn. But once, during the last spring that I was making kachina heads, my mother came to the kitchen door and called my father into the still-empty dining room of the Tsil Café. She told him she was going to close Buen AppeTito for a time and go somewhere new to find fresh ideas and rethink her food. I'd never heard her talk about leaving. I turned off the boiling pot and moved closer to the door.

My father reminded her that the first time she'd gone somewhere for fresh ideas she'd met him, and ended up rethinking a lot more than food. He sounded nervous. "You shouldn't go," he said.

"For two weeks?" she said. "It's my business, my money, my life."

"What happened to our life, our money? Us?" he asked. "What about Wes?"

"Wes is fine," she said. "This has nothing to do with Wes."

"Then it has to do with us," said my father. "Leaving doesn't deal with us."

"Sometimes, you have to follow your heart," said my

mother. "My heart is telling me to learn more, travel a little, do something fresh."

"Everything we do here is fresh," insisted my father. "We're unique—your catering, my restaurant. We invented fresh."

"Once, yes," she said. "Don't you ever want fresh ideas? You ever wonder why Carson doesn't do a new review of the Tsil? He told me until you change your menu, he can only mention you."

"Tell Carson I stick with things. My food. The way I eat. My marriage. I don't flirt to get my name in the paper."

In the silence, I held my breath, afraid of being discovered. Already, I'd heard more than I wanted to. But I couldn't leave my place beside the door.

"You can be so self-righteous," my mother finally said. "And hurtful. You don't care about anything but yourself."

"And my food."

"I was hoping you might include me," she said. "But, no. You're just like the father you try so hard to be different from: stubborn, closed-minded, unadventurous."

"My food is adventurous!" my father yelled.

"Ten years ago!" my mother yelled back.

"I have specials!" yelled my father.

More silence. I stood in my father's kitchen, surrounded by corn, cayenne, and achiote seeds. I'd make his kachina heads while my parents lost their heads.

"You don't treat *me* like I'm special," said my mother. "I need an adventure. Give me some breathing room."

"You're true to type yourself," said my father. "Just like *your* father—can't quite stick with anything but yourself. The little orphan, afraid to get too close, got to have your precious breathing room."

"I don't have to ask you for it. I can just take it," she said. Her footsteps took her up the stairs, to her kitchen. I turned on the burner under the water again, to bring it to a boil. I began to cut cayenne into little whips.

My father finally came back into the kitchen to work on a special. He whistled between his teeth, something he did only when he was nervous. He was a terrible whistler.

"Where do you think Pablito is?" I asked.

"Why do you want to know?"

"I don't know. Is Mom going to leave?"

"You heard her," he said. "You know as much as I do."

"Doesn't she love us?" I asked.

"She loves you, very much," he said. Then he smiled, as though the joke was on him. "Me? Well, she's still wondering."

The following week, my mother was gone. "For a week, Wes," she told me the day before she went. "Remember, I'm not leaving you. I'm not leaving your father. I'm just going away for a time. Your father and I had a fight. We have before and we will again. But we love each other."

"Thanks," I told her. I appreciated hearing her say it, but I knew I'd be worried until she was home again.

"San Francisco," she said the next day when she hugged me good-bye. "I've never really mastered seafood."

A taxi honked, and she was off, nothing but her purse and a shoulder bag for luggage. My father and I stood in the doorway of the Tsil Café.

"Is she still mad at you?" I asked.

"I don't know," he said.

"You're supposed to tell me everything's going to be all right," I said.

"Sorry," he said. "Maybe it's just seafood, like she says. She's crabby. She's coming out of her shell. She's flexing some mussel shells. Who knows?" He clapped me on the shoulder. "Everything's going to be all right, Wes. If you can keep your sense of humor."

He kept his sense of humor when he read Carson Flinn's food note:

> **Note:** We are empty with the word that Buen AppeTito—Maria Tito Hingler—has flown to San Francisco for an infusion of knowledge about shellfish. Our only solace is the anticipation of her return, and those first bites of the new experiments she's promised.

"The old dog," my father said. "Someday he's going to be When Available."

Our week went very well. I thought my father would be cranky, irritable, worried. I thought I would be, too. But we had fun. We ate together, planned together, played games—things we hadn't done for a long time. "We make pretty good bachelors," said my father.

"Don't you miss Mommy?" I asked.

"Of course," he said. "But you can have a good time even when you miss someone."

My mother returned with her sense of humor intact. She had hugs for us both, genuine kisses for my father. I was relieved. She was tanned from time on the beach. She forced us to the airport the next day where we picked up a barrel of shellfish on ice. My father had little experience with seafood himself, so she unpacked the barrel in her kitchen and showed him what she'd learned. They talked food, which they always had in common, and they cooked together, and they ate, and drank wines she'd brought home from vineyard tours. For a brief time, all seemed right with the world.

BUEN APPETITO CRAB CAKES WITH PINEAPPLE-MANGO SALSA

CRAB CAKES

1 stick butter, divided

½ cup red and green bell pepper, diced

Garlic, minced, to taste

¼ cup red onion, chopped fine

1 pound or more crabmeat

½ cup artichoke hearts

¼–½ cup Parmesan cheese

2 large or 3 medium eggs

2 leaves fresh basil

Cayenne, black pepper, and salt, to taste

1 cup bread crumbs, divided

Melt half the butter into skillet and add peppers, garlic, and onion. Sauté until soft. Add crabmeat and artichoke hearts and combine. Add the cheese, eggs, seasonings to taste, and half the bread crumbs. Make into cakes using about ⅓ cup of mixture, and refrigerate for at least half an hour.

Melt remaining butter until almost smoking, dredge cakes in remaining bread crumbs, and cook for a short time, until golden brown and the egg is done. Serve with Pineapple-Mango Salsa.

PINEAPPLE-MANGO SALSA

1 cup pineapple*
1 cup mango
4 cloves garlic, minced
Jalapeño, minced
½ cup cilantro, chopped
½ cup chopped scallions
Small amount cider vinegar

Put pineapple, mango, garlic, and jalapeño in food processor and blend just enough to mix. Add cilantro, scallions, and vinegar and let sit for an hour. Serve with crab cakes.

*Pineapple (pine-apple): *Called piña de las Indias by Columbus for its physical resemblance to the pine cone, the pineapple actually originated in Brazil. Columbus found it in Guadaloupe on his second voyage to the New World, on November 4, 1493. A courtier of Spain's Ferdinand wrote: "In appearance, shape, and color, this scale-coated fruit*

resembles the pine cone; but in softness is the melon's equal; in flavor it
surpasses all garden fruits. To it the king awards the palm." Sweet,
syrupy, equally tart fresh or dried, raw or cooked, the pineapple quickly
found its way around the globe and was incorporated into many cuisines.

Then my mother hired Pablito to help her deliver large catering jobs. My father objected. "Buen AppeTito is my business," she said. "I can hire whoever I want. He desperately needs the work. When he's driving, he's promised me he won't drink."

I avoided Pablito. My father did, too. Like Carson Flinn, Pablito was a wedge between my parents.

All through my thirteenth year, my father was irritable. Sometimes, I asked my mother about him.

"He misses the old Pablito. The one who jollied customers. Who could help them negotiate the Tsil Café menu. And look at Cocoa."

Cocoa was angry. When she demanded yet another raise, he gave it to her. "About time," she said. He was irritated with her, too.

When my mother was irritable, I asked my father about her. "You reach a certain age," my father said, "and you question yourself a little. You want things different, but you don't know what. You question everything—your marriage, your food, your friends, where you live."

"Do you?"

"Not as much as your mother. But it's a natural thing."

My father had been in the restaurant business for twelve years. He spent more time being irritated with things outside the Tsil than he was with me or my mother. He disliked finicky eaters. And people with conventional food tastes. And the assistant cook so drunk when he showed up at four o'clock he risked putting pieces of his fingers and thumbs in the dishes. And city inspectors. And liquor distributors who thought his selection too small to bother with. And women who left the food on their plates covered with lipstick-smudged linen napkins, the food and cosmetics hell to remove until he changed his color scheme to burnt orange, almost brown: "Like a pumpkin with a tan," he said.

He was happiest when he was cooking, or visiting with customers like Ronald, who admired his unique food. He liked people who were generous with his help. He liked artists and musicians and writers, and the Bohemians among the students at the nearby medical school, and the young who enjoyed his food but couldn't afford it very often, and the old who dined at the Tsil for its reputation.

Most of all, my father liked the chileheads who craved the heat, the pain, the sweat, and finally the actual endorphin rush that kept them eating hot peppers. Like the *tsil* of the Hopi, he'd challenged everyone to a footrace, had ended up stuffing hot peppers into a lot of mouths. Of all the chileheads, a few could not be outrun: the habanero eaters.

The habanero, a two-inch Chinese lantern, shines orange in the garden, a little bell that clangs in the mouth and vibrates the skull. In late summer and fall, my father kept a basket of home-grown habaneros on the bar of the Tsil Café. If anyone asked, he would call the habanero "the little pepper with the sweet heat."

"How hot?" the uninitiated might ask.

"Not very," he'd say, and he'd pluck one from the basket, hold it by the stem above his head, and lower it toward his mouth. "How *sweet* it is," he'd say, and bite off the bottom.

He never suffered from this macho display, or he never let a customer see his pain. His eyes would light up, his lips part in a smile, and he'd hand the habanero over. "Go ahead," he'd say, "the next bite is yours."

The guy might take it, the second third of it or so, and begin to chew, hesitate as the searing heat burned from tongue to throat. Finally, his sinuses would catch fire, and his nose might run. Some sneezed in uncontrollable fits. Some spat the habanero onto the bar. Some gasped for water, the semi-aficionados begged for salt. But all of them, and everyone watching, would slap my father on the back in admiration. In those moments, he forgot his irritation. He was the *tsil* hero.

In the late summer of my thirteenth year, after I'd burned my hands, after Juan and Conseca had gone home, when I was no longer cutting corn or making kachina heads, I often sat in the restaurant, reading a book, playing cards with whoever came by, listening to my portable radio.

The food distributor showed up. For the Tsil, my father needed fruits like pineapple, tomato, and strawberry; vegetables like potato, sweet potato, squash, and corn; and lots of chiles, all year-round. He was often unhappy with the quality he received. My mother, who used the same distributor for Buen AppeTito that he used for the Tsil Café, made do. My father switched companies often, like a gambler switches horses: not because he expects to win, but because he needs fresh hope.

Santori Produce usually delivered high-quality goods. But the delivery man, a little guy, not much taller than I was at thirteen, with a puffy chest and a light wisp of a beard, irritated my father.

"He's a sweet boy," I heard my mother say once.

"You're sweet on him," said my father.

"No," said my mother.

"Then he's sweet on you," said my father.

"I'm probably twice his age."

"I'm twice his age," said my father, "and he pays me no respect."

Around and around they'd go.

That late summer afternoon, after the young man had spent an hour upstairs delivering to my mother, he came into the Tsil kitchen with the few boxes my father had ordered. My father opened the chile box and raked through the habaneros.

"Brown spots," my father complained.

"I just deliver the stuff," the little guy said.

"And gab. You gab upstairs while my order grows brown spots."

"Hey," said the produce man, "tell it to my boss. My customers like me. My boss likes me."

"Even my wife likes you," said my father. He picked up a habanero. "But you're not earning a living being liked. You're earning a living delivering food. And it's not good food."

"I deliver what the guys pack," said the young man. "I don't do quality."

"You don't *know* quality. You're not even man enough to eat one of these, let alone know its quality."

"What?"

"Sure," said my father. He held the habanero up in the air, let it dangle like a little bell. "You see this? My boy there can eat this and not flinch. But you'd be begging the saints for delivery from the fires of hell."

"You're talking to a guy who likes peppers," said the produce man.

"Let me guess," said my father, "pepperoncinis, like you deliver to my wife upstairs? The ones shaped like your shriveled little self."

The produce man took a deep breath and set his jaw.

"Pepperoncinis," said my father. "They're for babies to cut teeth on." My father often made challenges like this, exaggerated boasting the preliminary to eating something really hot. But this time he'd included me. I reached for my radio, to leave, but my father pointed me back into my seat.

The little Santori man, all red-faced now, did not know the game. "I'm no baby," he said, looking back and forth between me and the habanero.

"Come on over, Wes," said my father. "Show loverboy how to eat something really hot."

I didn't want to, but I approached the bar. My father poured two glasses of water and brought out some salt. My experience with cayennes had taught me how peppers could burn. I went behind the counter and whispered, "I've never eaten one."

"Only the bottom. Just below where it starts to thicken. Swallow your bite whole," he whispered.

"What're you saying?" asked the Santori man.

"He wants a hotter one. A bigger one," said my father. "But this one'll do, I told him." He held the habanero high in the air, as he did for himself, and lowered it into my mouth.

I bit. Anything else would have been a betrayal of my father. I felt a flair of heat on my lips, then tongue, and swallowed. My throat burned, like when I'd tried tequila, but no worse. And then the pain was gone.

"Salt?" asked my father. "Water?"

I shook my head. "It's sweet," I said, and smiled. I found it easy to play his game. "Sweet heat."

My father clapped me on the back. "Your turn," he said to the produce man. "If you think you can out-eat a thirteen-year-old."

The Santori man grabbed the pepper from my father, bit the second third or so, and chewed.

I'd seen every kind of reaction in the Tsil Café, but I'd never seen what this man did. He froze, then buckled onto his knees and fainted. My father ran around the bar and threw a glass of water on him. He woke up spitting seeds and pulp. He reached into his mouth and pulled out pepper flesh. My father handed him the other glass of water, and the man drank. "Flush it with salt," said my father. The produce man shook salt onto his palm and licked like an animal. I felt sorry for him.

My father did not. "Some people call themselves men," he said. "Tell your boss I don't want to clean up after you again. My wife and I have a new distributor coming next week. Someone who knows food. Hot and mild. Quality or crap." He put the habaneros with the brown spots in a little box on the floor next to the man. "Maybe you and your boss can eat these. Learn how to be men."

The little Santori man stood up. "Fuck you," he said. "And your little boy, too. Cauterized mouths, both of you. Can't taste nothing. I don't need hot peppers to be a man. Ask your wife." He hurried out before my father could find something to throw at him.

The Santori truck roared down the street. My father clapped me on the back. "You okay?" he asked.

I shook salt into my mouth, let my saliva turn it to salt water. "I am," I said. "But tell me *why* I am."

"You didn't get the real heat," he said. He explained what most chileheads know. The heat of any pepper is not in the flesh or the seeds, but in the membrane that holds the seeds to the flesh. The bottom third of the pepper has almost no membrane. "Anyone can eat the tip of a habanero," he said.

"I shouldn't be proud?" I asked.

"You helped me out. If that little man knew anything about the food he delivers, he wouldn't have fallen for that trick."

"You trick a lot of people," I said. "That's not fair."

"I only trick people who need tricking," he said. "I've never played a trick on you. You're my son. You can know me, tricks and all. Like your mother does. Now go on up and tell her what happened. Tell her I've switched us back to Lombard's Vegetables. She'll want some company about now. A guy like you, who knows peppers. Ask her to give you some cottage cheese."

I started away, but turned when he called my name.

"You want to finish this habanero?" he asked. He held the deadly top third above his mouth.

"No."

"Then I will." He took it into his mouth and pulled out only the stem.

I waited for him to show the heat, but he just smiled. "I don't need tricks," he said. Whatever else I felt—awkward because he'd used me to get at the produce man, bewildered because he'd revealed his jealousy so plainly, embarrassed because he'd been so macho—I was proud to see him eat the top part of that habanero without flinching.

When I went upstairs, my mother wasn't there. She didn't have a catering job, and her van was parked in the alley. I went down to tell my father I couldn't find her. "Maybe she took a walk," he said. "Let's walk, too." I leashed When Available, to give him some exercise, and we started out.

We didn't get far. We saw Pablito's old truck parked down the street, right around the corner. "She wasn't upstairs?" my father asked. "Did you look in all the rooms?"

"I shouted for her," I said.

"And she didn't answer. Of course she didn't answer.

Damn it!" He turned and ran back to the Tsil. I followed him, dragging When Available behind me. I turned him loose into the garden lot. My father bounded up the stairs.

"Maria?" he shouted. I climbed the stairs behind him.

Only silence answered. A waiting silence. A silence that said something terrible was going to happen, and that I couldn't avoid it, or my part in it. My father and I stood in the kitchen, holding our breath, listening to nothing. But something was there.

Then I saw the pots on the kitchen counter, where my mother never put pots unless she was cooking. The cabinet under the counter was ajar, and I went to it. I opened it, bent over, and looked inside. It was empty. But of course it was full. Of memory and foreboding.

I pushed down the thin backing of the cabinet. My mother screamed. My father dived for the floor. Through the little doorway, we saw the naked legs of my mother and of Pablito. The little closet room was littered with their clothes. "No," said my father.

I left the room, went to the basement, and locked my door in spite of my father's rule. I had seen too much, been party to my father seeing too much. I hated the sight of Pablito's thin brown legs, my mother's thick white ones, tangled together, hopping for clothes. I had betrayed my mother, just as she had betrayed my father, and me. I had betrayed Pablito again, too. I felt doomed to be the one who saw things, the one drawn into dramas to play a part I had not auditioned for. I sat on my bed and imagined myself sitting on the stairs, watching myself, wondering about the large forces shaping my life. I hadn't asked for any of them: Teresita's pregnancy, Pablito and Cocoa's sex, my father's jealousies, my mother's sex with Pablito. *Did anyone control these things?* I wondered.

I decided to watch more closely. For over a year I'd sensed an undercurrent in my parents' marriage. But I hadn't studied it, learned it, understood it. And so everything had been a surprise to me. I vowed not to be surprised again.

INFIERNO:
REVENGE IS HELL

*M*y parents made up gradually. My father pulled a cot downstairs and slept in the basement, though not in my room, for a couple of weeks. Sometimes he seemed like Teresita: full of something. Sometimes like Pablito: tired of something. My mother stayed upstairs in her kitchen, my father in his. If they talked, I didn't hear them.

One night, I woke up and went upstairs to the bathroom. When I came back down, in the light from the lamp in my room, I saw my father's face, asleep. I wondered when he'd wrinkled under his eyes, where he'd found the deep line between chin and bottom lip, the one that spoke of grimness. His forehead, too, was lined: a stepladder of worries climbing his skull. His hairline had retreated and the hair on his temples had thinned. I was going through puberty, and finding new hair all over. He was forty-something, and losing things, I thought.

My mother's eyes seemed always pooled with tears. I wondered if she was sleeping well. Her first gray hairs straggled out of her braid. Her neck had thickened, puffy and wrinkled. Her strong and capable hands had spots and the skin on the tops of her fingers bagged slightly, as though one size too big.

Alone, they looked their age. Together, they were always too busy, animated, conspiratorial, and argumentative to judge. I wished they were back together.

One night I went upstairs for a little help with homework. I stopped at the kitchen door. My mother stood looking out her south-facing window. My father saw me and tried to smile. He poured two glasses of red wine. He clinked them together, and looked at me. "To what we have together, Maria. The catering, the restaurant, our Wes. Let's not destroy them."

She turned quickly, saw me, and turned away. "I wasn't trying to destroy them," she said.

My father took her a glass. "I'm trying to understand, not accuse," he said.

"Wes," said my mother. "Leave."

I left. I didn't see my father on the basement cot that night, or for the next several. I wanted that to mean they were making peace. We ate together, and I didn't see much evidence in their measured statements, their polite *please pass*es, or my mother's *I'll be catering a reception downtown tonight*.

One morning—when she'd been awake long enough to prepare my father a crab-filled crepe—she said, "Pablito will not be working here anymore, in case you want to know." She looked at the floor.

My father took a bite of crepe. "These are wonderful," he said.

"I'm glad you like them," she said.

Neither of them mentioned what still haunted me: my mother's scream when I kicked in the cabinet panel, the sight of bare legs, a clothing-strewn floor.

One night, as we finished some mushroom soup, my father asked my mother if she thought he should add salmon to his menu.

"How can you talk about fish?" I blurted out.

"What do you mean, Wes?" asked my mother.

"I don't know," I said. I wanted to say, *What are you doing talking about fish when I need to know if everything is going to be all right. That I'll have a mother and a father, and a place to live.* "You're talking, but I don't know what you're saying," I said finally. "About our family."

"It's going to get better," said my father.

"I'm truly sorry, Robert. And Wes. Sometimes I do things impulsively, like I'm looking for what I never had."

"You've *had* sex," said my father.

"Attention and love. I've had those, too," said my mother. "But I'm so hungry for them sometimes. I don't know what to do." Her face curled with pain.

I didn't know what to say, or to do. Whatever she was *looking for,* as she called it, I couldn't be the one to give it to her. But I could comfort her, and I did. I hugged her, pulling on her braid, as I had when I was a child.

"Thank you, Wes," she said.

The following week, something happened that I'd never seen before. My mother marched into my father's kitchen, where he was glumly cooking a special designed to give his customers something they'd never had before. I was snacking after school. She carried a glass of wine and some endive soaked in basalmic vinegar. "To what we have," she said. "Our appetites."

"May we use them on each other sometime?" asked my father.

"I'll drink to that," she said. She took a gulp of wine, swallowed it, and kissed him.

I cleared my throat, embarrassed by my mother's passion and my father's obvious delight.

"You want us to make up?" she asked me.

"Not in front of me," I said.

"Don't worry," said my father. "This is just the appetizer, not the meal."

His smile angered me. My mother had been indiscreet already, with her infidelity with Pablito. I'd had my nose rubbed in their sexual feelings, misfires, seductions, and jealousies. "I don't find it very appetizing," I said. I pushed hard on the doors of his kitchen, let them swing back like the doors in a Western bar room.

Fact is, I was curious about their making up. I wanted to see it, to know about it, but I was embarrassed by it, too. This awkward time became more awkward one night when I started up from the basement to say good night. My mother and father were laughing over a late dinner at her kitchen table. "Like a little piece of corn," shrieked my mother. I stopped short.

"Friends, Romans, countrymen, lend me your tiny ear," my father said. They both laughed again.

I was certain they were talking about Pablito's penis. But they didn't know I'd thought it a piece of corn myself, and I knew if I went into her kitchen and interrupted them, somehow they'd know. "Good night," I yelled from the top step. I left them to themselves. I wanted them to make up, but as they became closer after my mother's infidelity, I found myself out in the cold, abandoned to the basement, coming up only to interrupt their intensity. I wanted them to quit making up and just be together again, like when I was a child.

One morning, we ate sweet rolls at the breakfast table. "Are you guys going to stay married?" I asked.

"I am," said my mother immediately.

"That's what we're working on," said my father.

"People can love each other very much, and still hurt each other," she said.

"And fight," said my father.

"But they stay together," said my mother.

"Because they want to be together in the long run," said my father. "And the longer you stay together, the longer you've been together, and the balance keeps tipping in your favor."

"How romantic," said my mother.

"I'm here," said my father.

"Me, too," said my mother. "And don't worry, Wes."

"Are we going to be like we used to be?" I asked.

"No," said my father. "You can't just go back to something. You have to move forward."

They moved forward, and backstepped, too. Some nights, I'd find my father down on the little cot in the basement. But we'd go back up to the family kitchen the next morning to eat breakfast with my mother.

Some days, I'd come home from school and find my bed wrinkled, and a couple of Lucky Strike butts in a coffee mug on the floor. "Sometimes," said my father, "I just need to get away, and rest. Your room is the perfect place. Hope you don't mind."

I did, but I didn't want to say so. Just when I thought they'd made up, I'd find him on the cot in the basement, or his cigarette butts next to my bed, or he'd start talking about a new special to stuff in the mouths of his customers.

Cocoa had to sell these almost impossible specials, all of them with names that included the words *incendiary* and *diabolical* and *fuego*. Without asking my father, she hired a friend, Misty, to wait tables. "I need help, even if you don't think I do," I heard her tell him. "I'll pay her myself if I have to."

"She looks thirteen," my father said.

"She's old enough," said Cocoa. "People like a young thing."

She looked sixteen or seventeen to me, and I certainly thought I could like her. She had big brown eyes, lips with a natural pout. She was thin, but moved with grace and balance, like a dancer.

My father shook his head. "Misty. Everybody has a nickname instead of a name these days."

"It's her real name," said Cocoa. "Believe me, she'll work hard. Leave her to me."

My father cheered up only when Cocoa proved to be right: Misty could sell specials. She'd announce it to a table, then wink, then say, "I'll just let you think about it for a minute." They couldn't help but watch her move gracefully back to the bar. When she returned, they wanted to do something to please her.

Cocoa caught me watching her one evening. "*She*'s the waitress, Wes," she said. "She waits on you. You don't wait on her. You're both too young."

After closing, I sometimes ate leftovers. Misty often joined me. She enjoyed eating unsold specials as much as she enjoyed trying to sell them. "Anything to eat is better than the not much I grew up with," she told me. She liked my father, and the Tsil food. Sometimes she seemed to like me.

Of course, some dishes were impossible to sell. I remember an afternoon cooking with my father in the kitchen of the Tsil several months after we'd discovered my mother's infidelity with Pablito. He talked to me as though he were talking to himself, and I wondered if he even knew I was there. "So I'm stuck with thirty chile-covered turkey breasts, ready to blacken. *Too spicy*, they complain. They come in here because they want spice. The menu says spice. I got more warning labels on my food than you can find on rat poison. They can't read?"

Customers didn't need to read to understand the menu. Flames flared up the black cover, and the letters of Tsil Café dripped, as melted as candle wax, in the heat. Inside, little árbol chiles, like the ones he hung in miniature ristras in the kitchen, served as a heat index. "These fiery specials," my mother asked him one day, "how can they help business? Even your new desserts aren't desserts. Habanero Pumpkin Pudding with Ancho Maple Sauce? It's spicier than some of your appetizers."

"It's good," I defended my father.

"I like a cool dessert," she sighed.

HABANERO PUMPKIN PUDDING
WITH ANCHO MAPLE SAUCE

PUDDING

2 cups pumpkin,* boiled

2 habanero peppers, seeded (½ for the sane)

3 allspice seeds, ground

3 tablespoons New Mexico red chile powder (1 for the mild)

Maple syrup to taste—usually ½ cup

Salt to taste

Blend the ingredients together and refrigerate. Top with sauce.

ANCHO MAPLE SAUCE

2 large anchos,** seeded and cut into small pieces
    (½ for the tame)

1 cup maple syrup

1 tablespoon hot pepper vinegar

Dash of salt

Combine ingredients and simmer until very thick. Spoon onto pudding.

*Pumpkin (pompions, to the Plymouth colonists): *Like other squashes, the pumpkin has been in cultivation for so long, and so pervasively, that its origin is unknown. The Middle East and Asia culti-vated it at the same time pre-Columbian natives counted it a chief crop.*

Plains Indians dried pumpkins and made the strips into mats, useful for sitting or sleeping on until needed for food. Pumpkin varieties are endless in color, shape, texture, and uses (from the shell as a storage container to the seed paste as an agent used to tan hides). Pumpkins helped keep the Plymouth colonists from starving and were part of the celebrated feast Americans imitate at Thanksgiving. Now pumpkins are more symbolic than they are a critical difference in survival: There is the occasional pumpkin pie, but of the millions of pumpkins sold every year, around 90 percent rot after they are carved into jack-o'-lanterns or set out on porches and byways for adornment.

**Ancho (mild chile, name is "wide" in Spanish): *Like a good wine, this chile has "tones": earthy, chocolate. Because it is fleshy, it adds body to any dish without overpowering with heat or bitterness. Available everywhere, it is the dried pablano and can easily be reconstituted by soaking.*

The day I cooked with him, my father pounded un-cooked turkey breasts, working the chile powder deeper into the meat, thinking of still another recipe. "What do you think, Wes, chili tonight—four- or five-alarm? Something pure, something colorful, something to make heathens have visions as their stomachs rot in hell? Yessir, our special tonight is *Infierno* Chili, made with turkey breast, pumpkin, posole. Or we could call it P's Porridge Chili: *pavo*, pumpkin, posole, and pain! We'll add chipotle peppers, too. You know what they say, *Where there's smoke, there's fire.*" I tried to imagine that much heat; he pounded the meat.

He was still trying to disprove my mother's accusations about his lack of adventure. Cooking was his creative proof.

One night he invited Carson Flinn to dinner. "On the house," he said, "for old times' sake." He promised a buffalo burger from the old Tsil Buffalo menu.

He started Carson with a free drink, specially concocted by Cocoa, who enjoyed the extreme spice in my father's food experiments. Cocoa made a wicked martini, which I tried only years later: hot pepper vodka, a jalapeño floating in it instead of an olive.

The Buffalo-Habanero Burger my father cooked for Carson was so hot nobody could have eaten it without a steel tongue, an asbestos mouth, and a legendary cast-iron stomach. Even When Available, who liked spice, let that meat rot in his dish for three days.

The simple sweet potato fries had been dredged in cayenne before being baked in my father's special chile-peanut oil.

Carson left before dessert. "He'll be too chicken to write about it in the newspaper," my father said to me. "He'll go crying to your mother."

He was right. But when Carson complained, my mother told him he was on his own. "I told Carson it was time to quit playing me against you," she said. "But that goes for you, too, Robert. Don't play with him, trying to hurt me."

"You're the one who plays," he said. "The one who hurts. I'm an amateur compared to you."

"It's not something you want to get good at," she said. "Especially in front of Wes."

I wish he'd taken her advice, but he didn't. I returned

home from school one day, feeling ill. I couldn't wait to find my bed in the basement. When I came through the alley door, into the kitchen, I smelled the acrid char of burning sunflower seeds. I turned off the burner under a skillet and went down the stairs. The door to my room was locked. I knocked, but heard nothing. "Anybody in there?" I knocked again.

I heard whispering hushes. "This door is not supposed to be locked!" I kicked at the door. I began to sweat with what I'm sure was a fever. I hoped against hope that I'd find my mother and father inside my room, finalizing the process of making up.

That fantasy buckled like my knees with my mother's voice on the stairs above me. "Wes?" she asked. Then she swooped down the stairs, concerned, because I had almost collapsed against the door. "What's wrong?" She felt my forehead, a motherly gesture that endeared her to me, even though I'd been angry with her, too.

Now I felt sorry for her, for what she would see when my father came out the door. I've wondered since what it was like for my mother when I pushed into her hiding place in her kitchen, what it was like for my father when I pounded on the door, demanding that he open up.

"Robert," said my mother. "I'm going upstairs. To pack my bag."

"I'm sick," I told her.

"I know you are, honey," she said. She went up the stairs, anyway.

I should have known that, just like me, when I sat there waiting for Pablito and Cocoa to begin their lovemaking, my mother sat on a step, to see what she could see.

Cocoa swung open my door. She looked neat, tidy, unwrinkled. My father sat on my bed, fully clothed. Not my worst fear. But that didn't matter to my mother. Cocoa looked at me, then at my mother up the stairs. "Misery loves company, honey," she said. "And there's lots of company around here. But not mine. Not anymore." She turned to my father. "I quit."

Cocoa swept by my mother without incident, and was gone. My mother stood up, finally, and climbed the rest of the stairs. She returned with the skillet of burned sunflower seeds. She threw the seeds into my room, pelting my father. "Damn you," she screamed. On her way out, she banged the skillet against my door.

"I haven't done anything you haven't done," said my father.

"That's the worst thing you could tell me. Because I wasn't setting the standard!"

She left me leaning against the little partition of a room that my parents had built for me. Cheap two-by-fours and thin plywood. She left my father on my bed. She went upstairs, packed a bag, and, true to her word, but without a word, she left.

My father and I wandered an empty upstairs. "Pack a bag," my father said.

"I'm sick," I said.

"The car is just as good as a bed," he said. "We're going on a trip."

I went downstairs and stared at the dent my mother had made on the door with the skillet. It would always be there, like the scars on my hands. These things wouldn't go away. They couldn't be taken back.

My father came down the stairs. "You haven't packed," he said.

"Where are we going?" I asked him.

"Wherever we have to," he said.

"Leave me here," I said. I threw a stray shoe at the scar my mother had made on my door.

"You're not old enough to stay alone," said my father. "You will pack a bag. We're in this together, like it or not."

"Not," I said. But I packed.

II.

LEAVING THE TABLE

Pawpaw (North American fruit): *A member of the cherimoya family, the pawpaw looks like a three- to six-inch pudgy banana. The dark skin is thick, while the ripe flesh is creamy, yellow, laced with button-like seeds. Juicy and very sweet, the pawpaw is sometimes called custard apple, which is accurate for texture, if not for taste. Because it is easily bruised and thus difficult to transport, it is gathered in season by local people rather than cultivated and shipped to marketplaces.*

Ripeness is all. We might look formed, grown, delectable. We might look ready to pick, to leave home, to understand our lives. But until one ripe moment we are too firm, too bitter, insubstantial, unappetizing. Picked too late, we are rotting, wrinkled, unappetizing.

In our lives, we are unsure of the moment: too soon and we long for the tree. Too late and we sour, hanging on the branch. If we are lucky, we ripen to give pleasure or we fall into the earth beneath us, ready to take root.

LO SABROSO DE LA VIDA:
COURTSHIPS

*O*n the way to St. Louis—because that is where my father went, looking for my mother—I shivered in the backseat, feverish, while he cursed slow drivers and told me, again, the story of his and my mother's courtship. I wanted to protest, but I was tired. He would have persisted, anyway. Childhood can be like that. You find yourself imprisoned in some backseat, with an angry adult at the wheel, headed where? You're not sure.

"Change," muttered my father. "That's what she said. She wanted something new. Different. For her food." Then louder, "But she got a lot more change than just her food. She got me.

"She was in this cooking school in Santa Fe." His voice droned through traffic, through a rainstorm. Sometimes I could hear him, sometimes not. It didn't matter, because I had heard the story from both of them.

After a week of cooking classes in Santa Fe, three days of nothing but learning new ingredients, followed by two days of touching, sniffing, and tasting, my mother was sent to Albuquerque to attend a food fair. Her assignment: create a menu, buy the very best ingredients, return to Santa Fe, cook, and serve the meal to one of the instructors by 9 P.M.

She wanted a main dish of fillet mignon, but with a rich sauce of gin, juniper berries, allspice, and serrano chiles. The steak sauce had to be spicy enough not to be overwhelmed by the posole and bean stew served before it, or the Spanish-style rice served with it. Being a practical person, my mother did not choose exotic ingredients. She liked to spend her time preparing, rather than searching for, her food.

She wanted allspice seeds, to grind for freshness. She knew her instructors would know the difference. But wherever she went at the fair—the indoor stalls for everything that needed to stay cool, the lean-tos, the tents, the open-air vendors—she heard the same thing: "We're not selling it this year. Everyone is using last year's, or the year before. Bad weather. Revolution. Most of it no better than dirt."

She couldn't stop her search until she had asked each vendor. Her last chance was a small tent with hand-painted lettering on the front flap, *Lo sabroso de la vida*, "Spice of life," but she didn't know that then. She did not lift the tent flap because, from inside, she heard the angry voices of men. When the flap furled open, out stalked a man her age, still throwing what she assumed were Spanish invectives over his shoulder. The man stopped when he saw my mother, and he silenced himself. There was something about her that placed her firmly where she was, as though she had grown there. He smiled and nodded, almost bowed. "Enter at your own risk," he said, and she did.

Inside *Lo sabroso de la vida* was heat and darkness. Two men sat before a table of dried chiles, herbs, seeds. Everything they sold looked dusty, as though it might all be made of earth. She asked for allspice, and they gestured toward a large bowl in the corner. She reached for a seed, rolled it against her thumb and nail, sniffed it, then put it in her mouth. It was allspice. "I need only a small amount," she said. "For one dish."

They sold only in bulk, twenty dollars' worth at the least. She pleaded. They refused. She slapped a twenty-dollar bill onto the table. One of the men rose and began to scoop fistfuls of allspice into a paper bag.

My mother was furious.

That's when my father came back inside the tent, walked past her, took her twenty-dollar bill and her arm, and led her away.

She was even more furious. "The only thing worse than overbuying is not having allspice at all," she said.

He said nothing.

"I need that!" she shouted.

"Poor quality."

"It's the only allspice at the fair."

Some distance from the tent my father let go of her arm. "Excuse me," he said. "I'm Robert Hingler. The Hispanics call me Roberto. Those *hombres* in there tried to sell me chipotles filled with soil for weight. They're not to be trusted." He began walking again, and she followed. "I bought allspice when it was good, about four years ago. The recent stuff's acidic. Not much oil. You're welcome to mine."

"Where?"

"The place where I cook."

"I need to be back in Santa Fe." She looked at my father.

He was a tall man, very thin back then, in his khakis and T-shirt, a pack of Lucky Strikes rolled into his sleeve. He had a funny little mustache she thought looked like a sick caterpillar.

He was intense. His hand at her elbow as he pulled her from the tent had been insistent. But he did not seem dangerous.

"You're from the cooking school?" he asked.

"You've found me out."

"I cook for a very wealthy man, a landowner with more cattle than most pueblos have people. He indulges me. And my food experiments. So I stay with him, even though he spends more on the food than he spends on me. Because of this, I have the best allspice in the Rio Grande Valley." My father folded his arms across his chest. "If you want it."

She agreed to drive him home. They went north, out of town, past the Sandia Mountains. "*Sandía*," he said. "Watermelon. You shouldn't be in such a hurry. As the sun sets, you see the pink that gives them their name."

"Some other time."

He said nothing, except to give her directions, west, ten miles from the main highway. Just as she was sure something was terribly wrong, he pointed to a windbreak of trees, green and stately, and the large adobe ranch house they flanked. He directed her to the back, and he jumped out of the car as soon as she stopped it. She waited, expecting him to return with the allspice. After ten minutes, she went under the archway where he'd disappeared. She found him in his kitchen.

"You'll need a snack. To nourish you for your cooking tonight." He handed her a small bowl and a spoon. "Eat," he said. "It's dessert for my dinner tonight. I've tasted it before."

She ate: fresh raspberries over chocolate sauce over a sweet green pudding. The sauce was earthy, slightly spicy, dark with chocolate, bittersweet with raspberries. The pudding, she guessed, must be pistachio, but it tasted more of vanilla, and tangier and richer than pudding.

"Guess," he said.

Like him, the dessert had an intensity, but was not overwhelming, not dangerous. She told him what she tasted.

"For the pudding," he said, "I blend avocado, gooseberry, vanilla, and marigold honey. For the sauce: cocoa, raspberries, ancho chile, more marigold honey, maple syrup, and one other ingredient."

She refused to guess.

"The best allspice in the Rio Grande valley." He held out a bag of large, full seeds.

"Thank you," she said. "And thank you for the dessert."

"My pleasure," he said. "Food is my pleasure. Watching people eat is my pleasure. When my food makes them happy." He moved closer to my mother.

"I have to hurry back," she said, and she left my father's kitchen.

AVOCADO-GOOSEBERRY PUDDING
WITH RASPBERRY SAUCE

PUDDING

3 large ripe avocados

1½ cups fresh gooseberries

Marigold honey to taste

2 teaspoons vanilla

Raspberry sauce (below)

½ cup raspberries

This will cool faster if these ingredients are refrigerated.

Blend the avocados, gooseberries, marigold honey, and vanilla until very smooth and light. Put in wineglasses or other glasses—best when seen. Top with Raspberry Sauce (below) and finish with layer of fresh raspberries. Sauce and berries will keep the avocado from discoloring while it stays cool in the refrigerator.

FRUIT SAUCE

½–1 cup raspberries or other New World fruit

2 ancho chiles

2–3 tablespoons cocoa

1 finely ground allspice* seed

Marigold honey to taste

Maple syrup for liquid and taste

Put the fruit and chiles (cut into pieces) into a saucepan with a small amount of water. Heat until the dried chile is fully reconstituted, and has fully flavored the fruit. Blend until smooth, then return to saucepan and add cocoa, allspice, honey, and maple syrup. Heat until thickened. Let cool, then pour over pudding. Top with more fruit. Watch other eaters for signs of pleasure.

***Allspice** (the cinnamon/clove of the New World): *The Spanish called this little black berry* pimienta de Jamaica *(Jamaican pepper). Though it looks like a peppercorn, it is the seed of a West Indian evergreen tree. It spices sweet dishes made with pumpkin or avocado, or sweetens hot pepper dishes.*

On the way back to Santa Fe, my mother reached into the bag on the seat of her car, pulled out a seed, held it to her nose, then her lips. She crushed it with her teeth. It was better than the allspice she'd tasted at the cooking school.

In Santa Fe, she presented her menu and ingredients to one of her teachers. "So," he said, "you've met Mr. Roberto Hingler?"

"The allspice."

"Be careful," he said.

The next day, Sunday, she returned to the ranch house. "A thank-you call," she always called it. My father was off for the day. She might find him in Albuquerque, at *Domingo's*, which was run by Domingo Saenz, the son of his adopted godparents, Juan and Conseca. It was open only on Sundays.

Near Old Town, they told her. She found my father at *Domingo's*, trading his cooking skills for food. He stopped when she came into the kitchen. They took a table and ordered beer. She told him that her first cooking school menu, her first experiment, had gone well. "He seemed to really like my food," she said of her instructor. "But then he said he would never want to eat it again, not the sauce."

"He is a chef, and not a cook," said my father. "They try for one experience. And it has to be perfect."

"You're a cook, then?" asked my mother. "What do you try for?"

"I experiment. I don't want a single experience of perfection, but a singular experience that needs perfecting."

"Your employer indulges you?"

My father explained to her everything he was trying to do. He cooked only with the ingredients that existed in the Western Hemisphere before European contact. He knew that his combinations, like avocado and gooseberry, or cocoa and blackberry, might not have been possible in the New World, where diets for most people were not varied and depended on very local staples. But he liked the idea of cooking with what was indigenous to a land unknown to the rest of the world for years, and of seeing what that food might taste like when not adulterated by European ingredients. "If I had to choose one over the other, Eastern Hemisphere or Western, I'd choose Western," he said.

"He knew my name," my mother always said when she told me the story, "and I told him I was three-fourths Italian. When he called my food—garlic, cheeses, wines, onions, olives, the seminola wheat in pasta—*adulterations*, I had to smile."

"I was trying to get her goat a little," said my father about that afternoon. "But we talked food, and ate food together that *domingo* at *Domingo's*, all through the afternoon and evening."

I know those conversations. I grew up with their arguments about taste, function, nutrition, spice, form, and life. They loved it.

Every evening after that, when my father was finished in the kitchen of the big ranch house, he drove to the small motel where my mother had rented a room by the week. He brought a dish, and she brought something from the cooking school, and they talked, ate each other's food, smoked, and drank beer and tequila.

"We debated the chile heat of the New World against the horseradish and mustard heat of the Old," my father said, driving to St. Louis through the rain. Perhaps he wished for the simplicity of such a debate, given what would face him when he found her.

My mother was used to cooking for many people, my father used to experimenting for a few. "I think we were jealous of each other, back then," said my father.

Back then? I thought.

"I only fed my rancher's family, but your mother had real pleasure in pleasing so many people."

All through their lives, they were attracted to each other

by envy and respect and what they had in common. They loved food and the pleasure it could bring, in the preparation and the eating. They shared childhoods: Both had felt neglected in some way. Both were influenced by people other than parents, my father by Juan and Conseca, my mother by her grandmother Tito. They shared a love of argument, usually for fun, for pleasure. The drive to St. Louis proved it could also bring pain.

"It was a chance meeting," my mother told me later. "The spice, and the spice of life. For my cooking. For me." My mother came back to her business in Kansas City. My father stayed at the ranch outside Albuquerque. They wrote, shared recipes, made trips back and forth for two years. Finally, she convinced him to move to Kansas City, where his cooking would be some of the first Southwestern cuisine. Truly unique, it would educate a meat-and-potatoes Midwest to new possibilities of taste. They could work together, she said. Her catering business was thriving.

They were each thirty years old when he packed his kitchen and ingredients into an old truck and drove the eight hundred miles northeast. They moved in together, took a blood test, applied for a marriage license, and three days later were married. Within a year, they were expecting me. "I've told you about the day you were conceived, haven't I?" asked my father.

"Yes," I said.

"I was experimenting with a sweet potato fritter, to see if the addition of more chile powder would keep the sugar in the potato from burning to a black crust so quickly. I was in our kitchen, on my third attempt, when your mother called me from the doorway. I was intent on that fritter. But the second time she said my name, well, there was something about her voice. I turned and there she was in the doorway, naked."

"Dad," I said.

"Okay, I'm sorry. But you're old enough to know you don't make babies with your clothes on."

"I'm old enough I don't need to hear about it from my father. Especially not today."

"Okay. But when I got back to the kitchen, the pumpkin fritter was black."

"Not today," I repeated. "Maybe I'm not interested in your sex life right now."

My father drummed his fingers on the steering wheel. I had finally silenced him.

I like my mother's version better. "Your father was figuring out a possible restaurant menu, and many days he cooked all day, ate whichever experiments worked best, and fell into bed, exhausted. One night, you were conceived, when we were both half asleep, like in a dream. And you are a dream, Wes," she told me.

Once pregnant, my parents had an official wedding, in St. Louis. My mother wore a white dress, but with a necklace of tiny red porcelain chiles my father had ordered for her as a wedding gift. So, another trip to St. Louis, and my father suddenly very silent.

"Do you like being different from most people?" I asked.

"I don't think about it," he said.

"I don't like it," I said.

My fever had broken around the time we'd crossed the Missouri River, halfway across the state. By the time we reached the city, I was hungry, and my father grudgingly stopped at the first café we spotted. He refused anything but water and an ashtray. I had a hamburger and french fries, smothered them in catsup, wolfed them down, gulped water, and we were back in the car. "Maybe I could have a cigarette," I said.

"You were sick coming, I don't want you sick arriving," he said. "Let's get there before it's totally dark."

I had never been to The Hill, but suddenly, out of the chaos of traffic and lights and mismatched buildings, we turned into an area of small, neatly kept homes. On the corners were neighborhood groceries, restaurants. A church spire vaulted from the center, black against a darkening sky. My father drove the streets up and down the hill of The Hill, trying to remember which would be the small home of Maria Tito, where he expected to find my mother.

"You don't even know where you're going," I accused.

He didn't answer. He simply pulled up to a curb, behind my mother's parked van. He lit a cigarette. "I'm smoking already," I said, "just being in the car. I might as well have a cigarette."

He gave me one. I had held one before, and pretended to smoke. The thin tube of tightly rolled tobacco, solid and delicate at the same time, felt like power. I lit up, inhaled, and coughed out my first lungful of smoke. My stomach turned a notch, and I saw what my father meant by courting sickness. I inhaled once more, without coughing, then blew a stream of smoke like a sigh, as I'd often seen my mother do. The sharp catch in my lungs was a welcome stimulation. The ashen tip reddened, flaring like my heart. I was smoking, and in front of my father.

"Don't start," he said.

"I just did," I said. He *couldn't* tell me what to do. I took another puff to celebrate.

"You don't have to be an idiot in every single way I am."

"Just this one way, I hope," I said.

"Don't be rude."

He opened his door, and left the car. I wasn't sure whether to follow him, but she wasn't just his wife, she was my mother.

Great-grandmother Tito met us at the door. She smiled. "Her tires are still cooling off, and you're already here. That's a good sign." Her large body was planted on the threshold.

"Can we come in?" asked my father.

"She says *no*," Maria Tito said. "She had the drive to think, but whatever happened, she needs more time."

"Where are we going to stay?"

"There's a separate door to the basement. I'll unlock it in an hour. Mario's just closing his shop. Go talk to him." She pointed down the street.

We walked to a corner grocery. In the bright light inside, Grandfather Tito stood alone in the middle of an aisle, posed almost, as though thinking about his next step, not knowing why he should take it, as though content to stand among the pepperoncinis and capers and anchovies.

"C'mon." My father nudged my elbow.

"We're not going to say hello?"

"He'll be around. Your mother isn't the only one who needs to think."

"Give me a cigarette," I said. He did. But he didn't give me a light. I didn't push him, just put the Lucky in my shirt pocket for later.

He walked fast, up and down streets, past lit and unlit houses, past little stores and restaurants and bars and lodge halls. Finally, we made our way back to the grocery where Mario Tito still stood, though in another aisle. "See him?" said my father. "That's me without your mother." We did not go inside.

On the way back to Maria Tito's house, he asked, "Can you imagine ending up like that?"

I couldn't.

"Tell her I'm ready to start again," my father said when Maria Tito met us at the side door. "I want to cook for her. A feast of love, but without any expectation."

"There's a kitchenette downstairs," she told him. "We used to rent."

We slept together in a double bed. Just as I was drifting off, my father said, "There's only one way to do it, Wes. And that's to do it all over again."

In the middle of the night, I woke up. I put on my pants and rifled my father's pockets for matches. I walked around the block, smoking the cigarette I'd bummed earlier. I wondered how long we'd be in St. Louis, wondered if my mother would come back to Kansas City. A full moon made its rounds through a clear sky. I went back to the house and fell asleep again.

At noon I stumbled into Maria Tito's kitchen upstairs. In the sunlight, a half dozen pots gleamed from the counters. Broth simmered on a burner. Eggplant, prunes, fresh raspberries, and cheeses littered the counters. "You're cooking?" I asked my mother. "I thought Dad was cooking something for you."

"We're cooking for each other, Wes," she said.

I nodded. I knew their meals of contrition.

"Food talks, too," said my great-grandmother Tito, returning with a bag of groceries. "The food reveals the heart."

"Will I get to eat?" I asked.

"Leave your parents to each other," said Maria Tito. "I'll take care of you."

All that day, I watched my mother upstairs, then my father downstairs, in separate kitchens, like at home. Each was quiet, contemplative. They couldn't have ignored me more if they were having an intense conversation that did not include me. "Are you still mad at Dad?" I asked my mother. She was stuffing a prune with shrimp and macadamia nuts.

"That's between your father and me," she said.

"Are we going to go home anytime soon?" I asked my father. He was grinding seeds for a mole.

"Wes," he said, not looking up, "I have to focus."

Even Maria Tito, who said she'd take care of me, spent her time between kitchens. She tasted my father's mole, and suggested a hint of vanilla. "For you," he said, and added two drops. In my mother's kitchen, Grandmother Tito gave unobtrusive advice: "Wine in that dish will sour, vinegar will sweeten." So my mother put basalmic vinegar into the sauce for her asparagus.

As if they knew what the other was doing, each of my parents made two appetizers, a soup, an entrée, a vegetable, a salad, and a dessert. As Maria Tito and I bounced between kitchens, we watched them prepare what could be set aside to wait. Then everything intensified to what needed immediate attention or eating. Soon, my parents sent me and Maria Tito back and forth for reports on timing. My mother's kitchen was rich with the dark smell of flesh and sherry. "I'll have my appetizers ready in twenty minutes," she told me. "Run see if that will work for your father."

"Twenty-*five* minutes," he insisted. "I'll bring my appetizers upstairs. Appetizers there, seven o'clock, if we can eat soup downstairs, in my kitchen."

"Soup downstairs, if at seven forty-five," she said.

"You will eat the entrées in the dining room," insisted Maria Tito. "At eight-fifteen. Wes, you'll prepare the table."

"Wes," said my mother, "you and your great-grandmother can serve, then disappear after the entrée?"

"Wes," said my father, "you will turn on the burner under this corn at exactly ten after eight."

"Wes," said my mother, "I've left a little of everything on the counter for you."

"Wes," said my father, "after you serve, you may eat what I've fixed your mother. There will be a plate in the oven."

Finally, my father came upstairs carrying his appetizers like a gift: anchovy guacamole with tortilla chips; and his *erizo** in black bean–chile paste.

My mother had set out her appetizers: asparagus in a frothy sauce of cream cheese, grapefruit juice, cilantro, basalmic vinegar, and beaten egg whites; and her wine-soaked prunes, stuffed with shrimp and macadamia nuts and wrapped in bacon.

STUFFED PRUNES OF BUEN APPETITO

12 prunes, pitted

½ cup burgundy wine

Bay leaf

¼ cup soy sauce

2 cloves garlic

*¼ teaspoon crushed red pepper***

12 shrimp

12 macadamia nuts

Dijon mustard

6 lean bacon strips, cut in half

---

*Erizo (sea urchin): *Eaten in South America as an aphrodisiac, this dark ball is covered with tongue-shaped genitalia, pale orange, of strong and salty flesh. The taste is of the sea, of the ocean in human blood, of the hope that comes with the pungent smell of the loved one under the sheets.*

Pit prunes and let soak overnight in wine, bay, soy, crushed red pepper, and garlic. Peel shrimp, uncooked, and stuff into prune with a macadamia nut and a dollop of mustard. Wrap in bacon, secure with toothpick, and broil until bacon is crisp and shrimp is cooked. Let cool and eat as an appetizer.

Eat slowly. Most people tend to eat too quickly. But food, to be enjoyed, needs time, just as a relationship does. Get acquainted with this recipe, one small bite at a time.

**Árbol (pod chile, related to the cayenne, long and thin, bright red): *This thin-fleshed chile is ubiquitous in world cuisines, the pod found in Chinese carryout, the crushed flakes in the shaker on the tabletop of every pizza joint, the little flick of heat in spaghetti sauce. Its real bite of flavor, hot and almost sour at the same time, makes it a staple of most restaurants.*

He served his appetizers with punch. "Mescal and mango juice," he said.

She served hers with champagne.

They sat across the kitchen table from each other. Maria Tito and I scooted out of the room. Every once in a while, I peeked in. "Well?" my great-grandmother would ask me.

"Nothing," I said at first.

"They're eating," I said the next time. "And drinking."

And the next: "They're hardly even looking at each other."

Maria Tito grabbed me by the shoulder. "Don't worry," she said. We went to set the table in the dining room.

"They're always jealous of each other's food," I said.

"Of course," she said. "But after what they've done, or thought of doing, they must learn to appreciate each other, in the kitchen and out. Even more important, they must like themselves."

When we finished setting the table, they were in the downstairs kitchen eating soup. I walked by the doorway. They were not eating with gusto. I felt angry. I had ventured hopefully between their kitchens all afternoon. They'd had stormy days before, then sat down to a good meal, with good cheer, everything forgiven. This time, they had done bad things.

Maria Tito sat in her living room. She, at least, seemed calm. "What did you mean they have to like themselves?" I asked.

"People have rough times," she said. "They blame themselves. Your father told me you were sick yesterday. Do you blame yourself for getting sick?"

"It's not my fault."

"What about when you get mad? Is that your fault?"

"Sometimes. Sometimes it's someone else I'm mad at."

"Are you mad right now? At your mother and father?"

"Yes."

"They're mad at each other. Or they're mad at themselves. They've hurt each other. They did things, even though they didn't have to. So they need to forgive themselves, first. Understand themselves. Then maybe they can treat each other better. But they're stubborn. Your mother always has been."

"My father said he was going to start all over again. Why can't he just tell her that?"

Maria Tito hugged me. "He *is* telling her that. With his food."

"If they want to be happy, they should eat their own food," I said. "They like their own food best." I knew *that* much from experience.

Maria Tito stood up. I followed her as she marched downstairs to the kitchen table, where my parents were trying to enjoy each other's soup.

She did something very simple. She switched their bowls. "Enough nonsense," she said. "Try eating your own meals tonight. Get things right, each in your own heart, then come together again." She stomped back out and up the stairs. I joined her in the living room. But not before I saw each take a bite of soup: My mother had scraped artichoke flesh from the leaves for her cream of artichoke soup; my father had simmered turkey livers in turkey broth with grated potato and green chile for his trademark soup. They smiled at each other like students who had been chastised by a teacher.

POTATO AND GREEN CHILE SOUP

Turkey neck, giblets, legs, thighs, and wings
Allspice
*Mexican oregano**
*Sage***
Salt to taste

2 golden potatoes, skinned and grated
Turkey livers, to taste, frozen so they can be shaved into soup
2 New Mexico green chiles, roasted, skinned, and seeded,
     sliced thin

Make a broth of turkey parts in water, with allspice, oregano, sage, and salt, to taste. Pour off fat, and bring broth to simmer. Add the potatoes, let cook for five minutes, then add the turkey liver shavings, let cook for an additional five minutes, then add the chiles and let cook a final five minutes, or until potatoes are thoroughly cooked.

*Oregano (Mexican): *A pungent and hearty oregano indigenous to Central America, the Mexican variety is more highly spiced than the Mediterranean oregano found in most tomato sauces, pizzas, and other Italian dishes.*

**Sage (from sagebrush): *Sagebrush,* Artemesia tridentata, *is a shrub native to the arid regions of western North America. A woody shrub, it has silver-green aromatic leaves and large clusters of small white* *flowers. Though unrelated to the herb sage, it has a similar flavor and odor, and has been used medicinally and as a food (flavoring and the eating of seeds) by Native Americans for centuries. Sagebrush wood ignites so easily it is the wood of choice for starting fires by friction.*

Their menus from that evening became yet another catechism in the Hingler household. My mother's lamb in sherry sauce, her tart combination of just-softened eggplant with onions, garlic, olive oil, cloves, and Gorgonzola cheese. My father's turkey meatballs in a mescal–chocolate mole served with corn on the cob dripping with hot peanut sauce. By the time they should have finished those entrées, Maria Tito sent me to clear plates and give her a progress report.

I didn't even enter the dining room. My report was delivered with some repulsion. "They're licking each other's fingers." I put my hands in my pockets.

She told me to go downstairs and eat. My father's food was good, but I didn't lick my fingers. I imagined, from watching their preparations, the rest of their meal. Their salads were simple. His was cold smoked salmon, quinoa, and watercress with his roasted sunflower seed–tomato dressing. Hers was crumbles of bleu cheese she'd hidden among a salad of baby greens. Their desserts: her crepes covered with chocolate-raspberry sauce and his pineapple sorbet covered in tequila-soaked, then chocolate-covered, cashews.

Maria Tito brought me bites of the desserts in my bedroom in the downstairs apartment. "You will be sleeping by yourself tonight," she told me.

I didn't sleep. I walked The Hill. Around eleven o'clock I

pushed through the door of a tavern, a small place, dense with wood and smoke. I went straight to the bar and climbed up on a stool.

"I suppose you want a drink," asked the bartender.

"You wouldn't give me one," I said boldly. "My father wouldn't, at his bar."

"Who is your father?" asked the man. He leaned over the counter.

"Robert Hingler. He's from Kansas City. My mother is Maria Tito Hingler. We're staying at my great-grandmother's." I saw what I wanted, cigarettes on the bar shelves, next to the bottles.

"And your great-grandmother is Maria Tito?"

"And my grandfather is Mario Tito. And my father sent me for some Lucky Strikes. My mother said to just tell everyone who I am."

The bartender smiled. Either he knew my mother and grandfather and great-grandmother, or he knew I was lying. Or both.

"You haven't told me everything," he said. He glanced back at the cigarettes, then stared at me again.

I was confused. I'd told him all the names he should know. I scooted down from the bar stool, ready to leave.

"You haven't told me your name," said the bartender.

"Wes," I said. "Weston Tito Hingler."

The man handed me a pack of Luckies. "Tell your father to come pay me tomorrow," he said. "I'd like to meet him."

I hurried away, relieved. Surely we'd be gone before the man would ask after his money. I spent the next couple of hours walking and smoking until I was exhausted and green in the stomach. I let myself into Maria Tito's basement to lie down. I didn't sleep, just *wrinkled the sheets*, as my father sometimes said. I thought about the food my parents had prepared for each other. For the next year or so, I figured, they'd talk about those menus and sigh with pleasant memory. I would sigh with discontent. They would be okay. All I had was a pack of cigarettes.

GREEN SAUCE:
DEVELOPING TASTES

We stayed in St. Louis another day. Mario Tito, my grandfather, had not been standing dazed in the late evening at his grocery because of hopelessness. He'd found love, a widow who shopped at his place every day. Each night he took special care with the shelves she would see. His neatness, his small attentions, attracted her. That, and his promise to drink wine only for "medicinal purposes," which meant two glasses a day.

The night my father and I walked by, Mario had been waiting for her, to walk her to the lodge hall. When he dropped by his mother's house afterward, she fed him the leftovers of my parents' meal of reconciliation. "Good food" was his judgment, "but spicy and rich. Hard on the stomach and bowels."

"Such is love," Maria Tito said.

"Why is love so hard?" I asked her the next day.

Maria Tito patted me. "Love means a drive to St. Louis. It runs away, you follow it, no matter what. Your grandfather's looking for comfort, not love. And with Mrs. Dolani's great bosom, he'll have all the comfort he needs. Wes," she said, "learn to give yourself comfort. Give others love."

My parents spent the day by themselves, talking. I spent it with my pack of cigarettes, walking around St. Louis, across Kingshighway to the Missouri Botanical Gardens, then up to Forest Park to the zoo and the art museum. I didn't stay anywhere long, just drifted, smoked, watched. If anyone asked me who I was, I vowed, I'd say *Wes Hingler*. Nobody asked. I went home for dinner. And nobody asked where I'd been.

The next day we left. I started the drive home with my mother. "Do you still love Dad?" I asked.

"I'm going home, aren't I?" she asked.

"But do you love him?"

"Of course I do. Even people who love each other have rocky patches. Someday, you'll understand."

"I hope not," I said.

I switched vehicles when we stopped for gasoline in Columbia. "Do you still love Mom?" I asked my father.

"I went after her, didn't I?" he asked.

"But do you love her?"

"Don't worry, Wes," he said. "Your mother and I have a history together. We're just making a little more, day by day. Love is always there—it's what you live by. It's like food. Sometimes it gives you great pleasure. Sometimes, you just eat it to live. Either way, it sustains you, and you're lucky to have it."

"Do you and Mom love me?" I asked.

"You shouldn't have to ask that question," he said.

I didn't ask it again, not aloud.

I worked, grudgingly, at the Tsil Café. My father made me the front person, the greeter, the one who counted menus, sat customers at the table and said, *Misty will be with you soon.* My grades slipped. When I brought home straight *C*s, my father complained.

"What do you expect," I said. "You've got me building character instead of building my life."

"You're building both," he said. "You just don't know it."

"How am I building my life?"

"If you don't know, you're in trouble," he said. "You're building your life even when you're doing nothing. You're just building a nothing kind of life."

My mother agreed. Together, my parents complained about my smoking, my grades, my occasional sips of wine and beer. Once, my wild self-expressions—like the time I kicked Carson Flinn in the shin—had seemed cute or clever. Not by the time I was fifteen. Flinn came to the Tsil Café one night and ordered the special. "The side," I told him, "is my favorite." He went home and wrote one of his little paragraphs.

> **Note:** We dined, appreciatively, at the Tsil Café this week. The special was salmon fillet with a mango glaze accompanied by a side of corn bread–stuffed red bell pepper that Robert Hingler claims to be an old family recipe. We suspect Wes, the Hingler son, of masterminding this creation. If it is his, then he has the ingredients of his father and the creative flair of his mother in his genes. Lucky boy.

I didn't appreciate his speculative mention of me. The corn bread was Juan's. Flinn was so smug. I mistrusted him as much as my father did. So I wrote him a note. He showed it to my parents the next time he visited my mother's kitchen.

We are glad that we ate at the Tsil Café and enjoyed our corn bread, but we weren't right about who created our creation and want to tell us to go to hell. Who is this "we," anyway, our pencil and our stomach?

—*Wes Hingler*

I shrugged my shoulders. "What do you guys care about what I do?" I stomped down the stairs.

That night, as the last diners and drinkers left the Tsil, I grabbed a cigarette and went to the alley for a smoke. Misty leaned against the building. We smoked together.

"How old are you now?" she asked.

"Sixteen . . . almost," I said.

"You seem older."

"If I was," I said, "I'd leave this joint."

"That's what I used to say. To *my* parents."

"How old are you?"

"Twenty . . . almost."

"What's it like to be twenty?" I asked her.

"Like sixteen, only you have to take care of yourself."

"I'd like that," I said. "My own place. Do whatever I wanted to do."

"I just got my first place. Costs me a lot," Misty said. "I

have to work even harder. My place is close to here. Want to see it sometime?"

"Let's go right now," I said.

"Don't you have to ask your parents?"

"Are you going to ask yours?"

Misty went inside to count out her tips and settle with my father. I made a big show of going down to the basement—slamming doors, clomping down the stairs. Then I sneaked back up and into the alley. Misty was waiting. "Won't they check on you?" she asked me.

"They stay busy checking on each other," I said.

Misty lived ten blocks away in a one-bedroom apartment in a brick building near Westport. The night was muggy, and by the time we arrived at her place I was ready for the beer she offered me. "You *have* had beer before?" she asked. "I don't want to corrupt you." She winked and handed me a cold can of Falstaff.

"I'm ready to be corrupted," I said.

"Now that you're here," said Misty, "I guess there's not much to see."

"It's yours," I said. "That makes it a lot."

"My parents gave me most of the furniture." She took me into her living room and we sat on a beat-up corduroy couch. I could see into her bedroom, a mattress on the floor, a sheet over the window instead of a curtain. Misty played with her long brown hair, twirled it into rings around her fingers. She was thin, with small features.

I touched her hand, and the hair.

"My hair is so thick," she said.

"I like your hair," I said. I combed my hand through it, brought it to my nose to smell it.

She was startled by my scarred hand. I was used to the shiny wrinkles of the old burn. Few people had ever seen such smooth, red skin up close. She didn't say anything.

"I like you," I said. I moved my hand away. "Are you going to show me your bedroom?"

"I'm hot," she said. She unbuttoned her blouse. I couldn't believe it. "Take off your shirt," she said.

From then on, I did as I was told.

Misty was no more experienced than I was. We both appreciated the pile of our clothes, the first liberation of being naked with another, the tentative touches, the self-conscious questions about what worked and what didn't. We shared the joy of lying, spent—I much more than she, because I had no stamina that first time—afterward. I liked the helpless power, the drained relaxation, the hopeful assumption that the experience would be the first of many. We smoked—Lucky and Kool—propped up on our sides, studying each other in the lamplight.

Misty hadn't commented on my hand, but she was fascinated by my body, as I was by hers. We traced our muscles, felt the bones in our shoulders, cupped the hollows in our backs at the bottom of our spines. I was amazed by the luxury of touch. I had always thought of myself as too thin, too bony, with not enough hair on my legs or chest. I had grown as tall as my mother, but still needed two inches to overtake my father. I had my mother's thick eyebrows, my father's blue eyes, my mother's sloping shoulders, my father's springy step, my mother's large ears, my father's thin lips. I was used to myself, but whenever I saw myself in a mirror—showering at school, or upstairs in the bathroom—I couldn't imagine anyone else finding me exciting. Maybe Misty felt the same way, because she let me touch her, rub her, nuzzle her small breasts and bony hips. Desire, I suppose, makes us all desirable. Misty inspected the three purple stains that were my birthmark. She traced them with her finger, as though drawing them.

"My father calls them corn, my grandfather wine stains," I said.

"And your mother?"

"Birthmarks."

"My mother says the more moles a woman has on her breasts, the more children she'll have."

I tried to smile. I hadn't thought about pregnancy.

"Don't worry, I'm on the pill," she said. "But you should have asked."

"I'll ask next time."

"What makes you think there'll be a next time?"

"Maybe there won't be, with you," I teased. "But that was too good not to have a next time with somebody."

"Make it with me," she said.

Misty asked me to spend the night, but I wanted to get home, sneak downstairs, and sleep the few hours before school. I leaned over for a good-bye kiss. I learned that two naked people should never say good-bye until fully clothed. After we'd made love again, I dressed quickly.

My key fit the alley door, and I pushed it open quietly. At the top of the stairs I saw the light from my bedroom. Had I left it on? By the time I was halfway downstairs I saw my mother and father sitting on my bed, my father with an impatient cigarette, my mother leaning against the wall, her eyes closed.

My father looked up. My mother, sensing the shift, sat up, shook her head, patted her eyes with her hands. "I was with Misty," I said.

"It's after one o'clock," said my mother.

"It's after one-thirty," said my father.

I looked at my watch. "Almost two," I said. "How time flies." I hoped humor would help.

"What do you mean, *with* Misty?" asked my father.

"She's got her own place. She just moved in. She asked me to look at it. She's real proud of it. She wanted to show it off. I could tell by the way she asked that I'd better go and check it out. She was just being friendly. She—"

"Wes," interrupted my mother, "stop talking."

"How long does it take to look at an apartment?" said my father.

"That's where I was," I said.

"We believe you," said my mother. "We're just not sure what you've been doing there. And why you didn't tell us where you were going."

"Do you tell me everything?" I asked.

"Just tell us when you're leaving," said my mother. "You're not even sixteen, Wes."

"When Dad was sixteen he was driving around New Mexico, exploring. And your father never cared what you did."

"You don't know how lucky you are," said my mother. "We've tried to be with you. To give you what we never had."

"Can I just go to sleep?" I asked. "I've got school in the morning."

"We didn't keep you up," said my father. "In fact, you kept us up. And your mother has a big catering job, and I have a restaurant to run."

"And I have to help," I said.

"Let's talk in the morning," said my mother.

We didn't. My father acted the same as usual around Misty when she showed up for work the next day, and my mother, later the next evening, said only one thing. "I don't want to control you," she said, "but I do want to know you."

"You already do. I'm like you and Dad." She shook her head, and sighed. I almost felt sorry for her.

I walked Misty home most nights, and often stayed to make love. Sometimes, I spent the night. Sex was magic: easy and fun, a gift. We were playful, gentle, content sometimes simply to breathe each other's breath.

Then I began to drink. From the time I was four and had eaten an anchovy, I was steeled to small, potent tastes. My first encounters with alcohol, though not pleasurable, were taken in the spirit of getting used to the inevitable. I was my parents' child in that: If something could be eaten or drunk,

I would try it. My father cooked with mescal,* that close relative to tequila, with its smoky richness, its bitter, earthy taste. Mescal gave his nopal tamales part of their bite. Since it was the distilled juice of the agave cactus, mescal was bottled with a maguey worm, drowned and pickled. My father bought *Dos Gusanos*, two worms. Once, he'd let me chew the rubbery inch of larvae and I'd swallowed it down. The experience, more memorable than pleasurable, began a symbiosis of sorts between me and mescal, which became my favorite of the hard liquors.

Two worms also meant one to share with a friend. One of my few friends at school was Lou Carmen, a kid whose parents ran an Italian restaurant in Westport. We understood the particular intensity and neglect in being the children of restaurateurs. We swapped horror stories about nasty customers, about taking over when a dishwasher quit in the middle of a shift, about our fathers going crazy in the kitchen. Lou had a great story about his father bailing out a waitress who had tried to be a hooker in her spare time. The cop who picked her up in a sting operation was one of Lou's loyal cus-

---

*Mescal (New World beverage of choice): *Called "nectar of the gods" by Cortés, mescal is a distillation of the agave cactus, sometimes called the century plant because it can live up to forty years before its single flowering and subsequent death. The agave has an edible heart in the middle of a crown of spiny leaves—like artichoke. The edible stalk grows rapidly from the center, sometimes as much as a foot per day. Mexican agave is the largest, and is cultivated commercially for its fermentation into the alcoholic beverages pulque (a sweet wine punch), mescal, and tequila. To show its authenticity, most mescal is bottled with one or two maguey (agave) worms, which have a symbiotic relationship with the plant, and which the Aztecs ate for protein.*

tomers, and they worked it all out: reduced charges for the waitress matched the reduced charges on Sergeant Boni's bill. Whenever he could, Lou came over to the Tsil. Around ten o'clock, we'd watch what we called the "get-a-lifes" eat the ice from their last drinks and decide to go home.

One night, when I'd noticed the fifth of mescal was only a third full, I challenged Lou to help me finish it and eat one of the worms while I ate the other. We told my father we'd finish the cleanup. We turned the chairs up onto the tables and mopped the tiles. We opened a couple of beers and called our shots of mescal "chasers," a word Lou had learned at his father's bar.

When we were hungry, we went back to the kitchen to see what we could find. Plenty of chips around, but no salsa. "Let me make something," I said.

I washed some tomatillos that were on the counter, found other green things—a jalapeño and pumpkin seeds—and went to work. In ten minutes, Lou and I were dipping blue corn chips into a warm green sauce.

WES HINGLER'S GREEN SALSA

*12 1- to 2-inch tomatillos**
½ cup pumpkin seeds, roasted
*1 jalapeño,** minced*

Unhusk and quarter the tomatillos and soften by heating in slight amount of water and chile-vinegar.

Blend with remaining ingredients in food processor until smooth. Eat with chips or serve as a garnish for tamales.

*Tomatillo (husk tomato, strawberry tomato, ground cherry): *This leafy, vining plant flowers white, yellow, or purple, then makes its fruit inside a husk that begins green and becomes like parchment when the tomatillo is ripe. Mexican tomatillos are an inch or more in diameter and are popularly used in green salsas. Others can be orange or rust in color, and very sweet. The only Native Americans not to eat them were the Pimas, who called them "old man's testicles."*

**Jalapeño (takes its name from Jalapa, in Mexico): *Broad and squat, with thick flesh, bright green to ripe red, the chile most common in the United States. Stuffed, sliced for nachos, diced into salsas, and eaten both plain and pickled, the jalapeño is versatile, with a clean and lasting heat.*

We sat at a table, polished off the chips with a couple more beers, and chased with mescal until the maguey worms floated into our shot glasses. We held them up, tinked the sides, and took the worms in our mouths.

"Gross," said Lou.

"Chew," I said, "it's probably loaded with alcohol."

"I'm getting an extra buzz," Lou bragged.

"I'm getting an extra bug," I laughed.

Lou, drunk like me, laughed, too. He fell off his chair, breaking his beer mug and shot glass on the floor. I laughed harder. "What a mess." Lou was surrounded by broken glass.

I dropped my beer mug and it shattered next to his. "My mother says it's a custom," I explained, "to let people know it's no big deal to break a glass."

"I broke my shot glass, too," said Lou.

So I dropped my shot glass next to his. The thick base of it exploded into hundreds of tiny pieces.

"Shit," said Lou, covering his eye.

I bent over him and pulled at his hand. "Let me see."

His eye was red. He fluttered the lid a few times. Whatever had hurt him was not embedded. He quit his high drama.

"Let's clean up," I said.

We swept, and I walked Lou out the front door of the Tsil Café. "If I go blind you've got to read me *The Scarlet Letter* for English."

"You mean you were going to read it?" I asked him. We laughed. I locked up and went to bed.

The next morning, my father yelled down the stairs. A dense, stuporous hangover clouded my eyes and swelled my tongue. As usual, When Available was curled on the end of my bed. I kicked at him. We'd both better be up: the dog and the one in the doghouse. When Available didn't move. I kicked again, then sat up and put my hand on his nose. Dry, and cold. His body was cold, too. He was dead.

"Wes!" yelled my father again. "You get yourself up here. You have some explaining to do!"

When Available weighed down the end of my bed. I didn't know what to do. I wondered when in the night When Available had died. Surely he hadn't been dead when I climbed into bed, drunk, almost passed out. I felt sick. I was in trouble, and tired, and my dog, who'd been with me all my life, was dead. I lay back and closed my eyes. By the time my father came down the stairs, I was weeping.

"What is it?" he asked, sitting on the edge of the bed.

"When Available," I said, between sobs.

My father touched our dog, the one he'd picked from the pound and named. "I'm sorry, Wes," he said. "You've never lost anything before, have you?"

I'd lost a lot, I thought, including my innocence. But he was right in one way. I'd never *felt* a loss like this: not when Teresita lost her baby, not when Pablito grieved in our basement, not when my mother left for San Francisco, not when I found my mother with Pablito, not when Cocoa walked out. Those were losses, but I didn't know how to feel them. When Available's loss was easier to express: pure weeping grief.

My father sat me up and hugged me, in spite of my size. "I came down here to give you hell," he said. "To tell you I'm sick to death of the way you're acting. To tell you to stop smoking so much. To tell you to watch yourself with Misty—you're just children, for God's sake. And stop thinking you're sneaking drinks when I know exactly what's in my bar, and my kitchen, down to the shot. You can't even sweep up after yourself worth a damn. You're not getting away with anything, Wes. Not really." He stood up. "But for now, let's bury When Available."

"Bury?"

"You want me to rename him Available? Put him on the menu?"

"He's not Available. He's Never Available."

"Let's bury him in the garden," said my father. "Where

he's spent so much time. Where you've spent so much time with him. I'll tell your mother. Get dressed and take some aspirin. You must have a hell of a headache."

"I do."

"You know how I know?" he asked. "It's the same headache you're giving me." He stomped up the stairs. As soon as I'd dressed, I picked up When Available. My father met me at the top of the stairs with a box.

My mother joined us in the garden. We took turns digging a grave, my mother encouraging us to dig deep. The sweat was good for me, and the early-morning time in the garden, the three of us doing something together. My mother and father were people of strong emotion, and that left little room for those weakest of feelings: nostalgia and sentimentality.

"We won't get another dog," I said when we laid When Available in the grave.

"Children need pets," said my father. "You're not a child."

We stood silently over the dog in the produce box. We took turns shoveling in the dirt.

"We didn't eat him, Wes," said my father when we scraped on the last clods, "but as he becomes earth, and as we live off this small patch of earth we've made ours, he will nourish us in his death as he did in his life." That's what passed for final words. I did not find them very comforting.

"I loved When Available," I said.

"I know," said my mother. "He was a comfort to us all."

I thought of Maria Tito's words: Love others, comfort

yourself. I'd followed her advice badly: I'd comforted myself, pleasured myself. But I had loved nobody, not even as much as I'd loved my dog.

We patted the earth and went into the Tsil kitchen. The phone was ringing. My father answered. When he hung up, he said, "Conseca's dead. Pack up. We're going to New Mexico." I headed to my room, and my mother headed upstairs. Our family time, it seemed, would last longer than the hour it took to bury a dead dog.

STEWS AND MOLES:
PAST FEEDS PRESENT

By afternoon we were on our way to Santa Fe. In the red station wagon, driving to New Mexico, I remembered Conseca: her brown hands on bread; the blood-red dresses she wore on every occasion from Mass to visits; her smile, and the small gap between her front teeth her smile revealed; the way she reached over to hold both of Juan's wrists, to be sure of his attention; her large body bent in the garden as she smashed squash bugs under the boards she'd put out for them to crawl under; her tender unreeling of the gauze on my burned hands the summer I was twelve.

My mother and father were alone with their thoughts, but just before we stopped for dinner, my father turned to me. "Wes." I looked up, and he shifted his gaze until he could see me in the rearview mirror. "I was mad this morning. But there was something else I wanted to say."

My mother turned in her seat. "We know why you were so nasty to Carson Flinn," she said.

"What?" I said.

"When you wrote him that sour note."

"You wanted credit for something. But he got it wrong," said my father. "Now I see you know what you're doing."

"What are you talking about?" I asked.

"The salsa you made last night," he said. "We both tried it. How did you do it?"

"I just did it," I said.

"Could you just do it again?" asked my mother.

"I want to use it," said my father. "With my nopal tamales."

"It'd be perfect with my goat cheese canapés," said my mother.

"Lou and I liked it," I said.

"Make it for Juan," said my father. "It'd be good with his corn bread–stuffed peppers. Comfort in a hard time."

"Since when did you want food for comfort?" asked my mother.

"I want to move in that direction," he said.

"You can't tell Carson Flinn it's my sauce," I said.

They drove all night and we pulled into *Agua Pura* just as day broke—yellow as an egg in a perfectly blue bowl. Juan was in his garden, hoeing corn rows. I had expected a grief-stricken man with a tear-streamed face, lying, as Pablito had for so many hours, in a rumpled bed. But Juan walked quietly to us. "All night, we have been together in the house, the candles glowing. This morning I heard her voice. *Take care,* she said. So I came to hoe in the corn and thank my fathers for the sun of a new day.

"Come," he said. We sat in shadow on the bench in front of the small house my grandparents had built for Juan and Conseca and Domingo years before. "We'll go inside soon. Today will be a day of mourning. Tomorrow a day to bury her in the earth." He hung his arm on my shoulder. The weight of it told me everything about the weight of his grief. I began to cry.

Conseca Saenz lay in her red dress on a table in the living room of the small house. Candles burned, and two old Mexican women, their hair braided and tucked under shawls, muttered in Spanish what Juan told me was the Rosary. My father went to the body, held Conseca's cold head in his hands, then kissed her forehead. My mother took a seat, and one of the women handed her a kerchief for her head. She put it on. Juan took my hand. "You are so big," he said. "The last she spoke of you she guessed you would now be taller than both of us. And you are."

I went outside and sat on the bench. I wished I could do something. I thought of the green salsa I'd invented, how my parents wanted me to make it for Juan. Soon, I hoped.

I had to wait until the day after the funeral. My father cooked a meal in his parents' kitchen. We would return to Kansas City the next day. Juan and Conseca's son, Domingo, cooked, too. I had hardly recognized him at the funeral. He'd gained weight, and his face was round as a moon, so puffy his eyes looked like achiote seeds in whole wheat dough. When he walked into the kitchen the next day, though, he looked more like the Domingo I remembered. He and my father embraced. "What's cooking, *hermano*?" asked Domingo. "Something to clear the sinuses after all the weeping?"

"My mother won't eat if it's too spicy," said my father.

"My mother wouldn't either," said Domingo.

"She always ate my food when she visited," my father said.

"Brother Roberto," said Domingo, and patted him on the back in mock sympathy. "She ate, then came home and complained. *I want the ice—to suck in my mouth,* she'd say."

Instead of being hurt, my father laughed. "My mother is always more direct," he said.

"My mother was the same. Nice to everyone but me. I'll miss her straight arrows."

"She complained about my spice, huh?" asked my father.

"Be glad you missed that," said Domingo. "With any person, there are many things, good and bad, to miss."

"You sound like Juan," my father accused him.

"I hope so," said Domingo. "He's a good man."

"Will he be okay?" asked my father.

"No. But he'll be okay. That's how he is."

I cooked and listened. My father used less than half his usual spice.

Grandmother Hingler was unhinged. "I like this food," she told my father, "but I can't bear to eat somehow."

"You've lost someone important to you," said my father. "The one who negotiated your Anglo life in this Hispanic world." His voice had the edge I was used to when he spoke to his parents.

"I've lost a friend," said his mother. "A very dear friend."

"She was happy to be your friend," said Juan.

Grandmother Hingler ate more after that. "You should go to Albuquerque and eat at Domingo's Sunday restaurant," she said to my father. "He's changed his cooking since his trip to the Caribbean."

"Caribbean?" asked my father.

"Mother came with me," said Domingo. "Didn't she write you?"

"She wasn't herself all this year," said Juan. "I didn't know until she died, then I saw back. The little strokes, they come before the big one."

"What should we notice about you?" my father asked Juan.

"I bend. But I don't break," said Juan. "Where I have ground, I am planted."

My grandfather had been quiet through the meal. His life was changed by Conseca's death, too. "You will always have ground here," said my grandfather. "*Mi casa es tu casa.*"

"*Gracias*," said Juan. Then he looked at my father. "But I will come with you. To Kansas City," he said. "For a visit. To get away. Perhaps when I return, and the corn is ready to harvest, I will be ready to accept what is in the earth. What has returned to the earth."

"We have to drive straight through," said my father. "We have to hurry back to business."

"And the boy?" said Juan. "He can come with me, to help me in my slower way."

"He could keep you company. But he doesn't drive," said my father.

"I'll teach him to drive. If he teaches me to make his good green salsa. It will be a trade. By the time we get to Kansas City, he will be driving. And I will know his recipe."

My mother almost laughed. Maybe she thought it was ludicrous that anyone could teach me anything. She stood up to clear the table. "That's a wonderful idea, Juan," she said.

"He needs a learner's permit," said my father.

"He has *my* permission," said my mother. She tapped him on the shoulder. They left for the kitchen. When they returned, my mother was still smiling.

"Only if you get a driver's manual to study on the way up," said my father. "So you can take your test right away once you get back to Missouri."

"I have a book," said Juan. "For New Mexico. Missouri is probably not so different. Last year, Conseca said she would learn. She was tired of asking every time she wanted to go somewhere. She studied the little book for one month. I was going to teach her."

"I taught her," said Grandmother Hingler.

Everyone stopped eating.

"We were going to surprise you, Juan. In the mornings, when we ran our errands, she drove and drove. We explored. She was so proud."

"She didn't tell me," said Juan.

"I asked her not to. I was afraid you'd be angry with me."

"You were her friend."

"And now you'll teach my grandson to drive?"

All that evening, I studied the booklet.

The next day, before we set out, Juan brought me into his small house to help him pack his bag. A bowl of stew sat steaming on the table. "Eat," he said.

"I'm not hungry," I said.

"You will eat," he said. "It is Conseca's. The last meal she prepared. We will eat it together, in her memory."

I ate, wondering why my father couldn't cook anything

like it—hearty, the spice only an undercurrent. The stew had common New World ingredients, but was uncommon in flavors and richness. It was Conseca's last gift to me.

CONSECA'S POSOLE STEW

2 ancho chiles
1 cup pinto beans*
1 cup lima beans
2 cups posole (dried corn—a Southwestern hominy)
Salt to taste
Turkey necks, or drumsticks
Leftover turkey, cubed

2 tablespoons pumpkin seeds

6 medium tomatillos, cut into half-inch cubes
1 cup pumpkin cubes, or other squash
New Mexico green chiles, as many as desired
1 tablespoon mild New Mexico red chile powder
Salt to taste

Cut up ancho chiles and place in large pot with pinto beans, lima beans, posole, salt, and turkey necks or drumsticks. Cover with water and cook (add water if necessary—this has to be the broth of the stew) until beans and posole are done. Take meat from turkey neck or drumstick bones, and set aside, along with any other turkey meat available (this is a good stew for the day or two after Thanksgiving).

Roast the pumpkin seeds until they pop and begin to brown. Set aside. Add tomatillos and pumpkin to broth and cook until pumpkin is soft. Add the turkey meat, green chiles, chile powder, and pumpkin and sunflower seeds. Heat thoroughly. Adjust broth by adding water. Salt to taste. Eat with reverence.

*Bean (green, wax, scarlet runner, pinto, black, tepary, lima, navy, etc.): *Whether Old World or New, beans are the poor man's meat. Combined with corn, the bean becomes rich in all the amino acids, and as nutritious and filling as any meat dish. Green beans, the immature pod of the kidney bean, were grown in the Americas as long as eight thousand years ago. Lima beans have been cultivated by the Peruvian people of the Andes for eight thousand years. The lima bean has been painted on pottery and depicted with stick legs as a warrior; lima images have been woven into textiles found at Paracas, along the Pacific Coast. This important half-moon bean was cultivated by all the peoples of the Andes.*

Known as the "musical fruit," the bean suffers in reputation because of the association with poverty and gas. Of all the food folklore that tells how to eat beans without experiencing gassiness, none really works. A truth: If you eat beans every day, your body becomes used to them; if that doesn't work, you'll simply learn to live with the bean effect.

Juan and I drove to Kansas City by a different route than I'd ever taken. "Back roads," said Juan. "They take you back."

We stopped first in Pecos, where the ruins of an old pueblo crumbled into earth: earth dwelling being reclaimed by earth itself. Nearby were the lofty peaks of the Sangre de Cristo Mountains, and broad mesas, and the gradual slope of the Pecos River as it made its way to the Rio Grande. On the old Santa Fe Trail, and on Indian trading paths before that, the pueblo at Pecos had once been a cosmopolitan place. Pecos was, as Juan said, "in the center, in the eye of the gods. All this was in fields." He moved his arm in a great circle. "Corn, bean, and squash—like the stew of our Conseca. Everyone should have a garden, and around them the world."

We found the hole of an old kiva. Mice had scattered cobs over the bottom. "Storage and worship, a place for both," said Juan. "Corn is a good teacher. She tells you everything dies, and that everything lives again. I am not a good student, just now."

"Can I drive when we get back to the truck?"

"You *only* will drive. It's how I learned. My family, we couldn't get anywhere until I learned, said my father. So I drove my whole family up from Mexico."

I took back roads to El Capulin, the extinct volcano. Sometimes faster, sometimes slower, sometimes grinding the gears, sometimes nearly losing purchase on the road, I drove. Capulin, too, seemed like a center of the world, with its old entryway to fire. The road up, narrow and steep, was frightening, but worth the climb. We looked out onto plains, miles in each direction, the mountains like thunderheads in the west.

By the end of the day, we had backtracked to Raton, the famous pass through the Rocky Mountains. A storm flung hail on the old truck as we sat in a little restaurant eating chicken enchiladas with green sauce. "Your sauce is better," said Juan.

After the storm, we wiped the water and a few pellets of

hail from the truck bed. "We go up a back road, put up the canvas, and sleep here in the back. I've brought the bedrolls."

We stretched a two-day trip into five, wandering up the lost creeks on the High Plains, walking into grasslands to find wildflowers, stopping in the midafternoon to dip into the North Canadian, the Cimarron, and the Arkansas rivers. I never had a gentler teacher. Juan was doing what he'd intended: He was teaching Conseca to drive.

I told him about Misty. About my experiments with alcohol. About smoking, which he refused to let me do. "The Indians first grew tobacco,"* he said. "They used it for ritual. Like all things strong, too many use it too much." He asked me to develop a ritual. We bought a tin of Velvet tobacco. Each time I wanted a cigarette, we took some from the can and put it in the back of the truck, on top of a cigarette paper. We lit the paper and watched the smoke. We cupped it in our hands and breathed, but couldn't inhale much.

Juan made me do things differently, and so I thought about things differently. "Do you remember when we slept in the corn, and heard it grow?" I asked him.

"Why do you ask?" he said.

---

*Tobacco (don't inhale): *Native Americans consider tobacco a gift from the gods. In fact, though it is probably indigenous to the American tropics, tobacco has been so long cultivated that no wild plant still exists. One legend among eastern North American tribes tells of Corn Mother, who, when her people were starving, killed herself and asked her husband and children to cultivate her flesh and bones into the soil. The next season, corn and tobacco, her gifts, grew, and have fed the bodies and spirits of her people since. Native tribes seem to have used it ceremonially more than daily, and to nourish the spirit rather than to deteriorate the lungs.*

We were in the Kansas Flint Hills, bare hills swelling like waves on the prairie. We'd be home soon. "I want to grow," I said, not looking at him, just at his hands, cupped over a tiny pile of tobacco.

He put his hand on my shoulder. He was smiling. "You think this is silly, this tobacco, this ritual. But to grow you must begin to be serious, even about little things. We eat, but when we eat in church, it is more than food. Same with sex," he explained. "To have sex is nothing. To have sex with someone you love, inside of years together, then it is something. It is sacred. This Misty, will you be with her always?"

"No," I said immediately.

"Then you are doing the things a boy does."

"Juan," I said, "I *am* a boy."

"You grow when you practice to become a man." The last of the smoke died away. Juan crushed the remaining paper. The tobacco blew into the wind.

"My parents want me to be a boy. They want me to work for them, live with them, do what they say."

"They let you come with me. And learn to drive," he said. "Are you ready?"

I climbed into the driver's seat and started the truck. Around me was nothing but space. But I didn't feel free. "I'll be driving Mom on catering jobs when I'm not working the front of the Tsil for my dad."

"You'll be behind the wheel, driving yourself," said Juan. "Your need is to move away from your parents. But your joy will be in returning. Just as we are returning, now. Someday, you will be glad to be a child, as I am."

We came into Kansas City the back way. At noon we were stopped at a light on Southwest Boulevard. "Look," said Juan. He pointed out the window to a small, hand-lettered sign: *Pablito's.*

We were hungry. And we were fed. I hadn't seen Pablito in two years. I hadn't seen Teresita for even longer. Together, they ran a busy *taqueria*, traditional to Mexico. People lined up, told the man behind the counter how many tacos, flour or corn tortilla, and what in the large ingredient tubs to put inside: beef, chicken, posole, pinto beans—whole and refried—jalapeños, sour cream, lettuce, onions, and so on. My father's influence showed in the sides of cactus, in an imitation of my father's habanero sauce, dubbed Roberto's XXX, and in the availability of turkey on the food line.

Pablito sat on a high stool, at the cash register, taking drink orders, directing people to the condiment and sauces table, ringing up purchases, speaking from his perch to all his customers. Teresita poured drinks, helped with large trays, bused tables, worked with incredible speed to ensure that customers kept moving through their small establishment. She didn't recognize us at first, but Pablito did. His excitement grew as we approached him.

Mine did not. He would hate me: for my awkwardness around the pregnant Teresita; my dislike of his grieving and living in our basement; my spying on his affair with Cocoa; my leading my father to his brown legs in my mother's secret closet. But when we reached the register, he stuck out his thin hand. I took it. "My friend Wes," he said. "The register is broken today. You don't pay, except in friendship."

Teresita brought us beer. Juan refused the beer for us and ordered Coke. Teresita bubbled with their new place, open just two weeks. "The Carson Flinn man has been here. He liked us! He doesn't look good. Too big."

Juan shared the news of Conseca's death.

"There is nothing happy but sadness is there, too," said Teresita. She hurried to a corner, where a child ate at a small table. She brought him to us, his hand in one of hers. In her other hand was a basket with a baby asleep inside. "We have so much to live for, Pablito and me," she said.

Both children, Francisco and Julia, looked like little Pablitos—thin, with beaked noses, and smiles that widened and opened at the same time. The children and Pablito and Teresita's obvious happiness relieved me.

By the time Juan and I left, Pablito had offered me a job on Saturdays, his busiest day, helping him prepare food in the morning. "If your father and mother will permit," he said.

"I'm greeting at the door of the Tsil, an evening job. I can drive. I'll be here next Saturday."

Juan nodded.

"Will my parents be angry?" I asked Juan.

"Maybe. But their anger will be about the past. We have to live today, as well. They know that."

My parents were happy to hear that Pablito and Teresita were back together, with two children. Maybe Juan talked to them, but they seemed ready to let me make changes.

I was not smoking, so I didn't go into the alley anymore.

"You haven't been walking me home," Misty said one evening. She rushed off to fill a customer's water glass.

"I need more sleep," I said when she came back to the bar. I told her about my weekend hours at *Pablito's*.

"He led Cocoa on. How can you even talk to him?"

"She knew he was married," I said.

Our favorite customer, Ronald, came into the Tsil with his wife. I seated them. "Misty will take your drink orders right away."

"He still led her on," Misty said in passing.

"Led her on?" I went back to the bar and waited for her. "Am I leading you on?" I asked.

"You're not married, are you?" she asked. She went to take Ronald's order, though she knew it by heart: gin, straight up; for his wife, a Corona. I had everything ready by the time she returned.

"I won't be married for a long time," I told Misty. "And I'm not going to take over my father's restaurant. I'm not even going to live in this town."

She said nothing.

The next night, she said, "I miss our times together."

"I do, too," I said.

"You have everything," she said. "Or you could have."

"You? The restaurant? Money?"

"That's more than I grew up with. Don't you care about it?"

"I care, but it's not my future."

"You're talking about me, too, aren't you?" she asked.

I was glad when a party of four came in. I wasn't sure what my future was, but I knew Misty wanted everything to stay the same.

By the time I was almost seventeen, I gave up another

thing: high school. I quit with one year to go and spent more time working for Pablito and Teresita, cooking and taking care of their kids. They spoke to me only in Spanish. Soon I understood most everything they said. I could get an education without the relentlessness of high school: the homework, the social positioning, the emphasis on sports, the stupid clubs, the need to dress like everyone else, think like everyone else, eat what everyone else ate. I had never been good at those things, and high school never neglected to remind me of it.

Pablito changed his food offerings constantly. He listened to me when I talked about food. One time, he wanted to create a mole, a stew for turkey parts: He used the breast in his tacos. We spent a week of mornings trying different combinations of tomatoes, spices, nuts, seeds, and chiles. Nothing came close enough to the mole his grandmother had made when he was a child, in Mexico. "What did she use?" he wondered aloud. "More garlic tomorrow," he said after Monday's attempt. And Tuesday: "She loved her nuts." He doubled the roasted peanuts on Wednesday. "Spicier," he said, "because she was a spicy woman," and Thursday he added a second chipotle pepper. "Sweeter," he said, but sugar didn't help.

We cooked unsatisfactory mole for two weeks. "It is because I was a child that I remember it so well. But because I was a child, I cannot now create it again," Pablito said.

I went back to *my* childhood, to the aphrodisiac meatballs I'd watched my father make for my mother in St. Louis. I went to *Pablito's* the next day and asked him which had been our best mole. He showed me his notes. "To this," I said, "let's put in some things my father uses." We added sunflower seeds roasted almost to blackness, a small amount of mescal, and equal parts vanilla and maple syrup. After an hour, once the mole had cooked down, Pablito tasted the pasty sauce. He shouted his joy. The tears in his eyes surprised me. "I will call it the Wes and Pablito's Pablano Mole." He clapped me on the back, then hugged me. "But I don't think she would have cooked with mescal," he said.

"It's smoky," I said. "She cooked over a fire?"

"That's it," he said. "This will be famous in my restaurant. People who come here will taste my past. They will know better who I am."

My mother and father congratulated me on the mole triumph. But always, when I spoke of *Pablito's*, my father said, "You want to cook, you should cook here."

"Pablito lets me use onions and garlic," I said.

"Part of your rebellion." He covered his face with his hands. "Cooking with Old World food. Why me? Why couldn't my son be stealing cars, running away?" I was glad he could tease.

WES AND PABLITO'S PABLANO MOLE

1 dozen tomatoes

6 ancho chiles (dried pablano peppers), reconstituted in water

2 chipotle chiles, reconstituted in water

½ cup roasted peanuts

3 onions

6 big cloves garlic

2 teaspoons ground achiote seeds

1 teaspoon cumin

3 teaspoons salt, or to taste

¼ cup cocoa

¼ cup sunflower seeds, roasted almost to blackness

¼ cup mescal

2 teaspoons vanilla*

2 tablespoons maple syrup

Cider vinegar, to taste, 1 tablespoon or more (trust Pablito on this)

Turkey** parts—dark meat, skin removed

Take all the sauce ingredients and blend together until smooth. Mole, after all, means mixture—from the Aztec *molli*. Heat until bubbling, and add turkey parts. Cook for two hours, until the sauce thickens, and the turkey is coming off the bone. Add water if mole is too thick.

Serve turkey parts (whole or deboned) with mole sauce over rice or wrapped in flour tortillas.

*Vanilla (called *tlilxochitl* by the Totonacs): *Of the 35,000 orchid species in the world, only the vanilla orchid (indigenous to the rain forests of the Caribbean, to Central America, to the southeastern coast of Mexico, and to the northernmost latitudes of South America) produces edible fruit. The vanilla vine climbs into the forest canopy and produces clusters of flowers. The buds take six weeks to mature, then open for a* *single day during which they must be pollinated or they will not develop fruit. That fruit, often called a bean because it is a slender pod, grows to as long as a foot in the next nine months. Then, after fermentation, the pod's vanillin makes it the desirable nectar it has become. The Totonac people, along the Gulf Coast in what is now Veracruz, Mexico, found that they could control the vining, hand-pollinate, and thus increase vanilla production for use as perfume, flavoring, insect repellant, medicine, and aphrodisiac. True vanilla will cost nearly twenty-five dollars a quart, and will contain at least 35 percent alcohol (used in the extraction process).*

**Turkey: *Benjamin Franklin lobbied for the turkey as the National Bird, writing: ". . . for my own part I wish the bald eagle had not been chosen as the representative of our country; he is a bird of bad moral character. . . . The turkey is a much more respectable bird, and withal a true original native of America. . . . He is besides (though a little vain and silly, it is true, but not the worse I hope for that) a bird of courage, and would not hesitate to attack a grenadier of the British guards, who should resent to invade his farmyard with a red coat on."*

My mother, though proud of my mole, said, "You're taller than I am now, why not try to be smarter, too."

I went over to her to check the tall statement. Face-to-face, all I saw were her eyebrows, thick and dark, unplucked as always.

"I quit high school, too," she said. "I went to a cooking school. I never told you that."

"You're doing all right."

"At least get your GED," she said.

"Maybe someday," I said.

Juan wrote me a card: "My Wes: Your father says you are

not finishing high school. I didn't either. But I want more for you, as I would my son. Love, Juan."

Everyone wanted to fix me, or keep building my character, or whatever they chose to call it. But I had quit drinking hard liquor and wine—occasionally, I drank beer with Pablito. I had quit sleeping with Misty. I had a good relationship with Pablito and Teresita.

Then I made an odd peace with Carson Flinn. He had a stroke, mild, but it affected the movement on his left side. Since he was a big man, he had trouble walking, so he was confined to a wheelchair. He could eat, but he couldn't write quickly, longhand or at the typewriter. He wanted to keep reviewing. Not long after he was released from the hospital, he came to *Pablito's* for the new mole and other fresh items. A young woman helped him in and went through the line with his plate. She took notes as he talked about the food. I assumed she'd type his review when he was finished.

She couldn't help him in one way: the trip to the men's room. I wheeled him there, through the door, then took his arm to heft him up. He urinated. He settled back into his chair. "Penelope doesn't know food," Carson complained. "And she can't spell. It takes me longer to correct her than to get her to put it all down."

"Who is she?" I asked. She looked around my age, maybe a little older. And she was attractive—long rusty hair and emerald eyes, liquid and energetic.

"The daughter of a friend. She likes food. And she's bright, but she needs a lot of help."

"My father always said the food business was hell when it came to help," I said.

"That's why he counts on you," said Carson. "That's why Pablito and Teresita like you. You're dependable."

"Until I leave," I said. I began to wheel him out the door.

"Until you leave, I need you," he said. "Wes, I know we've not always gotten along, but you know food, and you're smart. At least that nasty little note you wrote to me was spelled correctly."

"I didn't drop out of high school because I was stupid."

"You were stupid to drop out," said Carson Flinn, "but I know you're not stupid."

On the way back to his table he made me an offer. He'd take me to the best restaurants and food parties in Kansas City. Give me some perspective, he said, on the business I'd grown up in. "In case you ever want to think about it for yourself," he said. "You'll learn to write better, to type, to file a story, to create a structure." If things worked out, he said, he'd share his byline with me. And I would have to work only three nights a week.

"What about Penelope?" I asked.

"She's starting school. An anthropology major."

"I'll talk to my father," I said.

"I already have," said Carson. "Cocoa's coming back three nights a week."

"Does my mother know?"

"Your mother is satisfied that nothing happened between Cocoa and your father. It might have, but it didn't, as far as she's concerned."

"You know a lot."

"Your mother and I are close friends."

"You're offering me this job because of her," I said. "I'm like this Penelope. I'm the son of a friend."

"We'll start at six-thirty tomorrow evening. I'll be waiting for you, in a cab, outside the Tsil."

He never answered my accusations. He was tough to work for, very exacting about food and writing. Although I had known him for years, I didn't know him at all. The little quirks of his personality, easy for the unpracticed eye to ridicule, turned out to be his strengths.

"This is a fussy business," he said once, as he complained about a broken mushroom cap and a comma splice in the sentence I'd just written for him. "Should I be less fussy than the people I review?"

"Of course I eat a lot," he said once, as I wondered how he could order another dessert. "Most restaurateurs know who you are. Sometimes they even know when you'll be visiting. They may even know that you'll sample a great deal of food. But you have to be sure to challenge them. So you consume as much as possible. In the long run, they'll feel the fairness of the review because they know you haven't narrowed your writing along with your selections."

"Of course I liked it better when I could at least try to disguise myself," he said after I asked why he had winced when a restaurant manager called him by his name. We were in Carson's living room, in his apartment by the Country Club Plaza. He had a beautiful view of Brush Creek. "Objectivity," he said, "is impossible. But the appearance of objectivity is an absolute necessity." He waved his hand. "Go into my bedroom," he said. "Look in my closet. I have everything in there but a clown costume." He had an amazing wardrobe, with scads of neckties, a dozen pair of glasses, six hairpieces. If I hadn't been coming to a respect for him, I might have laughed.

Three weeks later we were in his study. He dictated from my notes, and I typed with improving skill. I had wondered why he wanted to note both the odd lighting and the missing button on a waiter's shirt at the end of a review. "Life," he said, "is in the details. Because they add up. They are the logic of the writer, the language of a critic's thinking. Details are the map of thought. You can tell someone anything. The details show him that it is so." In this way, I learned not only to write what Carson Flinn told me, but to take notes for myself, and to ask him later, as I typed, whether he wanted to use them. The first time he said, "Yes, we need to say that," his use of *we* changed to include me. And he shared his by-line with me.

"I believe in fortunes," he said after we'd sampled the elegant opening of Shanghai Palace. We'd eaten a custard and a caramelized banana flambeau and a black bean cake dredged in cinnamon and nutmeg. But he insisted on our opening and eating the obligatory fortune cookies that came with the bill. Coincidentally, we both had the same fortune: *God has given you one face, and you make yourselves another.* "What does it mean?" he asked me. I told him we were born one person— our parents' child—but we become another person—our-selves. "That's a young person's interpretation," he said.

When I asked him for an older person's interpretation, he said, "All of life is striving for perfection." Later that night, I was typing in his apartment. I asked him what he meant. He waved my question away. He wheeled over to the hi-fi, putting on yet another record from his collection of Kansas City Jazz.

"You're a goddamned idiot," he told me after I had been with him for six months. "Your mother is right this time. Get your GED, and get yourself out of this town."

"My mother said that?"

"It is her fervent wish," he said. "I told her how talented you are. She's proud of your byline. You have a future. But you're stuck."

Carson Flinn was right. I was stubborn enough not to give him the pleasure of knowing it. Without telling anyone, I studied for and took the GED test. Only when I found out I'd passed, doing best on the parts that required written skills, did I share my good news. To celebrate, Carson took me to the best restaurant in Kansas City, and on a Monday, so my mother and father, who didn't work that day, could be with me. They allowed me to have a drink, and toasted me. I smoked with them after the meal. What next? they each asked me in a different way. I didn't know.

Juan came for another visit. I had just turned eighteen. I drove him around Kansas City in his old truck. On the way home I went past the hospital where I had been born. As we parked in the alley behind the Tsil after our drive, he showed me a train ticket, to Albuquerque.

"You want me to go to New Mexico?" I asked him.

He pulled the title to his truck from the glove compartment. "The truck is old," he said, "like me. But, like me, it is yours." He handed me the title. "The ticket is mine. The title is yours." On the back of the title he'd signed the truck over to me. "You learned to drive in this truck," he said. "Now maybe you can learn to go somewhere."

"What if that somewhere is New Mexico?" I asked him. "Could I go to college there?"

"Domingo went to the university, in Albuquerque," he said. "He could help you find out."

"I'm driving you home, then," I said. "We'll cash in your ticket. I'll find out what to do when we get there."

NUTS: FILLING UP

My Albuquerque apartment was hot in the day, cooler then colder each fall night. It was sparsely furnished: like Misty's place, when she first moved near Westport. I'd packed the truck, but moving from a bedroom to an apartment left holes. Juan gave me a dresser, my grandparents a table and chairs. I hung my father's menu on the wall, and the cover of a brochure my mother had designed for Buen AppeTito. On my coffee table was Ronald's dental plate. He'd had a new one made when he heard I was leaving, and gave me the one I'd worked so hard to find in that hot Dumpster years before. I displayed it like a totem.

Life away from home wasn't easy. I'd never been expert at making friends. I'd never had expenses, paid bills, maintained a vehicle. I'd never made a long-distance telephone call. I'd never been to a restaurant or a movie by myself.

College was structured, like work and family. But away from school, especially weekends, I drifted, unsure of myself once I'd finished reading, research, lab time, and studying.

For my first year, I cooked: because I knew how, because I missed my parents and their meals. I sometimes imagined what they were cooking or eating. I'd go to a store, find the ingredients, spend Saturday afternoon cooking an elaborate meal, then eating. Usually by myself. Usually with great feeling, but little pleasure.

One Saturday, maybe three months into school, I sat at my kitchen table and looked around me. Without thinking, I'd nearly re-created my father's kitchen.

Wide-mouthed jars of cornmeal—yellow and blue—and tiny pearls of quinoa.

Bottles of honey and vinegar, with spices mixed in them—sage, Mexican oregano, chiles.

Dried chiles, red to purple to black, next to fresh ones of every shade of green, orange, red, and brown.

The firm fruits—tomato, tomatillo, guava, mango, and pineapple.

Nuts—cashew, pecan, peanut, piñon.

Seeds—pumpkin, achiote, sunflower.

Dried beans, wild rice, pumpkins, winter squash, yucca root, jícama.

I'd re-created home. Pablito needed the mole of his grandmother. My mother cooked one meal a week exactly as her grandmother prepared it. Juan and I had eaten Conseca's stew, remembering, just days after her death. I often ate my father's signature salsa. "A tribute to orange," my father had always called it. I brought the orange of pumpkins, the orange and heat of habaneros, and the light of honey together, as he always had. The taste lightened my heart and saddened me at the same time.

SWEET HABANERO
PUMPKIN SALSA

3 ancho chiles, chopped fine, reconstituted in boiling water

½ cup lightly mashed roasted pumpkin

1 habanero,* or two for real heat, diced fine

3 tomatoes, cut into lengths and roasted

1 tablespoon mild red chile powder (or to taste)

Cactus honey to taste

Sage-infused pineapple vinegar to taste

Tomato juice to adjust liquid

Salt to taste

¼–½ cup roasted pumpkin seeds

Combine ancho chiles, mashed pumpkin, habaneros, and tomatoes together. Heat slightly and adjust taste and consistency with chile powder, honey, pineapple vinegar, tomato juice, and salt. Roast pumpkin seeds until they pop, or until slightly brown, and add just before serving on or with anything screaming for heat.

*Habanero (closely related to the Scotch Bonnet and Jamaican hot pepper): *The habanero ("de Havana") is probably the hottest of the hot. Take the jalapeño and times the heat by 30, even 50. The sweet flavor of its heat makes it good in fruit-based salsas and relishes. Watch for the habanero in the cooking of the Yucatán.*

Sundays, as my father had once done, I went to *Domingo's* to cook and earn dinner. Domingo was more relaxed than my father. "You need to learn *mañana*," he told me. "It's the feeling that anything rushed won't turn out well. It's why I cook on Sundays only. *Domingo's*, people come here with only one thing in mind—to eat. They're not on their way to a concert or a movie. Church is over, their big thing done for the day. They bring the newspaper, and their children or their grandchildren, and they know they'll eat. It is more like the old way, like when I've been to Mexico. Not the American hurry, hurry, hurry." Domingo worked for the state of New Mexico—social services—weekdays.

Sometimes, Domingo let me cook from the Tsil menu. "Special," he'd tell those he knew well, "very special." I'd take my imitation of my father's food to a table. Usually, my attempts were worth the effort. My disasters taught me that I didn't know all my father's secrets.

I became expert at his Black Bean and Gooseberry Enchiladas. Domingo encouraged me to cook them often. "I ate them soon after your father said good-bye to Old World ingredients. I thought he was *loco*, until I tasted them. Then I knew he could do what he wanted."

BLACK BEAN AND GOOSEBERRY ENCHILADAS

FILLING

1 cup dried black beans
3 ancho chiles (dried)
1 16-ounce can gooseberries (or 2 cups fresh)

1 dozen corn tortillas (preferably blue)
Corn oil

ENCHILADA SAUCE

4 large red tomatoes
1 tablespoon medium-hot Chimayo chile powder
3 big, fresh jalapeño peppers
Salt

GUACAMOLE

3 ripe avocados*
2 medium yellow tomatoes
2 tablespoons sage vinegar (crumble sage from American
*   sagebrush in vinegar and let sit overnight or longer)*

Cook black beans in water with the dried ancho
chiles until they are tender. Add drained, slightly
rinsed gooseberries in equal amount of black beans.

Make enchilada sauce by buzzing the four large
red tomatoes in a blender. Put them in a saucepan
with the chile powder and two of the jalapeños, cut
into fine pieces. Salt to taste. Cook for at least an
hour, until sauce thickens.

Quickly heat corn tortillas in hot corn oil, but do
not cook to crispness. Dip tortillas in enchilada
sauce, lie flat, and spoon on 2 tablespoons of the
black bean and gooseberry mixture. Roll to make a
tube. Set on plate. When all 12 tortillas are on plate,

cut in half and push out to the edges of the plate to form a circle.

Make a guacamole from the avocados, yellow tomatoes, sage vinegar, and remaining jalapeño pepper, everything chopped fine and mixed together. Put guacamole in small bowl and place in the space in the middle of the plate. Spoon guacamole onto enchiladas.

*Avocado (alligator pear—for the Hass's black lizard skin): *Native to the tropics of Central America, and of three types, West Indian, Mexican, and Guatemalan. Americans mostly eat Hass, shaped like a black alligator-skin baseball. It ripens well, peels with ease, pits well, and tastes rich and nutty. Great for guacamole (Spanish for avocado is* aguacate *or* palta). *The Fuerte avocado, with thin green skin, slim pear shape, and a lighter taste, is better for dessert or in salads, for texture rather than taste.*

I wasn't sure what I was doing that freshman year:

Sunday—*sleep late, go cook for Domingo, drink beer, eat, go to bed early.*

Monday through **Friday**—*attend class, drink beer in the late evenings, try to sleep eight hours.*

Saturday—*sleep late, plan a big Tsil meal, grocery-shop for the week, cook alone at apartment, hit bars on a full stomach. At student bars, find fellow student to drink with. Alternate shots of mescal with draws of beer, cheapest possible. When lubricated, tell stories about life: injuries and indignities especially good. If in class with fellow student, talk university. Don't mention grades—people don't like anyone who does better than they do. Try to end evening with a grand gesture, by eating the maguey worm.*

Go home alone. Wake up with pounding head, with smoky taste of mescal in mouth, with half-memory of a good time in brain. Take as many aspirin as necessary and go to Domingo's *to cook* Tsil *food, feeling like a failure. Note: Every once in a while, any day it's unavoidable, think of drinking as a secret, like the unknowable distance a father puts between himself and his parents. Or think of it literally, like a secret place, like a little room behind a cabinet in a kitchen. Experience the pleasure and terror of that, when necessary.*

My schedule might as well have been published in the *Albuquerque Journal*: Both Domingo and Juan seemed to know it. Early spring of my freshman year, Juan showed up at my door one Saturday morning. My head pounded, light lanced my eyes. My tongue was a swollen lizard. My skin was still creased red from the folds of my sheets.

"*Buenos días,*" Juan said with a smile that told me he was bent on something. I'd find out what when *he* was ready. "Come for a drive."

"I'm asleep," I said.

"Sleep in the truck."

I stepped over beer bottles, dirty clothes, dirty dishes, and my piles of school notes, each pile representing a class in which I would receive an *A*. I put on pants, a T-shirt, and my sandals. "Where?" I asked, though I knew he wouldn't answer.

"You're tired," he said.

"Studying," I said.

"Books," he said. "You have a mind. You use it well. Some of the time. Get in."

"Where are we going?" I asked again. I climbed in the passenger seat of his new truck.

"You know what time it is?" he asked.

I'd forgotten to put on my watch, and I held up my wrist to show him.

"Time of year," said Juan.

"March," I said.

"No," he said. "Spring. Full moon. We must prepare the earth."

"What earth?" Shovels and hoes—those old shapes that spell work—lay in the bed of Juan's truck.

Juan drove silently. He stopped in front of a vacant lot in an older neighborhood. The walls around the corner were smattered with graffiti. "Domingo owns this lot," said Juan. "He said we could use it." He turned off the car. "Potatoes and peanuts," he said.

"You've come a long way from Santa Fe to garden," I said.

"I didn't come to garden," Juan said. "I came to wake you up. To watch you plant. I'm going to show you how."

"I've planted potatoes," I said. "I've worked for other people. My father, for example."

"Have you planted peanuts?" Juan asked.

I shook my head.

"Then you don't know everything," he said.

"And you do?" I asked.

"I know about plants," he said. "I know when people need tending."

"Tend to someone else," I said.

He opened his door and climbed out. "Who do I have, except you?"

I slid out of the truck and helped with the tools. One day

couldn't hurt me, I thought. I didn't know we'd stop only for water. I complained of hunger. Juan told me to think of the earth. We turned over the soil, all by hand, and dug deep rows. Juan went to his truck for the blue potatoes he had there. He cut them into small pieces, an eye in each piece, then spat on each eye and laid the seed potatoes into the rows we'd dug. We planted four rows, each forty feet long. Then we planted four rows of peanuts, doing the opposite as for the potatoes: We mounded the soil. "As they sprout, they send out tendrils. Some tendrils bear leaves, some we will cover, to build them into hills. Many, many peanuts."

The sun finally set and I was blind in darkness by the time we sowed the last of the peanuts. "Every day, you water," said Juan. "Every other day you move through with the hoe, if it needs hoeing or not."

"This isn't *my* garden," I said.

"You said yourself it's too far from Santa Fe." Juan gathered tools and walked slowly to the truck. His stoop shamed me. I admired his ability to work, at his age.

"I could tend it every once in a while," I said. "Weeds don't grow that fast."

"You are not fighting weeds, you are building the habit of the gardener." Juan clattered the tools into the back of the truck.

"Now you sound like my father," I shouted from the dark garden.

"Good," said Juan. "He learned well, too."

I went to the truck, exhausted.

"I'll check on you next week," he said when he dropped

me off at my apartment. "And, Wes," he said, calling into the darkness, "the potatoes are very rare. They will fetch a good price, the ones we can't eat. Domingo wants his cut for the restaurant."

I went into my apartment sunburned, sore, exhausted, too tired to prepare dinner. After a single shot of mescal I fell into bed. I vowed never to get up. I vowed not to go to the garden until Juan took me there the next week.

But by the middle of the week, I wanted to see the garden again, to make it real. I drove there, watered, and made a quick tour between rows with the hoe. Then I went about the business of school, library, lab, homework. I went back that evening for another watering.

I liked having something to hurry to in the morning and after school. Perhaps I was too obedient to the requirements of others, or to plants and foods. I'd learned those habits in my childhood, and, like bad ones, they are hard to break. Besides, time passed more quickly. Juan visited each week. Domingo spoke proudly of the potatoes he'd feature in his restaurant. I was less homesick, less self-pitying. I received my second semester of straight *A*s, and spent more time in the garden. In the few places we hadn't cultivated I planted tomatoes and green beans. As the green beans ripened, I picked them by the bagful and cooked another of my father's recipes at *Domingo's*.

SWEET POTATO AND GREEN BEANS WITH PINEAPPLE-CASHEW DRESSING

Sweet potatoes,* and
Green beans,** equal amounts

Peel sweet potatoes and cut into pieces the same size as the green beans. Wash and break stems off green beans. Steam just until the sweet potato pieces are no longer crunchy, but not until they are soft. Serve with Pineapple-Cashew Dressing.

PINEAPPLE-CASHEW DRESSING

1 teaspoon achiote seeds
Corn oil, small amount
½ cup pineapple
½ cup honey-roasted cashews
1 jalapeño, diced

Grind achiote seeds into a powder, and cook in oil in small pan until orange.

Put pineapple, cashews, jalapeño, and achiote in blender and make this into a sauce. Serve over steamed vegetables.

*Sweet Potato (ages, camote): *Of the same family as the morning glory, the sweet potato is native to the New World tropics and was culti-*

vated by the Aztec for its tuber as early as 2475 B.C. It was among the first new foods encountered by Columbus on his 1492 voyage, when it was known as ages. Cultivated all over the Western Hemisphere, it is a staple of fall meals (though it was never meant to be served with marshmallows—not a New World food, since the original marshmallows were made from the root of the marsh mallow, of European origin). Like peanuts, sweet potatoes were shown by George Washington Carver to enrich soil depleted by the overplanting of cotton and other crops. Sweet potatoes are not to be confused with the yam, which is the rhizome (sometimes weighing up to 30 pounds) of the Dioscorea plant, native to the Far East and America.

Green Bean: *The green bean, often called a snap bean, is the unripened pod of the kidney, and pod fibers from Mesa Verde (southwestern Colorado) show that Native Americans ate them in the immature state. But green beans, matured into kidney beans, provide much better nutrition, are easier to store and much more highly prized. Cortés introduced kidney beans as "haricots" to Spain in 1527, and they quickly spread to northern Italy, where they were called fagioli. The dark, brown-red skin, creamy flesh, meaty flavor, and firm texture make kidney beans excellent in soups, stews, salads—any dish in which a bean needs its shape, color, and texture.*

After my peanuts ripened, I promised, I'd make the same recipe with peanuts instead of cashews. My father wouldn't have to know about the substitution.

By midsummer, my potatoes flowered, then the vines began their slow withering: The green paled, then yellowed; the leaves curled into themselves like an old man's arthritic hand.

Once they wilted completely, the wind blew the leaves away. The stems lay on the earth like old snakeskins. "Soon you will see nothing," said Juan, "but they are there. Waiting for the one with a memory. When the Spaniards came, potatoes were the best crop. We knew where true treasure was buried. We could always stay alive."

Juan told me not to dig until the earth in that part of my garden looked dormant: I experienced the miracle of abundance where nothing grew. Domingo took his share, then paid me well for the blue potatoes Juan and I didn't save for ourselves.

The peanuts would not ripen until fall. That semester I enrolled in a course called Edible Plants of New Mexico, and, while I waited for my peanuts, I began to eat the earth where I found myself. My teacher was a graduate student, Maria Standing Tall, a little older than I and, in spite of her name, shorter. On the first day of class, she said, "Shoots, tubers, seeds, stems, and roots. Some fruits. If you want what's tender, enroll in the spring semester. We're going after the tough stuff. Most everything will need baking, boiling, roasting. We'll be digging and hulling."

Having just dug potatoes, I understood. I waited impatiently to dig peanuts, too. Juan and I watched the green leaves begin to wither one week, die the next.

"Dig one peanut," Juan said the following week. In the earth was a perfectly formed peanut shell, brown and tough. Juan took it from me. He opened it between his thumbs. "Nothing inside," he said.

"What's wrong?" I asked.

"Impatience," said Juan. "The nut has not formed in the shell."

"How long will it take?" I asked.

We walked to his truck, and he drove me home. "I have something to show you," he said. He picked up a folder from between us. We went inside and sat at my table. Juan opened the folder and showed me a piece of paper with a map on it. "Your father's first garden," he said.

My father couldn't have been much more than ten years old, from the looks of the loopy letters, and the odd proportions of sections and rows he'd drawn. In his boy's hand, he'd written *Pintos, Potatoes, Peanuts, Pumpkins, Peas.* "He called it his *P* garden," said Juan. "He'd laugh and laugh. I did most of the work. But look at his pleasure." Juan spread some photographs on the table. My father as a boy: thin, tall for his age, leaning on a hoe. My father: hose in hand, watering potato vines. My father: his arm around Juan's waist, smiling at the camera. Two shadows crossed the ground in front of my father and Juan.

"Who took these?" I asked, thinking of the shadows.

"Conseca," said Juan.

"And the other shadow?"

"Your grandfather," said Juan.

"My grandfather didn't have time for my father."

"Your father doesn't want to remember." Juan pushed another picture at me. My father stood beside his father. They looked so alike they might have been twins. Next to them stood, I guessed, the young Domingo, the same smile on his face as on my father's. My grandfather had his hand on both the boys' heads, as though measuring their growth, as though he'd grown them both in the garden. "They looked alike, then," I said.

"Your father and your grandfather?" asked Juan.

"My father and Domingo. They could be brothers. Except for skin color."

"Half-brothers," said Juan.

"That's a good way to put it," I said. "Almost brothers." I thought of all the time they'd spent together, how both of them gardened, had restaurants, loved food and beer, had their hearts in New Mexico. Domingo had given me the land to plant peanuts and potatoes.

"Half-brothers," Juan said again, more firmly.

I stopped thinking and paid attention to Juan's sudden intensity.

"They *are* half-brothers," Juan repeated.

"How?" I asked.

Juan was silent while I weighed the possibilities. Either Juan had impregnated my grandmother or my grandfather had impregnated Conseca, who gave birth to Domingo. The shadows on the ground told the truth: my grandfather and Conseca. "You raised Domingo as your own. You stayed with them?"

"We tried and tried, but we couldn't have children, Conseca and me," said Juan. "At first, when she was with child, I believed in miracles. Then I demanded the truth. Then I left. But each day I thought of her, the swelling of her belly. I cared more for life than for who was the father. Than for my pride. I made peace with your grandfather. We have tried always to be a family."

In the photograph, my father looked so happy to be with his father. Something must have changed, sometime.

"In their hearts, the boys knew," said Juan. "But when we told them, at sixteen years old, your father took it hard. He became jealous of Domingo, of the attention your father divided between them. He blamed his mother, too. And Conseca. He clung to me, though I tried to teach him differently. Just as I've been teaching you differently."

"What are you teaching me?" I asked.

"To be different from your father."

"I am," I said.

"So different," he said, "that you might be brothers. You cling to me. You drink too much because you are not comfortable with who you are. You think of yourself as special, as different. It is tiresome." Juan showed me one more picture: my father, holding a plant, vine and roots, the roots full with peanut shells, and on my father's face a smile of ferocious accomplishment. "He waited and waited for the peanuts to come into the shell. Every day he dug. Finally, almost overnight, the energy of the dying plant transformed itself into the seed that we eat. The nuts filled the shell.

"You and your father are alike. Neither of you waits patiently. Neither of you understands where your life comes from, what you owe to the vine, to the leaves above you. There you are, the twin peanuts, filling the shell, fat and proud. But blind as the earth that surrounds you."

Juan put the photographs away, along with the primitive map of the *P* garden. "You will wait for the peanuts to mature. I will wait for you to mature." He left.

That night, I could not sleep. Juan's story had left me bewildered, vulnerable, like a butterfly crawling out of its co-

coon. I walked the streets of Albuquerque, watched the moon slowly arc across the sky. My grandfather wasn't who I thought he was. My father—jealous and stubborn—still burned with his father's infidelity. Juan had been cuckolded, but had helped raise two boys, neither a son, to manhood.

He'd helped raise me, too, in spite of my resistance. He'd said I was like my father. He wanted to shock me like my father had been shocked. I was nineteen. My father had been sixteen. My father had run from his parents as though his life depended on it. I was running, too. Maybe I was being stupid.

In the morning, I dialed Juan's telephone number. But it was my grandmother Hingler who answered. I didn't know what to say, so I hung up. When my phone rang, Juan said, "You just called."

"How did you know?"

"You've been thinking?" he asked.

"We'll talk more, soon?" I asked.

"Of course. Your grandmother wishes you well."

Maria Standing Tall, like Juan, pushed me. She not only knew plants, but she knew their stories, their whims, their meaning. We took field trips into the Rio Grande Valley, or into the Sandia and Jemez mountains. With Maria Standing Tall, everything that surrounded us became a sign, and took on meaning. "We are growing things, too," she said, "surrounded by growing things. Look around you. Look at your lives."

I did something I'd never done before. I wrote letters to my grandparents, telling them what I was doing: gardening, going to school, learning about New Mexico. When I wrote, I spoke to each differently. My grandfather was not the man my father had created for me, but the man I knew from my experience: Juan's friend, someone who had worked all over New Mexico and knew the landscape well, someone who probably loved me. My grandmother was a woman who had taught her friend Conseca to drive, then lost her, a woman who appreciated Juan, who had, over the years, acclimated to New Mexico.

My grandparents wrote back, each differently, in voices I hadn't known before. My grandfather: *Nothing is better than a New Mexico mountain pasture, with a spring bubbling up so cold you imagine the water in it thawed from snow melted only moments before. To drink from that spring.* My grandmother wrote: *We think of you every day, though not with concern for you, as though you were a child, but as a life going on like ours, discovering new things, happy to be alive.* These were not the grandparents I'd been taught to know.

My peanuts matured, *fat and proud.* I salted some in the shell, hulled some for roasting, ground some into peanut butter, and sold the rest to Domingo. I cooked with them on weekends, as I'd promised. Domingo created a salsa like one he'd eaten in the Caribbean, on the last trip he took with his mother. He taught me to make it, and I sent the recipe to my father along with ten pounds of peanuts. I thanked him, and my mother, for all they'd given me: *More than peanuts,* I joked.

My father wrote back that he was serving the sauce on his vegetables, instead of his pineapple-cashew dressing.

GUAVA AND
CHOCOLATE DRESSING

½ cup guava* juice
2 tablespoons powdered chocolate
1 tablespoon habanero pepper sauce (El Yucateco red is excellent)
2 tablespoons sage vinegar
¼ cup roasted cashews**
¼ cup roasted peanuts

Heat the guava juice and add the chocolate powder.
Cook until mixture begins to bubble. Then put
everything together in a blender and blend until
completely smooth, adding more guava juice for
thinning or more cashews for thickening.

Serve in half an avocado, the dressing filling the
cavity where the seed used to be, and surround the
avocado with watercress on a plate.

Or serve as salad dressing, or with fresh vegetables like black beans, corn, green or red peppers, or
any combination of these.

*Guava (Psidium guajava L.): Part of the myrtle family, native to
tropical America, the guava was misnamed in its scientific classification,
as were many New World plants: psidion, which is from the Greek for
pomegranate, and guayabe, which is Spanish for guava tree. Gonzalo
Hernandez de Oveido called the guava a guayaba apple when he visited
Haiti in the mid-sixteenth century. Guavas have six times the vitamin

C of oranges, concentrated in the skin and outer mesocarp. Guavas were being grown by the Chinese as early as 1592, just a century after Columbus sailed the ocean blue.

**Nuts: *The New World nuts include cashew, Brazil, pecan, and peanut. Cashew and Brazil are both from the South American tropics; the pecan from the American South; the peanut was first cultivated by the Andean people and is not a true nut, as it grows underground (legume-like) rather than on trees. Pecans, which grow on a kind of hickory tree, have remained as American as, well, pecan pie, which makes that an appropriate dessert, along with pumpkin, for that New World feast, Thanksgiving. Cashews, sweet and buttery, have been adapted to Chinese cuisine, and for limited uses in other parts of the world. Brazil nuts are almost never seen except as most people pick past them in the cocktail nut tin. But peanuts are everywhere. Cortés first heard of them in 1519, when he sailed from what is now Cuba to what is now Mexico. Peanut butter was supposedly first introduced as a health food for the elderly at the St. Louis Exposition of 1904 (which also saw either the introduction or rising popularity of ice cream cones, hamburgers, puffed rice, iced tea and Dr. Pepper). American George Washington Carver found uses beyond peanut butter and foods, thus keeping the peanut one of the New World's most important crops.*

Part of my final exam for Maria Standing Tall read: "The spirit of a place, and of a people, comes from the land. We express the interaction between land and people in our foodways. When we eat, we are one with the land, and, by extension, one with all its people."

PUFFBALLS:
FINDING THE INSIDE

I had written to my parents about the Edible Plants of New Mexico course, and the spring semester sequel as well. I did not write what Juan had told me about Domingo, about himself and Conseca, about my Hingler grandfather. But his telling had made things different for me: Seeing one thing differently, I saw many things differently.

Maria Standing Tall and I began to cook together, everything from cattails to yucca cactus. We made teas from dandelions, mints, and rose hips. We gathered piñon* in the mountains, roasted them, shucked the thin shell of skin, and gorged ourselves.

Maria refused alcohol. She cooked for the pleasure of tasting food as it was, without beverage, sauce, spice, flavoring. I tasted with her, but I was enough the son of my father that I experimented, as well. One day I spent all afternoon creating a new soup.

*Piñon (pine nuts): *Nut pines, found at elevations between 4,000 and 7,500 feet in the western mountains of North America, are short-trunked, small trees that yield their seeds/nuts in the fall and early winter. These seeds, rich in protein, have as many as 3,000 calories per pound. After harvesting them, Native Americans roasted them, then shelled them for eating or for longer storage.*

YUCCA SOUP

1 quart turkey broth, finely strained
2 good-sized yucca* roots, and stalks, peeled and cubed
Half a grocery bag full of yucca flowers, bitter centers removed
2 good-sized zucchini, cut into small cubes
4 tomatoes, sliced
1 tablespoon Chimayo chile powder
Salt to taste

Heat turkey broth and simmer yucca roots until softened. Meanwhile, boil yucca flowers for ten minutes and drain. Add flowers, zucchini, and tomatoes and cook just until zucchini is soft, but not clear. Dust with chile powder and adjust with salt.

*Yucca (*Yucca eleta*, also Soap tree, Our Lord's Candle, narrow leaf): *Native to the grasslands and deserts of the Southwest, from Texas to Arizona, and as far north as Kansas, and at elevations from 1,500 to 6,000 feet. Also known as palmilla yucca, it has a thick stem covered by yellowed, dry leaves. The leaves are spiny, thin, and grow in a crown-like cluster. The white, hanging-bell flowers bloom from spring to early summer. They, along with yucca stem (baked) and root, are prized as food among southwestern Native American tribes—Hopi, Tewa, Hano, Navajo, Ute, Apache, Zuni.*

I was more delighted than she was. When I pressed her, she said, "It's good. Not authentic, but good."

"You don't really like it," I said.

"My gift is in knowing foods," she said. "Your gift is in creating new things to do with food."

Maria Standing Tall reminded me of Juan: She used what she knew very directly. Once, after a late-summer rain, we gathered puffballs, a mushroom some people call stomach fungus. Puffballs are not poisonous. I was happily walking through a pine forest in the Jemez, gathering, even eating, an occasional find. Maria knew I had seen puffballs, so told me to pick generously and meet her at the stream we heard in the distance. After I'd filled my pack, I went toward the sound of rushing water. She sat on a rock, a long knife in her hand. "We'll check them now, to see which ones to keep," she said.

My stomach turned sour. "Check them?" I put my pack next to hers.

She cross-sectioned a puffball.

"I have a knife," I said. "What are we looking for?"

"See?" Three rejected mushrooms lay next to her on the rock. She picked one up. "This stuff looks like gelatin. That means it's a baby stinkhorn. I wouldn't want to eat one."

"Why not?" I asked, trying to remember if one of the mushrooms I'd eaten seemed gelatinous.

"They taste terrible," said Maria Standing Tall. She picked up another mushroom. "This yellow-green color means it's past its time. And look at this one." She showed me another puffball, again sliced on its longitude, this one full of holes. "Worms," she said.

I pulled out my pocketknife, sat down, and reached into my bag. "This one good?" I showed her a creamy white half.

"Perfect," she said.

I was relieved when the puffballs, one after the other, were fine, only two with holes and one past its prime.

"Uh-oh," she said, nearing the bottom of her bag. "This is why you cut them." She held up what looked like a puffball. "See this shape? Like a shadow of another mushroom inside?"

I nodded.

"It's a baby, of the *Amanita* mushroom. You never want to eat one. Highly poisonous. You can die."

"What are my chances?" I asked. "I ate two or three of these without checking them."

"Chances are good you're a fool," she said. "In the plant world, you have to know at what stage you find anything. Same with the human world." She stopped when she saw how frightened I was. "That was a half hour ago," she said. "You'd know by now."

Maria Standing Tall threw the poisonous mushroom as far as she could into the woods. Then she ate a perfect puffball. "In three weeks, we'll go to a corn dance."

Before the corn dance, Grandfather Hingler died of a heart attack. I drove to Santa Fe to meet my parents. Their trip had been hot and tiring. I'd seen my father angry at his father, but had never before seen him sad about him. I watched my father and Domingo mourn without letting the others who attended the viewing, the funeral, and the burial know about their separate but equal connection to their father. That was hard enough, and though they were friendly with each other, neither was able to get beyond the performance of the ritual. On my parents' last day in New Mexico, we all ate at *Domingo's*, and neither brother truly acknowledged the connection until we left to return to Grandmother Hingler's home for a last good-bye. Then, in an almost mocking show of emotion, Domingo saw my father to the door, hugged him, and shouted, *"Hermano!"* And my father saw the convenience of the show, and broke from Domingo and shouted, *"Hermano, para siempre!"* The extravagance of their declarations made everyone in the restaurant think they were exaggerating a feeling, not revealing a bloodline.

After a last night with my grandmother, my parents left for home. They were going to take me back to Albuquerque first, so I could help deliver some furniture to Domingo. Just outside Santa Fe, my father pulled to the side of the road. "Damn," he said. He'd forgotten the envelope his mother had put on a table by her front door for him, the one that contained his father's and her wills. "There's a copy in there for Domingo, too. She wanted him to have it," he said. "She made a special trip to her safe deposit box."

"How could you forget it?" my mother asked him.

"You expect me to be thinking of her death so soon?"

"Can she mail it?" my mother asked.

"It's only twenty minutes back," he said.

We turned around. My father hit the steering wheel a couple of times and swore. Once, he parked on the side of the road again, his eyes too full of tears to drive. My mother patted his back and rubbed his neck. "It's okay," she said. I sat in the backseat and, to tell the truth, was happy to watch his heart do a little melting.

We pulled into the drive at *Agua Pura*. Juan was carrying a box across the courtyard, from his small house to the big one. He looked surprised. We piled out of the car, and he stood, expressionless. The box was full of personal odds and ends, his photographs, his toothpaste, the old clock he kept on his mantel. My father reached for the box. "You want some help with this?" he asked.

"Your mother," Juan said, "she says the house is too big to be in it all alone."

My father went inside for the large envelope. He said nothing to Juan about the box. When he came out the door, he called back over his shoulder. "Love," he said. "Love you both." My mother and I climbed back into the car. My father walked over to Juan's little house. He peered into the windows, then came back. He started the car and we left.

"Well?" asked my mother.

"Nothing left in there but old furniture, and the bed where he used to sleep."

"They deserve some happiness," said my mother.

"They deserve whatever they deserve," said my father.

We delivered the furniture and the will, and then I said good-bye to my parents. I wasn't certain what to think of Juan and my grandmother, about all I'd learned and seen about the odd arrangements on *Agua Pura*.

In fact, by the time I attended the corn dance with Maria Standing Tall, I needed a ritual—something to make me see and feel and come to terms with who I was and what I might do. We went to one of the pueblos north of Albuquerque, along the broad river valleys that had made an agricultural habitat possible for the earliest Americans. We arrived "before the tourists," Maria said. She asked me to park my truck a respectful distance from where the ceremonial dancing would take place. The sky was that perfect blue known only to people who have lived in the Southwest, a land of both tremendous beauty and difficult sustenance. Difficulties were forgotten for the corn dance, and the peaceful sky was soon full of sound. Cars gunned for parking places, blaring their horns. Dogs barked, roosters crowed, children screamed, cried, laughed, shouted. Drums began what would be hours of steady rhythm. They were joined by the jangles, the beads, and the deep-throated humming of men.

Sound enriched what I observed. Homes, decorated with pine branches, wreaths, and hanging ristras of red chiles, and totems offered to sun and wind. Small tents with hand-lettered signs offered tortillas and fry bread, skewers of beef, venison, and chicken. Some dancers were in full dress, beaded and feathered. Others, mostly children, wore primitive but proud imitations of their parents, and danced with pop-can tabs for necklaces, bottle caps for rattles.

The dancers, Maria told me, thanked the sun and the rain, beseeched the elements, too. I had no sense of the language, the music, of why people stood, sat, danced, gave voice to feeling. Maria Standing Tall was my interpreter. Nobody was allowed to photograph, so memory, she told me, must document what I saw, heard, and felt.

I didn't see, hear, and feel what she did: everything chaotic but purposeful, jangled and pure, patched together but smoothly run. One image stuck in my head: little corn-husk dolls, lined up in a booth, for sale, for children. Their heads, a loop of husk, had achiote seeds for eyes, a piece of blue corn for a nose, a straight strip of cayenne for a noncommittal mouth. Had my father ever seen a corn dance? Why had I never asked?

For six hours I stood next to Maria Standing Tall, watching her rhythmic swaying, aware of the humming and mutterings and catches in her throat. I did not know her.

I went home for Thanksgiving, the Anglo harvest ritual that consists of gorging the gut instead of communicating with ancestors and gods. In New Mexico, I had harvested a bounty to bring to Kansas City. Great-grandmother Maria Tito had moved into my basement room, giving up her house after she'd fallen and broken her arm. My parents had put in an elevator chair, and she rode up and down with a delightful smile on her face. She'd lost just enough of her mind to be fun, not enough to be terribly difficult. Every time she saw me, she said, "You're Wes? So big." She'd lift her bushy eyebrows in mock disbelief. I slept on a couch my mother and I hauled into my old bed closet.

We had our usual gigantic Thanksgiving. Carson Flinn was there with Penelope, the young woman who had first helped him take notes after his stroke. "She spells better, now," Carson told me when she was in the kitchen. "And she's even more beautiful."

I agreed. Her rusty hair had grown even longer, her eyes greener and more intense. She had square shoulders, graceful movements, a contagious giggle. I'd asked Cocoa to make sure I sat next to Penelope. I guessed she was just a year or two older than I was. "Last year of college," Carson Flinn confirmed.

Cocoa, though a guest for this dinner, still helped seat, water, and feed the others, like Ronald and his family. I'd brought everyone except Penelope a ristra as a gift. Ronald drank too much and draped his string of chiles around his neck. Carson Flinn, who had recovered some of his mobility and lost some weight, said the rusty pepper chain would have a place of honor in his kitchen. "Eat it, too," I reminded him.

Cocoa wondered when she'd find time to eat so many peppers. I gave her a possible recipe, from a tent at the corn dance. "Nothing but four or five of these peppers—they're fairly mild—ground into beef, until it's about half pepper, half beef. Like grainy beef, and scooped up into tortillas. I'll make some tomorrow."

"Not tomorrow," said my father. "We're going on an expedition tomorrow."

"What about the restaurant?" I asked.

"Closed for pawpaws," he said. I thought he was making a joke, but I'd heard of pawpaws. "You may know your New Mexico edible plants, but you need to visit an oak-hickory forest instead of a pine one."

He roused me early. I wasn't sure which of us was more tired. He'd developed lumpy shadows under his eyes. He carried a carton of cigarettes and a thermos of coffee. I knew if he was tired, he'd at least be alert. We drove northwest out of Kansas City into the Missouri River bluffs. He parked the car off the road near a rusted iron bridge. We walked along a creek, into woods. I had no idea what to look for. We walked for half an hour, stepping around buckbrush, over wild grapevine, avoiding prickly gooseberry bushes and poison ivy. I was ready to give up. I had to urinate, and I sidled up to a hickory tree and unzipped my trousers. Just before I started my stream, my father yelled at me. He hurried over. "Our first find," he said.

Sure enough, just a few feet from the hickory tree grew what looked like its miniature. On the leaf-covered floor of the woods lay several pawpaws, and in the tree were three or four more. He picked one from the tree, wiped it on his pants, and ate it. I finished my business elsewhere, and he handed me my first pawpaw: slickly sweet, mango-like in texture, as soft as an overripe cantaloupe, a little pulpy around the hard buttons of seeds deposited randomly in its stubby banana shape, but rich throughout with a little nut taste from the skin.

PAWPAWS

One oak-hickory woods, preferably well watered
A diligent hour of search
A quick eye
An appetite
As many pawpaws as possible
A handkerchief

Search woods for an hour until you spot the small tree, broad leaves like a cross between hickory and catalpa. Look for the greenish plug of fruit, sometimes on the ground, if late in season, preferably on tree, just ready to fall. Eat immediately, and wipe hands on handkerchief when finished. Return to car without fruit in hand—the memory of gorging on pawpaws in the woods is better than trying to do anything with your harvest once in your kitchen.

※

"You like them?" my father asked.

"I like being here, eating, with you," I said.

"Everywhere in the New World," my father said, "are simple but completely rare foods, like these pawpaws. Few people have eaten them. I wish I could say I've eaten every one of those New World foods." He picked another of the soft fruits, another elongated, olive-colored pear, and put it in his mouth. He gave me one, too. When we finished the fruit from that tree, we found another, and another, until our appetites gave out.

Back at the car, my father turned to me. "By the way," he said, "some people say pawpaws give them the shits."

"Juan told me about Domingo," I said.

"About Domingo?" he asked. He was quiet for a time. "You mean about my father and Conseca," he said.

"That's what I mean. I wonder how that made you feel. Growing up."

We climbed into the car and drove for some time without saying anything. "Water under the bridge," he said. "Once, it really bothered me. Because nobody said anything. But it was always there, inside the families, like we were different from what everybody thought we were. Domingo and I never talked about it. He went to Catholic school, I went to public. We handled it.

"Mostly, I just wanted things different for you. I mean, your mother and I have had our problems, but at least you know everything, right?"

"I didn't know about Domingo," I reminded him.

"When Juan told you, did it bother you?"

"Of course," I said. Then I was quiet for a long time. "I realized you'd always kept me from my grandparents. I've gotten closer to them. Juan said I was too much like you," I said. "I wondered why I was in New Mexico, doing the things you did. Maybe I shouldn't be. Maybe I should be home."

"You want some Kansas City time? Because I could use you, after your spring semester, for maybe a month or so. Just long enough to help me with something I have up my sleeve."

"I'm gardening there during the summers."

"There's a garden here," said my father.

"I don't even have a bedroom anymore," I reminded him.

"Wait'll you hear," he said. "It's a party. A big one. My fiftieth birthday. We're going to make it the biggest restaurant event in the history of Kansas City. A meal like no other, ever. We'll eat things like pawpaws. Things that are local, or rare, or not usually done. We'll break all the taboos."

"Do you have a menu already?"

"A few things, because I want to say I've eaten them once in my life."

"Like?" I asked.

"Dog. And guinea pig. And insects."

"Dad, I thought When Available was just a joke."

"This isn't a joke. Will you help? It's a culmination, for me. And I'd like you there."

I thought about trying to live at home again. About leaving New Mexico and the garden Domingo would let me plant.

"Put your garden in," said my father. "Get your crops up. Then get some help watering and weeding, and come up here June fifteenth. You'll be back in Albuquerque by July fifteenth, the day after my birthday. I'll pay you."

"I don't need pay," I said. "It'll be my birthday present to you."

"Tell your mother," he said.

"Does *she* like the idea of this big party?" I asked.

"Tell her you know about Domingo, so she'll know you do."

"She knows?"

"Everything I know."

The next day, I found my mother in her kitchen, drinking coffee and spreading bleu cheese over croissants. I began my day by saying, "Juan told me about Domingo."

"Oh, that," she said. "That was before I was married."

"Of course," I said. "Dad just told me I should tell you I know."

"He knows?" she asked.

"Sure he knows. He said to tell you, so you'd know that I know."

She was confused. In her confusion she looked around her kitchen, and then directly at the cabinet, the one with the hiding place. I knew she had something to hide, something about Domingo. "So Juan told you. *How* did he? Or *why*? I mean . . . you must have become very close."

"We gardened together. We talked. He wants to tell me about himself, and about Dad, and about Domingo, and Grandfather Hingler. He's trying to grow me, like a plant."

She smiled. She was relieved, and her relief bothered me. "That's good," she said. "You always need information. That's what my grandmother Tito always gave me."

"And you'd do it for me?" I asked.

"Haven't I?" she asked.

"You haven't told me about you and Domingo," I said.

My mother was generous and expansive in her cooking. Carson Flinn once told me that my father served food with heat, my mother with warmth. But on that day she served her information cold, with no meat on the bones. Perhaps that's as it should have been.

When she and my father were courting, mostly by letter for those two years after their initial meeting and evenings tasting food and getting to know each other, my mother took one trip to New Mexico my father never knew about. She'd been struck by how alike the two of them were: Domingo a browner version of my father; Domingo a more relaxed and less intense version of my father; Domingo an already settled, already confident version of my father; Domingo, who offered her a different version of life.

"We were intimate on that trip. I'm not just talking about sex, because when you get older you realize that's not everything. But we shared everything, as I had with your father."

"Did Domingo want to marry you?" I asked.

"I told him I couldn't. I corresponded with your father, and then I made the right decision. Your father and I married. That's all. Subject closed."

"Why didn't you marry Domingo, if he was like Dad without the problems?"

She smiled. "Your father and I were meant for each other. We like problems."

"Does he know? About Domingo?"

"It was my trip. Like research. Your father and I have kept our New World foods and Old World foods, the Tsil and Buen AppeTito, separate. We have a life together and separately. Domingo wouldn't have allowed that."

"He's too much like Juan? Too open?"

"You don't have to carry my secret," she said. "Tell your father about Domingo. Or I'll tell him, if you want."

"I'm coming back to help, next summer, for his fiftieth birthday," I said. "I'm just not sure about New Mexico."

"Good," she said. "I've missed you."

III.

RETURNING TO THE TABLE

Xi-Tomate (the word *tomato* comes from the Aztecas): *A true fruit, though often not sweet enough to be a fruit, so it's also considered a vegetable, but without the firmness and texture of other vegetables. It's the New World relative of the deadly nightshade, and now is the most common and indispensable fruit in any kitchen.*

The base of two American condiments, catsup and salsa, the tomato was once viewed with suspicion, even hostility. Although brought by explorers of the New World to Europe in the early 1500s, the fruit did not appear as an ingredient in any European cookbooks until around 1692, when Antonio Latini, an Italian, included several recipes for Spanish-style tomato sauces in his Lo Scalco alla moderna. As late as 1820, Europeans who colonized the United States remained fearful of eating tomatoes.

Many have debunked the story of a Colonel Robert Johnson, said to have stood on the courthouse steps of Salem, New Jersey, and publicly eaten a raw tomato and survived, thus proving its lack of venom.

Few cuisines now shun the tomato, and its presence is ubiquitous on this globe.

You have young traditions, old ones, from the New World and Old. You are both the vegetable and the fruit, a goer-between-worlds. You are various, negotiable, capable of thickening, a good base for sauces, a fine garnish of salads. You are bright as blood, big as a heart, sweet and acidic. Ah, life!

THE AVAILABLE TAMAL:
EXOTIC APPETITES

When I returned to Albuquerque, I stayed in better touch with my parents, and they with me. I didn't tell my father about my mother and Domingo. *It's not my secret*, I kept telling myself. Someday, my mother would open up her little room. I wasn't going to lead my father there again.

Postcards began to arrive, progress reports on the big meal from my mother and father and Carson Flinn. Carson's easy conversion surprised me until my mother told me that Penelope's undergraduate thesis in anthropology was on Aztec foodways. Besides, my parents and Carson had a history together. My father was going to turn fifty, the Tsil Café twenty. My mother had known Carson Flinn for twenty-five years—since she'd started Buen AppeTito.

My correspondents were excited. Their cards punctuated my coasting through the rest of the fall, then spring semester, still making good grades, still drinking a little too much, still wondering if I should be in New Mexico.

Dear Wes: We always joked about the dog tamal, but why turn fifty if you can't experience what you've always wondered about? If you have any ideas about how to proceed, help me. Can a per-

son get in trouble for raising a dog for food? Maybe I'll find out. Love, Dad   P.S. We'll name him Available.

Dear Wes: Your father is nearly fifty years old, and still research-ing and reinventing the New World. Possible headline: OLD MAN: NEW WORLD. I continue to learn from him. He put me in charge of huitlacoche, the corn fungus eaten by the Aztecs: Am I slighted or honored? And, in true Robert Hingler fashion, he's calling it an appetizer! Penelope is bringing me along with this. Glad you're on board. I won't make you take notes for this one. Until summer, C. Flinn

Dear Wes: I've said no to everything but vegetables—I may eat guinea pig, and llama blood and insects, but I won't help your father cook them. Look out if he lives to be 100! By the way, don't be surprised to know we've invited Pablito and Teresita to the big day—they're going to help with the cooking, and a bever-age—something to do with chia seed—and they'll get credit, too. You helped us find them again, when we were more calm. Thanks, Your Mother

Dear Wes: You drank your mother's milk, so how about your mother's beer—Chicha? It's traditionally made by women and children (supposedly pure ones, but let's not get picky here) who masticate corn—their saliva converts the starches to sugar. We'll be home-brewing for the next several months, if I can keep your mother chewing. Love, Dad

Dear Wes: We've started putting out some publicity, and besides our group (Mom, me, you, Carson, Pablito, Teresita, Cocoa,

Misty), we've got Ronald and ten others signed up. Maximum is fifty. I found a place in Peru that sells guinea pigs in a market, and I can get them hairless and gutted, ready to cook, quick, frozen and shipped. I don't want to tell you the cost. How many times do you turn fifty, and need fifty guinea pigs? Love, Dad P.S. They sell dog, too, fed only on corn and avocados.

Dear Wes: Does one look forward to cooking the root of the scarlet runner bean, harvested at $8 a pound by people God knows where? I get to make any sauce I want (as long as it's New World). Maybe allspice and juniper berries with passion fruit, to remind your father of our earliest days together? More bulletins later, Your Mother

Dear Wes: Your father seems to assign me anything with an Aztec name. From huitlacoche I've graduated to tecuilatl, a slimy algae that dries into a black cake (dirty soap) that supposedly tastes like cheese rather than mud. We'll see, won't we? I've heard you are continuing your food education in Albuquerque. Native American and New Mexican and Mexican are great—but do they have Spanish restaurants there, too? Let me know, C.

Dear Wes: Opuntia, the fruit of a cactus the Spaniards called tuna, supposedly turns the urine red as blood. What a way to remember a meal—even more shocking than the asparagus smell that lasts for hours. Should we tell our guests in advance about it or not? Sorry to sound perverse. I'm just having fun with this. Love, Dad

Dear Wes: Menu is now official, and invitations sent out. We've got restaurateurs, food people through Carson, regulars like

Ronald, some anthropologists from a few colleges, thanks to Penelope. Looks like it'll run about $100 per person, but nobody's complained about the price. Once you're home, we'll talk specifics—much to do. I'm closing the Tsil the night before and the night after. Love, Dad   P.S. Mom told me about her Domingo experiment.

Dear Wes: I didn't want to bother you before your semester was over. But now that you'll be home in two weeks, I have a favor to ask you. Please encourage Juan and Domingo to come up for the 50th. Your grandmother Hingler looked at the menu and declined. I'm sending you one in an envelope so you'll see why. Can't wait to see you, Your Mother

Here's what she sent:

MENU

BEVERAGES:

Chia seed punch (Pablito's), served with appetizers

Chicha, corn beer as made by the Incans (Buen
   AppeTito's), w/ main course

Hot chocolate,* Aztec-style, without milk (Tsil Café),
   w/ dessert

APPETIZERS

Tamales, as made in South America,** with corn mushroom (huitlacoche) sauce

Tecuilatl—Mexican algae (obtained by Carson Flinn)

Maguey worms, roasted and salted (Tsil Café)

SALAD

Amaranth*** greens, with sweet amaranth seed dressing
    (Tsil Café)

SOUP

Quinoa leaf and green chile, flavored with llama blood
    (Tsil Café)

MAIN COURSE

Guinea pig stuffed with Mexican marigold (Tsil Café)

Scarlet runner bean root (Buen Appe Tito's)

Chayote squash with iguaxte sauce (Buen Appe Tito's)

DESSERT

Opuntia fruit—Spanish called the cactus tuna
    (Tsil Café)

White sapotes in palm nut (coquitos)/ honey sauce
    (Pablito's)

*Chocolate (cacao): *Chocolate is made when cacao beans, split, are fermented, then roasted, cracked open, the outer shells thrown away, and the cocoa heart ground into a paste, or "liquor." From there, the unsweetened chocolate can be powdered (by removing cocoa butter), can be flavored with vanilla, chiles, or other spices, or can be made richer with the addition of cocoa butter. Indians drank it, liquified and spiced, as observed by Spaniards new to the New World and to chocolate:*

> [Chocholaté] is a drink very much esteemed among the Indians, where with they feast noble men who pass through their country. The Spaniards, both men and women, that are accustomed to the country, are

very greedy of this Chocholaté. They say they make
diverse sorts of it, some hot, some cold, and some
temperate, and put therein much of that "chili"; yea,
they make paste thereof, the which they say is good
for the stomach and against the catarrh.
—*The Natural and Moral History of the East and West
Indies,* by José de Acosta, Jesuit missionary to Peru,
1590

**Dog (New World dogs—no pets allowed): *The Conquista-
dors of Spain found the Aztecs eating dogs fattened on avocados and corn.
In 1609, destitute and starving, the Virginia Colony subsisted on horses,
dogs, cats, rats, and snakes. In 1769, James Cook feasted on Tahitian dog,
and his chronicler wrote: "South Sea dog was next to an English lamb."
Lewis Garrard, traveling in the American West before the Civil War, was
served a stew of dog meat, rose hips, and corn.*

***Amaranth (grain, used as cereal by the Aztecs and Incas;
leaves are eaten as greens): *The mustard-size seeds are 16 percent
protein, surpassing wheat, rice, and corn. Over 50,000 seeds can be
shaken from a seed head that grows to be a foot long. Nutritionally, amaranth enhances other grains because it has what they lack: plenty of the
amino acid lysine, as well as high quantities of trace minerals. The lowly
pigweed, that broad-leafed occupier of vacant lots, is amaranth's second
cousin and can be foraged for greens.*

The menu had my father's appetites—for friends, and
food, and perhaps fame—all spelled out. I could see them
on the telephone, or sitting at the table with their cigarettes,
discussing the menu. With each new item, probably, Carson
Flinn shuddered, questioned, was cajoled, was told to talk to
Penelope, and then was converted. I imagined my parents
talking finances, Cocoa and Misty wondering about the timing, my mother questioning the quality of shipped food.

From a distance, the menu seemed crazy. Had fifty people signed up to eat llama blood, maguey worms (though I'd eaten them, mescal-soaked, plenty of times), dog meat, and guinea pigs, let alone *huitlacoche* and *tecuilatl*? When I showed the menu to Maria Standing Tall, she read my mind: "All these things were eaten, yes. So were human beings, by the Aztecs. But that was all within a cultural context, not a restaurant in the Midwest."

Nothing I could say or do would stop the meal, of course. I wondered why I'd agreed to help. I'd left home once, and though I wasn't exactly sure what I was doing away— being myself or my father—I was not in the kitchens of my youth.

"You don't *have* to go, do you?" asked Maria Standing Tall the second time I complained to her.

I didn't answer. She would think me strong if I stayed in Albuquerque, weak if I went home for the big out-of-context meal. I'd feel disloyal to my father if I stayed in Albuquerque. "Look," I said finally, "it's my family. Not many can understand them. I wish I did sometimes. But they're my family."

"So go," she said. "For your parents. Your father. It's his fiftieth birthday. Just do it with yourself in mind, too. Get some more experience doing what you do best."

"And what's that?" I asked.

"You're a cook," she said. "You just have to learn to cook for yourself."

I took Maria Standing Tall's advice. I told my father to assign me some of the dishes. Carson Flinn agreed to let me stay in the spare bedroom in his apartment for the month. He gave me Penelope's address, saying that if anyone could convince me the menu was worthwhile, she could. I wrote my mother and told her that she and my father should be the ones encouraging Domingo and Juan to join the celebration. I wrote my father, explaining that I'd be staying with Carson, and I hoped he'd understand. I wrote Penelope, and, after her reply, I called her. Not only was she excited about the menu, she was planning a trip to Mexico to buy some of the ingredients. Her eagerness was infectious, and, I admit, her warmth attracted me. "I really want to spend some time with you," she said, "get to know you better."

I planted my New Mexico garden, recruiting some boys from the neighborhood who had first ridden by on their bicycles, then come into the lot, then asked about the plants, then become helpers in exchange for vegetables. They would watch the place for a month. I planned my next semester at the university, so I'd be certain I knew where to go after my brief time in Kansas City. I wished I had more friends to say good-bye to, more people I needed to tell I was leaving. I called Maria Standing Tall. "It's that time already?" she said. "Happy cooking."

I told Juan I wasn't sure where I belonged. He said something like I thought he would: "Life is nothing but being in between." He said he'd be in Kansas City on July 14. "And, *hijo*," he said, "however it goes for you, think of what's next and not what is now."

With that advice, I headed home: called by two kitchens, by Pablito and Teresita, by Carson Flinn, and by Penelope. I arrived at the Tsil before five o'clock. My great-grandmother Tito met me at the door of the restaurant. She wore a bright blue dress, and carried menus. "Special today," she whispered, "the little pigs and the pond scum and the cactus berries." She handed me a menu.

"Great-grandmother Tito," I said. "It's me, Wes."

"Wes?" She looked closely, as though my name might be written on my face. And maybe it was, because she brightened up. "They said you were gone."

"Dad!" I yelled. I started across the restaurant, which was empty except for Maria Tito.

My father burst out of the kitchen in his stained apron and hugged me. He saw Maria Tito. "She try to seat you?" he asked.

"And told me some very exotic specials."

"She's not exactly impressed with my birthday plans."

"I've been worried myself," I said.

"Don't eat anything you don't want to," he said loudly.

"Llama blood," said Maria Tito to nobody in particular. "*Special*, they call it."

My father took the menus from her and sat her in a chair. "Your mother lets her come down and greet customers when there aren't any," he whispered to me. "Cocoa should be here soon. Go see your mother."

My mother hugged me, then sized me up. "You need food," she said.

"Blood?" I asked, imitating my great-grandmother's disgust.

"Your father's cooking tonight," she said.

We didn't eat llama blood or pond scum or "little pigs." The special was my father's cranberry-chile pesto, but beefed up with oven-dried beefsteak tomatoes, and served over smoked turkey.

CRANBERRY-CHILE PESTO

½ cup cranberries*
3 New Mexico dried red chiles
2 ancho chiles
2 tablespoons pine nuts, roasted
2 tablespoons sunflower seeds, roasted to taste
Sunflower oil (for texture—begin with ¼ cup)
Chile-dried tomatoes,** ½ cup

In a small saucepan, put dried cranberries and seeded and finely chopped chiles in a cup or so of water. Cook until they are swollen, and enough water has evaporated to leave you with about ½ cup. Put in food processor with the pine nuts, sunflower seeds and sunflower oil, and the chile-dried tomatoes. Blend until smooth. Add water if necessary, or more pine nuts and sunflower seeds to thicken. Eat with meat, or by the spoonful.

*Cranberry: *In 1768, Benjamin Franklin, from England, wrote his daughter a letter in which he longed for the foods he missed: cornmeal and cranberries, among them. First memorialized in an English language cookbook in 1795, with a recipe for cranberry sauce, the cranberry was*

*long harvested by Native Americans and then the colonists. Cultivation
began in Cape Cod, Massachusetts, with the discovery that wild cranberries grow more vigorously in "bogs," places where swampy water has been
replaced by sand or organic matter. Though cranberries have a year-round
popularity as a juice, most Americans buy them once a year, frozen or
canned, to serve with the Thanksgiving turkey.*

**CHILE-DRIED TOMATOES

*Tomatoes, sliced in half lengthwise if plum or Roma tomatoes, or sliced
widthwise if large tomatoes, or whole if cherry tomatoes
Sunflower*** oil
Medium-hot ground chile powder, preferably Chimayo
Allspice, ground*

Lightly oil a cookie sheet with sunflower oil. Place tomatoes skin side down as close together as possible. Sprinkle
liberally with chile and allspice. Put in very slow oven,
200°F, until tomatoes are nearly dry, between six and eight
hours: Do not let them brown; do not let them toughen
and begin to lose their flavor. Use within a week, or pack in
a sterile jar and cover them with sunflower oil to keep for
several months, or freeze.

*****Flos Solis maior** (sunflower; Spanish name is *girasol,*
which can also mean social climber): *Both seeds and root are
edible. The seeds, nutritious and nutty, have become a favorite snack,
especially salted in the shell. Sunflower oil is light, with no cholesterol.
The root, also called Jerusalem artichoke, shares the same nutty taste and
fibrous texture as the true artichoke (not native to the Western Hemisphere). Jerusalem artichoke (also known as sunchoke) has more in
common with the potato: Both must be dug, both discolor when peeled,
both have a similar taste, but the sunchoke is nuttier and sweeter. Raw,
Jerusalem artichokes crunch up a salad or salsa. The French called it*
poire de terre *(earth pear). Can be cooked by boiling, baking,
steaming, broiling, or smoking.*

The food was wonderful. "I've missed your cooking, Dad," I said.

"I'll feed you as much as you want. But I'll work it off of you, too."

My father was serious that he needed my help. I'd never seen him look so tired, yet so intense. For weeks, he'd been haggling with suppliers of the exotic food he'd promised his party guests. For weeks, he'd been tasting chicha beer, experimenting with sauces to go with the opuntia cactus fruit for dessert, developing an amaranth seed dressing, wondering how to best cook what wouldn't be shipped to him until the last minute.

He banged on Carson Flinn's door early on my first full day home and soon I was in his kitchen sampling tuna cactus, the one that would turn my urine red. "It's good," I said, "but I'm no expert."

"Taste is what matters," he said.

"I like it. But don't rely on me." He was trying to make me his partner in the meal. "I'm just here to help," I reminded him.

He scowled. "You can help by telling me what tastes good."

I had a moment of regret: I shouldn't have returned home. My father was overexcited and nervous about *his* project, *his* party, *his* food, *his* birthday. He liked having my help—hadn't he always?—but he hadn't asked me a single question about my life. "You have to treat me better than most of your temporary help."

He smiled. "I forgot," he said, "you're family." He patted me on the back.

My mother had already made peace with the menu. They ignored Maria Tito, even though her reticence probably represented the norm in Kansas City. "Maybe I'm a little nervous about this menu," I said one day.

"Me, too," said my father. "But I've got an idea."

"For me?"

"For you. A big favor. I want you to find a guinea pig. I need to know what they taste like."

"No," I said.

"You're going to eat one eventually, why not now?"

"They'd all be babies in the pet stores," I said.

"Look in the classifieds." He threw the paper across the kitchen table at me. "Penelope's coming over to help you."

"When is she going to Mexico?" I asked.

"Closer to the party. So everything will be fresh. She wants to get to know you better." He smiled.

"You *are* desperate here, aren't you?" I asked.

He didn't answer because Penelope walked into the kitchen. She took my hand, and held it. Her reddish hair was freshly washed, and frizzled. Her lipstick was bright red. "Ready to hunt and gather?" she asked.

How could I have said *no*? My father left the kitchen.

He knew what he was doing. I welcomed the chance to spend time with Penelope, even if on this weird mission. Heads together, we scanned the classifieds. Penelope found an ad asking for a nice home for a guinea pig. The family was moving and didn't want to take the pet. "When you eat," said Penelope, "you *do* take it with you."

"That's terrible," I said.

"And morbid," she said. "In ancient cultures, and our own, there is worship, sacrifice, sadness, and courage in finding, killing, and eating food." She took an opuntia cactus from the bowl where my father's experimental sauce was congealing. "Red urine." She laughed. "We're so far removed from food rituals these days. That's what I'm studying. I'm used to it by now."

"Used to what?"

"Being a little morbid."

"I once got beat up for saying I ate a dog tamal," I confessed. "Third grade, I think."

"Is someone going to beat you up for eating a guinea pig?"

"I could get arrested."

"I won't tell." Penelope leaned toward me, put her face near mine. "Now let's go," she whispered.

I was an easy mark. For her, I made the phone call. For her, I got in the car. For her, I knocked on the door. For her, I stood stone-faced while three children, behind their mother, sized me up. They offered me the cage, some food, and some extra wood chips. They called the guinea pig Mikey, and insisted that Mikey say good-bye to each of them. I took everything. If I hadn't, they might have suspected what I thought they suspected anyway: that Mikey would be hairless, eviscerated, rubbed thoroughly with Mexican marigold,* slow-baked and eaten by the end of the day.

---

*Marigold; Marsh Marigold (*Tagetes erecta; Caltha palustris*): *All marigolds, though some are called African, some Aztec, and some French, are native to Mexico.*

I wished I had borrowed one of Carson Flinn's hairpieces, a mustache, anything. When I climbed back into Penelope's car, I was rewarded with a soft kiss. "My hero," she said.

Seduction and food always came together in the kitchens where I was raised. No surprise, then, that I did as I was told as long as Penelope was at my side, her lips near mine, her appreciative breath in my ear.

She said I should be a student, open, as she was. In the kitchen of the Tsil Café, she quickly broke Mikey's neck, cut him from neck to anus, removed his innards, singed off his hair, and turned him over to my father. By then, he didn't resemble Mikey anymore. He was meat, and not much meat at that. He was a thinly muscled skeleton, small arms and legs. He might have been a breastless game bird, pigeon, or dove: he was that small. *Ah*, I thought, *that's me. Sacrificed on the altar of my father's fantastic fiftieth.* Penelope handed the little body to my father, and we left him to do what he did well: transform meat into food.

An hour later, my father pulled the "meat" from the oven. After a half hour of roasting, the little pig was even smaller. My father cut off a hind leg, held it delicately to his nose, then took a bite.

Strongly scented, with bright yellow and orange flowers, marigolds are often grown in vegetable gardens both for color and to repel pests. Tagetes lucida, also known as Mexican tarragon, was used to spice chocolate and meats.

Marsh marigolds, also called cowslips, can be eaten as greens while young, picked in the bud and pickled like capers, or allowed to flower and made into beverage. Captain John Smith instructed the Virginia colonists in 1609 to forage for marsh marigolds, cattail roots, and Jerusalem artichokes.

"Excellent," he claimed. He washed it down with some of the chicha beer he and my mother had bottled.

I refused to taste the pig, but the beer was wonderful, light as a pilsner, but as deeply flavored as a bitter beer—almost sour, with a hint of the allspice my father had added when he bottled it.

Penelope went for my mother, who also tried the pig, though with some trepidation. "At least we have a standard," she said.

"A delicious standard." Penelope picked a bone from her mouth.

"You see, everything will be fine," my father reassured my mother.

"Both of you have wonderful experience, and wonderful food," said Penelope.

"We'll keep you," said my father.

Penelope offered to drive me home. We didn't go to Carson Flinn's. We went to her place, a farmhouse she rented from a retired farmer who was a client of her accountant father. She wanted to show me the place in case I'd be willing to house-sit while she went to Mexico. The farmhouse was old, with faded clapboard siding, but it was snug inside, full of books, with a large, sunny kitchen.

"Stay for dinner," she said. "Carson will be going out someplace, no doubt."

We cooked together, a simple pasta with red sauce, with salad and a good bread Penelope had bought. I wondered how spontaneous her invitation was, but I didn't question her, especially once she began to unbutton my shirt before dessert. Soon, I was as naked as a singed guinea pig, but very alive. Penelope was passionate, eager in her own appetites and eager to please, as well. After we made love, she had that satisfied look she'd had in the afternoon, removing a guinea pig bone from between her teeth.

In the morning, she served me coffee in bed. I knew I would stay. "I'll tell Carson," she said, before I even mentioned it.

"I'll tell my parents," I said.

"Of course," she said.

They weren't surprised. They liked Penelope. She was going to great lengths—all the way to Mexico—to please them. She was on a research grant for the summer, making my father's fiftieth birthday the focus of a paper. "I'll study you, too," she said.

"Your guinea pig?"

"Be careful," she said.

The week before she left for Mexico, we spent all our time together, either at her farmhouse or at the Tsil Café. My father might have been having his fantasy fiftieth, but I was having a fantasy of my own—living with a woman of sexual and sensual appetite, someone who didn't seem interested in attaching strings, someone who understood food and my parents as though she'd known them all her life.

When Penelope flew to Mexico, my parents kept me too busy to feel sorry for myself. My mother's chayote squash arrived the same day I took Penelope to the airport, and I waited there for it. My mother's California contact had assured her it would keep nicely, and serve well. "How do I cook it?" she had asked him over the phone. When he told her he didn't eat it himself, she went to the library, where she found information under the common name of custard marrow. She discovered that chayote had a large edible seed in its middle, which she could use in her *iguaxte* sauce—a paste of toasted, mashed squash seed and tomato. She also read that she should peel the skin after baking, because it toughened dramatically.

She did not read all she should have. We opened the box of what looked like individually wrapped, lime-green, creased pears. She baked one, then began peeling the skin. A gelatinous substance oozed around her knife and soon covered her hands. Within fifteen minutes, as she was toasting the large button of a seed, her hands turned red and swelled. Some kind of allergic reaction, she was told by her doctor.

"I remember reading about that," said my father.

"You could have told me," she complained.

"When you get close to fifty, you can't remember everything," he said.

"Try remembering what your wife needs to know, okay? Or you'll be cooking and eating this meal by yourself." Her hands burned all night. When she woke up in the morning, though, they were normal, even softened.

"Aren't you glad I didn't remember?" he asked. "You wouldn't have made a discovery."

"Next time I cook chayote, I'll put some juice on your face," she said. "Burn away the wrinkles."

Two days before the big meal, Carson Flinn pulled up in a taxi, and was wheeled inside just in time to join us for lunch in the dining room of the Tsil Café. He handed my father a sack. "Take this stuff before it spreads."

My father peeked inside. "*Huitlacoche*," he said. He might have been a chef, for once, with the world's finest truffles.

"Penelope's back?" I asked. "I didn't expect her until tomorrow. The place is a mess."

"She's back, but she's *flat* on her back," said Carson. "A little Montezuma's revenge, I think. Or perhaps just the wear of the trip."

"I'd better go clean things up." I stood up.

"Don't," said Carson. "If you ever want to be a romantic, you won't. She's not in great shape." Carson pulled some *huitlacoche* from his bag. "Look at this instead," Carson told us. "It's nearly as bad as the one who brought it from Mexico." We saw the misshapen, grayed, puffed, almost dusty ends of corn, diseased with this highly touted, edible fungus. "I hope you know what you're doing," Carson said to my father.

"I know what I want, a dog tamal in a *huitlacoche* sauce." Carson made a face.

"Carson, be a gourmand," chastised my mother. Her loyalty to my father's meal surprised me, given her crisis with the chayote.

Another special delivery followed Carson's: fifty dressed guinea pigs, just beginning to thaw in their diabolically smoking dry ice. With them, at the very bottom, in white butcher paper, were the hindquarters of a dog. My father held one of them up like a club. "Fed only on corn and avocado."

"Please spice it well, Robert," said Carson Flinn.

Maria Tito leaned over in her chair to look at the guinea pigs. She dropped her water glass. Then she followed it onto the floor. My mother rushed to her and pinched a little garlic in her nose. She revived immediately, but had to be helped back into her chair. "You're cooking rats?" she asked.

"Guinea pigs, Grandmother," said my mother.

"The blood," said my father. "There's supposed to be a bag of llama blood in here." He tore into the big box again, but found nothing.

Lunch was cut short. My father made a series of phone calls. I worried that he'd cook up some harebrained scheme involving me, the Swope Park Zoo, and a very nervous llama. But another delivery came at the end of the afternoon, and more dry ice encased a plastic bag of frozen llama blood mixed with papaya juice to keep it from clotting. "Your ingredient," my father said to me. "You're hired to make the soup."

"Recipe?" I asked.

He handed me a book. I scoured it. Here's all I found: *Llama blood was often used in Peruvian stews.*

"You said you wanted some dishes to yourself," said my father. "I'd suggest a potato base, with plenty of green chiles. The quinoa leaves are in the downstairs refrigerator when you need them."

I called Penelope. She wasn't worried about the mess I'd left at her place. She didn't feel like talking, she said, though she was confident she'd be there for the big meal. "I *have* to be," she said. "I still have to bring the *tecuilatl.*"

"The what?" I asked.

"The Mexican algae."

"Have you tried it?"

"Don't worry. That's not what gave me the stomach bug."

"I'll see you tonight," I said.

"No," she said. "I'm in no shape. Stay with your folks."

I waited through two days of my parents' anticipation. Two days of phone calls to Penelope. Two days of reassuring Maria Tito that we were not in cahoots with the devil. Two days of fielding phone calls from anxious guests who had doubts: Either they'd double-checked the menu—"You're really serving dog? Where did you get it?"; or they sounded like they'd talked to Maria Tito—"Is it safe to eat worms, guinea pigs, blood?"

My father told them everything he could: These things have been eaten for centuries; his suppliers were reliable and everything had arrived unspoiled and wholesome-looking; they'd signed up for an exotic, one-of-a-kind meal, a lifetime experience, and that's what they'd get. "By the time the ingredients are cooked, nobody will think of them as the ingredients anymore. Food," he said, "is more than ingredients."

When the big day arrived, we were nervous, anxious, excited. We were already full of the adrenaline and exhaustion of elaborate food preparation. In the morning, we found Maria Tito in my mother's kitchen. Huge pots of water boiled on the stove, pasta noodles hung from counters and cabinet doors, from the table and chairs. She sat in front of a bowl of her own linguini, stuffing rolled forkfuls into her mouth.

"How much have you eaten?" asked my mother.

"I'm hungry," said the old woman. "I've never been so hungry."

We bagged as much of the drying dough as we could, but Maria Tito ate for another hour before she stopped.

"I need my kitchen," my mother finally insisted.

Oddly enough, I felt at home again. Then Pablito and Teresita came, greeting me warmly, with pictures of their children, and pictures drawn for me by their children. They had closed their restaurant for the day and left the children with a baby-sitter. They began cutting the sapote into elegantly thin sections, the mottled green skin making a fine contrast with the sweet, almost black flesh. They cracked the coquitos for the coconut-like flesh, to mix with honey for a sweet sauce for dessert. And they helped wherever they could, upstairs in my mother's kitchen, or downstairs in the kitchen of the Tsil Café. Their chia punch—chia seeds and flowers and pineapple liqueur, to be served with the appetizers, with frozen pineapple instead of ice—waited in the basement refrigerator.

Carson Flinn arrived to oversee preparations. He brought Penelope, slightly pale, but ready for the day.

"Can you cook?" I asked her. "I have to begin the soup."

"Did you get everything I ordered over the phone?" she asked. She'd consulted with her anthropology professors, and we had a plan.

"Right this way," I said. We went to the basement. Maria Tito lay on her bed, taking her usual nap, in her slip, her fancy dress hanging over the door. We went past the small bedroom to the refrigerator and loaded our arms full of quinoa leaf, the bag of llama blood, a bag of dried green chiles. We went to the bin for some purple potatoes I'd asked my father if I could use. We planned to leave the skins on in hopes of teasing out a royal color with the blend of skin and blood.

"Everything else is upstairs," I said. We passed by Great-grandmother Tito. Her eyes were wide open. Most likely she'd be up to criticize and supervise before long.

"I can't believe the day's finally here," said Penelope. "This amazing meal. It's so . . ."

"Bizarre," I said.

"I was going to say exotic. And experimental. And perfect. Of course, it's just what I needed for my special project. And your father's making it all possible."

"Thank you, Father," I said, in a mock prayer, "for dogs and guinea pigs, worms, and blood." I held up the bag of llama blood. "Don't tell him," I said, "but if you hadn't convinced me, I might not be quite up to the challenge."

"Where is your father?"

"Down the street, at Branner's. They have a huge roasting oven. Perfect for his guinea pigs."

"Don't take your father for granted." She began washing the quinoa leaves in the sink.

"But this menu, it's not really true or authentic to any one culture, or place. It's a gimmick. We're making this soup based on almost zero research into Peruvian stews." I joined Penelope at the sink, to scrub potatoes.

"Who else would do anything like this?" she asked.

"Who else would want to?" I asked.

"Lots of restaurants in Mexico. Now how do we begin this soup?" I handed her a huge pot, the one I'd used to boil the corn pieces for the *tsil* kachina heads, the one that had burned my hands years before. She filled it half full with hot water.

"You liked Mexico?" I searched my father's cabinets for Mexican oregano.

"Mexico City is polluted. But I found everything I went for, and the markets are incredible." Penelope cut the potatoes into small cubes and dropped them into the water.

When they had barely lost their crunch, we blended some for thickener. We used some of the potato water to soak the green chiles. I'd managed to find some wild onion and garlic that Penelope said were native to Central and South America, and I added them to the soup. Penelope tore the quinoa leaves—because they're related, they look like lamb's quarters—into small pieces. They, and the llama blood, would be the last additions. We wanted to serve the soup at room temperature, as I assumed the Peruvians would have.

Penelope told me more stories about Mexico, about the *huitlacoche* corn fungus and the *tecuilatl* algae cheese. She was warming to me. What was it about soup? I remembered back to the green chile, potato, turkey liver soup that was supposed to be an aphrodisiac. Maybe llama blood was one, too. Cooking itself could be an aphrodisiac. Unless, as happened that day, a father returns to the kitchen.

"How is it going?" he asked.

"Soup looks fine, we'll taste soon," I said.

He left. Once prepared, the soup took on a royal purple

worthy of a Peruvian ruler. My father puréed corn to mix with *huitlacoche* and jalapeño for the dog tamal sauce. The tamales themselves had been steaming for an hour. They smelled no different from his buffalo or turkey tamales. Penelope seemed as interested in watching my father as she'd been in cooking with me.

I frowned at her once. "I have a paper to write," she whispered, "and it's not about you."

She helped my father prepare the opuntia fruit in bowls for dessert. Once he had her doing that, he called me into the bathroom to show me the results of eating opuntia all morning: The toilet water was tinged red. He laughed as he flushed, and I didn't know what to say. His excitement about the meal made me uncomfortable, even embarrassed.

Juan and Domingo arrived late in the afternoon. "Brother," my father called Domingo. "Father," he called Juan. The two were tired from the long drive, and they went upstairs to rest in my parents' bedroom. "The guests will be here in one hour," said my father. "Dream yourselves some appetites."

"Your great-grandmother," said my mother, "has she been upstairs after her nap?"

"She was waking up," I said. "A couple hours ago."

"I'd better help her," said my mother. "She's been a little crazy about the big meal. Wes, taste the *iguaxte* sauce and give me an opinion."

Penelope and I tasted it. "Salt," we both said.

"Take care of it," said my mother. "We all know as much as each other about what we're doing here."

"We're celebrating," said my father. "I'm fifty. Let's go break into the chia punch!"

We went downstairs. The guinea pigs arrived from the ovens down the street. Carson Flinn sat in front of the bar shaving shards of *tecuilatl* onto appetizer plates.

"Shit," said my father, "the maguey worms!" He ran into his kitchen. I followed him. He hauled baking sheets out of the oven onto the counter. He threw a worm into the air and caught it in his mouth. He chewed. "What did I tell you," he said. "Perfect!"

They resembled the grub worms I'd once dug up in the garden, with little puffy sections strung like beads down their length. I had thought cooking would transform them into something more appetizing. They *were* golden brown, with a light dusting of salt and chile powder, but they still looked exactly like worms.

My father put them into a large basket and carried them to the bar. The dog tamales would join them soon for the appetizer buffet. "Who wants to help get fifty salads ready?" my father asked.

My mother climbed the last stair into the Tsil dining room. She was pale. I wondered how tired she'd made herself that day. Domingo and Juan clomped down the stairs from our living quarters. No matter how tired, our party was converging. My mother took a chair and waved at the air. We all stopped to look at her. "Grandma," she whispered. "Grandma Tito is dead. On the bed. In the basement." Her voice rose: "She's dead."

We turned to each other, shocked. My father knelt beside

my mother's chair. "Maria," he said. He reached up to hold her head in his hands. Juan and Domingo stood nearby. I went to the top of the stairs, but couldn't look down. Pablito and Teresita, standing in the door of the Tsil kitchen, punch and glasses in hand, turned to set things down. Penelope went to Carson, to wheel him to my mother's side. None of us knew what to say. Then the Tsil Café door opened, and three guests clamored in. "Such a smell," said one. "Better than I expected," said another. "I've been debating all day long," said the third.

They stopped short, noticing the stillness, the sober faces. "What's wrong?" asked a woman I recognized as a restaurateur who specialized in tapas on Southwest Boulevard.

My mother stood up. "We were conferring about last-minute preparations," she said. "You know, last-minute surprises. And we were blessing this meal. Everything's ready. The meal is ready to go on. The birthday boy has turned fifty, as though he could help it."

"Help yourselves to appetizers as you're ready," said my father. "Pablito, the punch."

Pablito brought the punch. Domingo helped my father bring the tamales and *huitlacoche* sauce. Penelope and I washed amaranth greens for the salads because I wanted to escape the crowd. I couldn't pretend everything was all right. I could think only of Maria Tito, lying as I'd seen her, eyes open and staring. Or maybe my mother had shut her eyes.

More guests arrived. Finally, fifty people drank punch, slowly bit through the masa of their South American tamales until they took their first bite of dog. I looked out once to see several guests work up courage enough for the crunchy maguey worms. My father came to report. "Tamales are tamales. They either love or hate the *tecuilatl.* Everyone loves Pablito's chia seed punch, just as they love him. Plenty of maguey worms in the baskets."

After the salads were ready, I stole down the stairs, braced myself, and walked into my old room. In what had been my bed lay my great-grandmother, once so expansive, once my mother's salvation. Her eccentricities had bothered me, then endeared her to me. Death had stilled her to a slight frown. I touched her cold head, her stiff hair. I took a deep breath. On the way back up, I met my father. "Just when you don't think you can do something," he said, "you find you have to." We went up the stairs together.

We ate a meal of meals. The amaranth salad was pronounced "incredible" by Carson Flinn. Others agreed. They toasted my father—his skills, his "advancing" age, his experience in the kitchen, his experience in life. My mother went to her grandmother's bedside for a brief vigil between courses, while Penelope and I served the soup.

My father stood to make a toast. "The soup was prepared by Wes and Penelope, our young cooks. The ones who will take what we know and learn more, and *be* more, than we are. Every man turning fifty should be so lucky, to have young people like these close by. Thanks, son, for the help." I heard the clicking of many glasses. I was happy and scared to death at the same time. What if people didn't like the soup, with its flavor like copper, fruit, and spice—like a chile-bitter-beer mixed with papaya juice, grounded in the earthiness of potato? I waited. Carson made his first true critique of my cooking. He raised his glass. "Exquisite," he said. "We think Wes is indeed the son of his father. And his mother." Some eaters clapped, others continued eating with gusto. Some politely moved their soup bowls to the side. I was the son of my mother and father, and proud of it, suddenly. I, too, could cook.

"Eat now and well if you are timid," said my father. "For we move into the heart of the jungle and the mountains of Peru." He disappeared to put together fifty plates, each with a guinea pig, a side of scarlet runner bean root, and a half of chayote squash with my mother's *iguaxte* sauce. She helped him, making sure the sides she'd prepared were presented well. She brought Carson the first plate, followed by Pablito and Teresita, and Cocoa and Misty. "You should have put little crab apples in their mouths," joked Carson Flinn about the guinea pigs. A few laughed.

Penelope and I brought out gallons of chicha beer. Those most tentative about the food fortified their courage with the exotic drink. As the main course was served, I heard a variety of comments. "I can't believe I'm doing this," said a woman my father had befriended after her restaurateur husband died. "Glad I'm not South American every night," said another, reminding me of all those years ago, when my friend Bill had been delighted he wasn't one of those Italian whores. One man leaned over to Penelope and said, "You're right, he's the real thing." I thought maybe she'd told him about me, but she answered, "You should come to the Tsil on a regular night, too." It was, after all, my father's party.

Robert Hingler was happy. He slipped away to the basement before the dessert of opuntia fruit and white sapotes, served with hot chocolate—strong, bitter, chile-laced, and perfect with the sweet fruit. The ceremonial part of the evening began then, the toasts, the giving of the small gifts that some had brought, the impromptu tribute Carson Flinn put together. It sounded like one of his reviews. I don't remember all of it, but Flinn was full of statements like "We approached Robert Hingler as we might a food we've never tried before—poking, sniffing, taking small bites, wondering when the pleasure of the dish would assault us. Hasn't he assaulted us?"

Others thanked my father for pushing spice into Kansas City. Others thanked him for a unique restaurant. Still others jokingly thanked him for assuring them more customers—those who would never venture more than once into a place that promised so much chile heat. Some had brought my father wine and champagne as gifts. He asked Pablito to open them. "Let none go home hungry or thirsty. I am full," he proclaimed. "Full of food I'd only heard of before, full of your generosity, full of the love of my family and friends and community. Let everyone fill up."

After dinner, as I helped clear plates, everyone declared the unprecedented feast a great success, even though I picked up many barely eaten guinea pigs. I had noticed a great deal of tasting, and found it a strange irony that my father—

Tasting is to eating what a dirty picture is to sex, he liked to say—had given a party in which so many people couldn't move beyond the picture and the taste of this pre-Columbian feast.

Penelope went with me to visit my great-grandmother Tito the second time I went. My mother sat on the edge of the bed, her head bent. "Wes," she said, "come." She held out her hand and I took it. "You must come with us to bury her properly, in St. Louis. I need my family."

"Of course," I said.

Penelope took my hand and my mother smiled at her. Pablito and Teresita came down, and Cocoa, and Misty, and my father behind them. "Is everybody gone?" asked my mother.

My father nodded. He took my mother's hand. "Thank you," he said. He reached down to stroke my great-grandmother's face. My mother began to cry.

Penelope rushed from the small room, once my bedroom, where my life crowded me into a corner. Maria Tito, who had been there when I came into the world, lay dead. My father, who had locked himself in my room with Cocoa, was fifty, flushed with appetite. Pablito, who had been with Cocoa many an afternoon during that hard time in his life, and with my mother in her kitchen during an even harder time in my life, stood next to Teresita, who took her siestas in my room even before it was my room. Misty, who had been my first lover, lit a cigarette, blew smoke into the air, as my mother and father had, as Cocoa had, as they all had. Even as I had. I heard footsteps. Juan and Domingo came downstairs.

My life was there: in flesh and memory. Perhaps everyone,

sooner or later, sees a collage of their life. The picture tells them who they are. I thought of what Juan had told me about the peanut. I felt like a shell, filling up. Everyone who had helped me fill was right in the tiny basement room with me.

Penelope had gone home. I called her the next day. She said she was busy writing up the meal. She wanted to let us mourn by ourselves. Perhaps, after the fact, she had become suspicious of appetite. After all, I had once been skeptical of my father and mother and their appetites. The extravagance of the fiftieth party was no exception. But appetite means you fill up. I was certainly full. The undertakers came for Maria Tito. They would embalm her, then send her to the funeral home on The Hill, where we'd have a service and burial.

Then, for two days, we filled up: leftovers, memories, togetherness. For two days our urine was as red as blood. "Thicker than water," my father joked.

Then we drove to St. Louis.

ROASTED CORN:
SECRETS, INGREDIENTS

*O*n the way to St. Louis, my mother sighed and fidgeted. Maybe she was nervous, or full of grief, or full of anger. Maybe all of it. Of her father, Mario Tito, she asked, "Why does he force me to make all the arrangements?" Of Grandmother Tito she said, "For so long she was the *only* thing I had in this world." She blinked away tears. "Grandmother Tito fed me. This was in the days before formula, before you weren't supposed to give cow's milk to babies until they were a year old. Grandmother Tito made a gruel, mostly milk, but with corn and rice. She fed me with a big wooden spoon. As soon as I cut teeth, I chewed up that spoon. I still remember how her lips puckered when she blew my food to cool it. Like little fish, they were."

"She was memorable," said my father.

"My father never really fed me. He couldn't cook, he said. We often ate the vegetables from his garden. We'd just pluck them, wash them in the hose, and eat them raw. When my grandmother picked me up after my stays with him, she would cluck her tongue. He'd tell her he hated cleaning dishes. And she'd yell at him that he had to dirty dishes in order to eat. *Or do you eat?* she asked him. *I eat, but I don't cook,* he'd answer.

"The best times were when his strawberries* came in. We would gorge ourselves. I often got sick, but I couldn't stop myself, they were so bright and thick and sweet."

The last time I'd seen Grandfather Tito, he'd fallen in love with Mrs. Dolani. "Comfort," Maria Tito had called it. Maybe my grandfather had found some happiness, with the help of Mrs. Dolani, now Tito. When I asked my mother, she said, "When I went to pick up Grandmother Tito, he spoke of nothing but moving into her house. Two of Mrs. Dolani's daughters live on that block. They were going to move the third into the basement apartment. On the phone, he seems as lost with his mother's death as he was with his wife's."

"Everything's the same, then," said my father. "You'll know what to do."

"Right. I'll do everything," said my mother.

She did. She met her father at the funeral home where he sat waiting with the new Mrs. Tito and her three daughters. He was a small man, and his suit looked big. But he smiled, and gave my mother a little wave. "Thank God you're here!"

---

*Strawberry (edible rose): *Indigenous to both Europe and America, the common strawberry was first found in the New World in Chile and in the mountains of western North America. Eastern North America was home to the wild strawberry (same genus, different species—the genus is Fragaria, in the family of the rose). Most currently cultivated strawberries were introduced from the New World to the Old, a single plant said to be responsible for all the strawberries grown in France. Colorful and sweet, easy to make into jellies, jams, preserves, and sauces, easy to dry, and easiest to eat fresh, the strawberry has been a favorite for everyone from Native Americans to Thomas Jefferson, who learned of the fruit first in France.*

Mrs. Dolani said. She stood up and held out her arms, extravagant in bulk and jewelry.

My mother surprised me by hugging her father's new wife, and the three daughters. "He's so confused," said Mrs. Dolani in a stage whisper. "I know how to please him in life. But he takes death so hard."

"Death *is* hard," said my mother.

"Of course," said Mrs. Dolani.

"I'm not confused," said Mario Tito. "I didn't want to rush decisions. I knew you'd want to help," he said to my mother.

"Let's go in the office," said my mother.

My father and I took a tour of The Hill. He walked much slower than the last time we'd toured the neighborhood. "Stiff from the drive," he said. Then we waited at a small restaurant for my mother to join us for dinner. She was cheerful for a woman who had just lost her grandmother and negotiated a burial with her father. "He's happy enough to do as I asked," she said. "I thought there might be big conflicts."

"What about?" I asked.

"You don't know Hill people," said my mother. "They have strong opinions on everything. Who will preside over the service, what scripture might be used, whether to have pallbearers, where the burial will take place, whether to extend the burial service beyond the usual Catholic ritual."

"So what's going to happen?" asked my father.

She looked over the menu, letting food, as always, be part of her comfort. "Nothing mattered to me except where she's buried. Turns out my father's already bought a spot on the other side of Mr. Dolani, in the churchyard. He never intended to be buried near my mother."

I didn't understand. "So where will Maria Tito be?"

"Next to my mother . . . next to her daughter."

"It's quite a drive," said my father.

"To where?" I asked.

My mother brushed the air. "The parmigianas are great here," she said, "chicken or eggplant. And the marinara is half Chianti, cooked to incredible thickness. I've tried to match it, and never can."

THE MARINARA SAUCE
OF BUEN APPETITO

8 plum tomatoes

2 cups chicken broth

3 cups Chianti wine

2 6-ounce cans tomato paste

12 ounces water

1 tablespoon sugar

½ cup chopped parsley

8 cloves garlic

2 onions

2-ounce can anchovies (save oil for sauté)

2 teaspoons basil

½ teaspoon fennel seeds

1 tablespoon oregano

Pepper to taste
Salt to taste
½ cup grated Parmesan cheese

Skin and seed tomatoes, blend, and add to chicken
broth and Chianti wine. Blend tomato paste, water,
sugar, and parsley and add to liquids. Chop garlic,
onions, and anchovies and sauté in anchovy oil, then
blend to a paste. Add to other liquids along with remaining spices. Simmer to desired thickness. Cool
slightly and add Parmesan cheese. Good over pasta,
or on pizza, or as dip for bread.

We let her order for us. "Mrs. Dolani invited us to the
house after the funeral tomorrow, for a dinner with her daughters and their families. Then we'll go back to Kansas City. In
the meantime, let's just get through this."

I tried to adopt my mother's attitude through the viewing, wondering about the false smile on Maria Tito's thickly
made-up face. I tried again through the profusion of flowers
and tears. Maria Tito had moved away to live with my
mother, and she'd lived longer than many of the women on
The Hill. Still, she was well mourned, in spite of her reputation as an outsider. "More opinionated, more tolerant,
more creative," explained my mother. "Less conventional,
less devoted to religion. You knew her, Wes." I smiled at my
memories of her appetite, her wine, her sense of humor, her
constitutionals with her magazines.

The priest knew her well and spoke the truth about her life: her dedication to family, her cooking, her generosity, her patience that was often peppered by frustration with people not as energetic, not as talented, not as able to adjust to the difficulties in their lives.

Still, Maria Tito's funeral was not focused on the death of a particular individual, but on the death of a member of a community. By the end of the service, the priest made only one mention of my mother, calling Maria Tito Hingler "the devoted granddaughter who learned to cook at Maria Tito's side, and who took her nurturing traditions and made a business of feeding and caring for others. We miss her on The Hill."

Later, my mother told me that true respect comes to those who stay. "I left because my grandmother sent me away. She knew what she was doing."

After the funeral my mother, father, and I drove north, almost ten miles, to a cemetery I'd never seen. The huge lawn, with flat stones, was designed to make mowing easier. The priest stayed on The Hill. My mother read the Twenty-third Psalm. The black-suited men from the funeral home, as attractive as flies, lowered Maria Tito's remains into the ground. We each threw a rose onto the casket. Then the cemetery personnel lowered the vault lid, and we each offered a shovel of dirt. Clod on cement, such a final sound. The funeral-home people scurried away.

I wandered the cemetery, looking for other Titos, or for DiPasquales, my great-grandmother's maiden name. I found only her daughter's flat stone, almost covered with the artificial grass laid out for Maria Tito's service. "Your mother's grave?" I whispered to my mother.

She nodded.

"Where's the rest of the family?"

"Tell him," said my father.

"Tell me what?" I asked.

My mother blinked tears. She shook her head.

"Can I tell him?" asked my father. She nodded. "Your mother's mother," he said. "She didn't die in childbirth. That's just what Mario Tito always said. She killed herself, when your mother was six months old."

I should have known there was another secret, the way my mother had been acting. I didn't know what to do, so I did what I thought Great-grandmother Tito would have done. I hugged my mother. "It's okay," I said.

"Nobody told me the truth," said my mother. "Until I forced Maria Tito to tell me. I had to know why my father changed so much. Why everyone on The Hill treated me differently than the other children. Why we had to go to this cemetery—not the parish graveyard—to visit her stone."

"You could have told me," I said. I bent down and peeled back the corner of artificial grass that covered my grandmother's stone. I read CONSTANTINA ALEXANDRA TITO. "I didn't even know her full name."

"How do you talk about what you can't understand?"

"You should have told me," I said. I thought of my mother, hidden from us in her little closet space. By herself, or with Pablito, or whomever else. Probably wanting to be found. Lost and found, hide-and-seek. Childhood games that most adults keep playing as long as they live. I thought of what I'd learned from her about Domingo. I thought of myself, another secret from her family when she and my father came to St. Louis for a church wedding. And then we'd come again, after my parents' twin infidelities. I was beginning to hate secrets, as my great-grandmother had.

"You feel you should have been able to do something," said my mother. "If you had said the right thing. Or done one little thing differently. Or if you had just been a better person. I was only six months old when it happened, but I grew up thinking something must have been wrong with *me*." My father handed her a handkerchief and she wiped her eyes.

"But you're over that now," I said. I traced the letters of my grandmother's name in the warm stone.

"Do I look like I'm over it?" she asked. She blew her nose. "You can't understand it, and you can't get over it. You just live with it."

"You're just living with it?" I asked. That didn't sound like my mother.

"I'm not resigned, Wes. But it's always there. It's part of who I am."

I thought of my mother's warmth with her customers. Her incredible gift with food. Her stamina. Her unflappable work ethic. I could see where it came from, with her need to stay busy, and connected. I could also see where that hidden part of her came from—her need for a private place, for a private life, for someplace where she didn't have to give. I hugged her, then tried to break for the car.

She held on to me. "Wes, I don't want you to worry

about me. I'm private about some things," she said. "And maybe you didn't need to hear it until now."

"Maybe," I said.

She was wrong. I should have been told because, like everything else, sooner or later I'd find it out. Sooner meant knowledge, like knowing the ingredients you have to work with before planning a meal. Sooner meant being creative with what you had. All my life, I'd been trying to figure out my mother and father, and, by inference, myself. Finally, I knew the ingredients I had to work with. At my father's fifieth birthday, just a few days before, I'd cooked. I'd been praised. I'd felt closer to him and to my mother. Carson Flinn had said I was indeed their son. But I needed to do him one better. I needed to become myself.

We drove to Maria Tito's house, where my mother grew up, where Mario Tito now lived. "He's in the back," yelled Mrs. Dolani from the kitchen. We walked around the small bungalow in what was a neighborhood of small bungalows. The summer afternoon was heavy with humidity. To my surprise, the backyard was completely converted into garden space, bordered by a profusion of perennials: asparagus, rhubarb, winter onions, garlic, raspberries, strawberries. The strawberries, in a raised bed four feet wide and twenty feet long, separated Grandfather Tito's yard from his neighbor's grass. Pathways in Mario's yard separated small squares of zucchini, green beans, eggplant, tomatoes, peppers, corn, carrots. The cool season plants—green onions, lettuce, beets, spinach—wilted toward their deaths.

Down the middle of his backyard, Mario Tito had built

a walkway overarched with awnings. Grapes climbed each support post. "I don't remember all this," I said.

"Around the time he met Mrs. Dolani, he started again," said my mother. "He'd gardened up until I left home. He spent hours among his plants." She pointed. "He had a little throne, like that one." Mario Tito sat on a stool, bare-chested, in a pair of shorts, under a profusion of grapes. He had tied a cloth around his head. A little man with a pot-belly, he looked like an underweight Buddha. We approached.

"Just deciding what to pick for dinner," Mario Tito said.

"You didn't come to the cemetery," said my mother.

"Please," he said, and held up his hand.

"Looks the same," she said.

"That's the trouble with life," he said. He stood up and strode across his garden. For a man I'd always thought of as lethargic, he was remarkably spry. "What do you suggest?" he asked my father. "You can see I have an overabundance of cherry tomatoes."

"I never grow them," said my father.

"Will you be cooking, either of you?" asked Mario Tito.

"No," said my mother.

"No," said my father. "We're still recovering from an extravaganza of cooking. My fiftieth birthday."

"We're still recovering from Grandmother's death," reminded my mother.

"I'll cook," I said. "I could make that roasted corn salsa you cook when you need to use up your midsummer garden."

"With cherry tomatoes?" my father asked.

"I'm cooking," I said.

"Okay," he said. He and my mother headed inside, and I was left alone with Mario Tito for the first time in my life.

"What do you need?" he asked. "We'll be cooking for the neighborhood."

I explained the recipe, and we gathered food together. "I didn't expect you to be so big," he said. He reached up and patted my head.

"I didn't expect you to be so small," I said, and put my hand on his shoulder.

"I'll help you cook, though I prefer my vegetables raw."

"My mother said so." I followed him back into the kitchen.

"Write the recipe down," he said, "if you have it in your memory."

"I do," I said. I wrote:

ROASTED CORN SALSA

Leaf of wild prairie sage

½ teaspoon Mexican oregano

2 tablespoons vinegar

3 dozen cherry tomatoes

4 ears of corn

2 jalapeños

3 red serrano peppers

1 medium zucchini, diced

1 teaspoon Chimayo chile powder, medium hot

2 tablespoons sugar, one in mixture, one over corn while roasting
⅛ teaspoon allspice
Shake or two of ground chipotle pepper
Salt to taste
4 roma or two medium-sized tomatoes, diced

Soak sage leaf and oregano in vinegar for at least an
hour. Cut cherry tomatoes in half and broil until
blackened in spots. Cut kernels from corn and roast
under broiler until blackened in spots. Seed and dice
peppers and zucchini, and broil until softened. Put
together in bowl. Add remaining ingredients, strain-
ing the sage leaf and oregano from the vinegar, and
stir well. Add fresh tomatoes. Adjust spices, sugar,
vinegar, and salt to taste. Serve with tortilla chips.

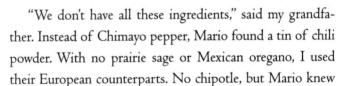

"We don't have all these ingredients," said my grandfather. Instead of Chimayo pepper, Mario found a tin of chili
powder. With no prairie sage or Mexican oregano, I used
their European counterparts. No chipotle, but Mario knew
his wife kept liquid smoke in the kitchen cabinet.

After an hour, we tasted. "He'll know," I said.

"Know what?" asked Mario.

"The substitutions," I said. "He likes his New World
recipes."

My grandfather ate a spoonful of the salsa. "What about
you?" he asked. "Do you never make substitutions?"

"Why would I?" I asked.

"Today, you are the cook," said Mario Tito. He looked exotic, with his cloth kerchief and his bare chest. "You can do as you please."

"What would you do?" I asked.

"We could go back to my garden."

He picked cilantro, more tomatoes, then onion and garlic, and we returned to the kitchen.

I sliced onion and garlic until the kitchen smelled more like my mother's than my father's. I chopped cilantro, blended the tomatoes to juice, added the new ingredients, stirred, and tasted. Even with more salt, the salsa was sweet. "What do you need, Wes?" asked Mario Tito.

"Lime. Or lemon juice."

So I added the juice from one of each, and we tasted. "Wonderful," I said.

"But what is a sauce without wine?" asked my grandfather. He went to his wine rack and opened a bottle of Cabernet. He poured a cup into a saucepan, salted it, and brought it to a boil. He stirred it in and we tasted again. He beamed. "Let us call the others in. Let them criticize you for straying from the recipe." He tasted the salsa again. "What do you know of me?" he asked.

"That you were sad a long time, after your wife's suicide."

"What do you know of me now?"

"You garden. You have good taste."

"I'm not only the man of the stories?"

"That's true."

He reached for a white shirt that hung on the back doorknob. "Wes, never be the man of the stories about you." He went for my parents. While he was gone, I adjusted the salsa with one more ingredient.

My father tasted, then immediately picked through my concoction. "You don't like?" asked Mario Tito, pouring him a glass of wine.

"It's wonderful," my mother said.

"I like it," said my father. "But I like to know what I'm eating."

"You are eating Weston Tito Hingler's Roasted Corn Salsa," said my grandfather. "You want to know what's in it, ask him."

"Wes?" asked my father.

"You tell me," I said.

He guessed well, all but the wine. My mother knew that. Neither guessed the one ingredient I'd reached onto Mario Tito's shelf to find, and added by teaspoons until I'd added a full tablespoon. "There's one other thing," I told them. "But I'll let that be my secret ingredient."

"Secret ingredient?" asked my father. "Wes, cooking is not about secrets, but about skill."

"Fine," I said. "But I've had enough secrets kept from me that I can keep this one for a while."

My parents were quiet, then. They simply ate what would become, in later years, one of my signature dishes. Then the neighbors arrived with the true comfort food of The Hill— spaghettis, lasagnas, manicottis, sausages, cubed cheese salads, olive salads.

I thanked my grandfather before I went to bed that night.

"You have a nice touch with the food," he said.

"Thanks," I said.

"I want you to have a present," he said. He went to his pantry and pulled out a gallon bottle of Greek olive oil. "Use it well," he said, "for your corn salsa and many other recipes."

"You saw," I said.

"Yes. And your mother probably knew your secret, too, but she let you keep it. She will let you be yourself. Your next self. Your father, he might be a little more stubborn."

SEMILLAS: THE COOK'S
APPRENTICESHIP

*W*here am I?" I asked. I'd startled awake and found myself in the back of my parents' car. For a moment, I was that thirteen-year-old kid who'd ridden home switching vehicles with parents after our last trip to St. Louis. Then, I'd been determined to be myself, to give myself some comfort. I wasn't sure I'd done a very good job of either one.

"We're about an hour from home," said my father.

"You were one tired young man," said my mother. "You snored, like your father."

I watched the Missouri hills slowly unfold around the car. "Did you like my corn salsa?" I asked.

"Excellent," said my mother.

"Very good," said my father. "You've got a way with salsas." He found me looking at him in the rearview mirror.

"Maria Standing Tall said I had a gift," I said.

"What'd you cook for her?" my father asked. "One of my recipes?" He lit a cigarette.

"Yucca soup. My own recipe."

My mother elbowed my father. "Sorry," he said to me. "You told me you were cooking Tsil food at *Domingo's.*"

"Your father was being vain." My mother turned to me. Her face was older than I'd ever seen it, lined with care and hard work.

I put my hand on her shoulder. "You look like Great-grandmother Tito. Same face, same hair as when I was a little boy."

"Old, you mean?" she asked.

"No, just family," I said.

"Hey, you two," said my father. "We were talking about cooking." His eyes found mine in the mirror again. "You're good," he said. "You've got recipes, you've got a gift, like your friend said. You made a hell of a soup for my fiftieth. I dragged you back for the big occasion. What'll it take to drag you back again, a little longer?"

The car came over a rise, and the landscape opened up until I could see for miles. I felt at home in the broad expanses, the slight, rolling hills. "I'd come back soon," I said. "If you wanted me."

"I want you," he said.

"And if you'll let me try some of my own recipes."

"It's a deal," he said.

"You're quitting school?" asked my mother.

"I'm quitting school," I said. "At least for now."

"I quit," said my father, lighting another cigarette. "You did, too, when you knew you were a cook."

"If Wes is certain about this," said my mother. She put her arm over the seat and touched my knee.

"I'm certain, at least for now," I said. I was quiet, then, watching the land go by, sensing the increase and intensity of traffic as we neared the city. Soon, I'd be headed back to Albuquerque, but not to live. To pack.

Before I left, I sat with my family at my mother's big table and read Carson Flinn's article about the fifieth, liberal with the conceit he'd promised—old and new. My father was getting older, as was his restaurant, yet he was trying new things. His recent event—the fiftieth—was to find old food traditions to try anew. Old restaurants all over the city should try more new foods, should push each other more to eat the old dog in a new way. He mentioned me, too, new to cooking, but older and more experienced with food, come back to his old home for a New World meal.

"What do you think?" asked my father.

"I'd rather be the young dog with the new tricks."

My father agreed. "I've done what I've wanted to do," he told me. "With my restaurant, with my fiftieth birthday. At my age, in this business, I need new blood."

"Llama blood?" I asked.

"Your blood," he said.

My father might have wanted fresh blood, and he might have wanted me, his own flesh and blood. But by the time I returned home two months later he seemed to have forgotten the promise of new recipes. Sure, he let me make up some recipes as long as I used his ingredients. That first Halloween

I made a buffalo* chili, baked for hours in a small pumpkin. He smiled like a jack-o'-lantern. I made a quinoa pilaf that passed his approval. For his next birthday, I even one-upped his desire for authenticity. I'd read that indigenous Americans valued the seed over the flesh of squashes, so I cooked squash seed tamales. We would have invited Penelope to my father's fifty-first birthday, but she had moved to Chicago for her graduate studies. We had a small celebration, intimate, with congratulations for my recipe.

Still, he resisted real change, and during this time I often complained to my mother. "I'd say you can cook with me,"

*__Buffalo__ (bison): *Native to both the mountains and Great Plains of North America, bison once ranged from Canada to what is now the southern United States in the tens of millions. Native Americans not only hunted the buffalo, but based entire cultures on this animal: They lived in tepees made of skins, sewn with gut, with bone or horn needles; they used horns for dippers and spoons and other tools; they used hooves for glue, bones for scrapers and hoes, hides for blankets; and, of course, they ate every edible part.*

Post—Civil War America was eager to rid the great agricultural west of Native Americans, and killing buffalo was seen as patriotic—a way of debilitating the Indian way of life, its culture, its livelihood. Buffalo hide, once deemed inferior to beaver and other animal skins, was given a boost because of scarcity of more valued hides and because a Pennsylvania tannery developed a better tanning method. Between 1870 and 1880, buffalo were hunted to near extinction, their hindquarters, tongues, humps, and hides shipped east, though hides were more often the goal than the meat, and the Great Plains were said to smell of rotting carcasses for many years.

With the building of herds in the twentieth century, buffalo meat is once again eaten. Mild in flavor, it surpasses beef: leaner, higher in iron, lower in fat and cholesterol. Buffalo contains so little fat it must be cooked at lower temperatures and for a shorter time than beef.

she'd always answer, "but this is between you and your father. Work it out."

I took Carson Flinn to dinner at a new Oriental place, very spicy. I wondered aloud whether I should just start my own restaurant. "Learn what you can," he said. "Maybe your father knows more than you think he does." He picked a cayenne from his noodle dish.

"I've been learning all my life," I said. "I've been in that kitchen since I was four years old. I've cooked with Pablito. And Domingo. With my mother and my father."

"Don't you remember that fortune we both got once?" he asked. "About making yourself another face instead of being content with the one God has given you."

"That was a mass-produced fortune, from a pretty bad restaurant, now that I think of it." I finished my mussels in garlic bean paste.

"That's not the point," he said. He waved for the check.

"I'm paying," I said, when the server came.

"Wes," said Carson, "both of us read that little slip of paper wrong. It wasn't a fortune, but a warning. Don't apprentice yourself to your father if you don't want to. Apprentice yourself to food, to the face you've been given. You'll know when you're ready to start your own restaurant."

My one problem with Carson: He was usually right. So, for the time being, I remained my father's child, my father's apprentice, my father's companion in the kitchen of the Tsil Café. At least we quit making the *tsil* kachinas out of corn. Instead, we twisted cayennes together for miniature ristras to put on each plate. "Does this mean I've finally built my character?" I asked.

"Such as it is," my father teased.

"Would you ever consider having a special that cheated just a little?" I asked.

"I guess I *haven't* built your character," he said.

"Maybe my character isn't entirely yours to build," I said.

"What do you have in mind?"

I cheated with flour. With cheese and butter. With onion and garlic. I served him my Shrimp and Mango Quesadillas, made with Sweet Potato Tortillas, and waited for him to wince.

WES HINGLER'S SWEET QUESADILLAS

TORTILLAS

1 medium sweet potato, baked
2 cups flour
½ teaspoon salt
2 tablespoons butter
Sunflower seeds

Squeeze pulp from the potato, add to flour, salt, and butter, and cut until dough forms. Roll out into thin circles. At last roll, push sunflower seeds into patterns—circles, stars, suns—and roll once more.
Cook in dry hot skillet until slightly brown in spots.

FILLING

8 shrimp, dusted with cumin, grilled, and cut in half
Fresh mango, cut into 16 pieces the size of the shrimp halves
White cheese—Jack, or any mild Mexican—cubed, 8 pieces
Sharp Cheddar cheese, cubed, 8 pieces
1 bunch green onions, diced fine
2 cloves garlic, minced fine

Mix filling ingredients together in a bowl. Spoon onto a sweet potato tortilla. Top with another tortilla and bake until cheese is just melted. Serve in a deep dish, surrounded by Wes Hingler's Green Sauce (made with sunflower, instead of pumpkin, seeds).

To my father's great disappointment, nobody complained when we served the special. Nobody even noticed. At the end of the evening, as Ronald was leaving, my father asked him if he'd had the special.

"Great tonight. Unique," said Ronald.

"You didn't mind the cheese? The onion and garlic? We've never served anything with cumin in it at the Tsil." My father threw up his hands.

"Spice is the variety of life, or so they say," said Ronald.

"That's not what they say," said my father.

"They should," I called out from the kitchen doorway.

I'm not sure my father would have ever let go. Our routines make us routine, our lives continue without interruption until we're interrupted. As we were when we had the phone call from Grandmother Hingler. Juan was ill. He wanted his family around him. In two days we were in her house, where Juan lay in the bed my grandparents had shared until my grandfather's death. He seemed unconscious, but with his eyes open. While we waited for Domingo and his wife and three teenage daughters, my father and mother and I cooked together. Everyone arrived, and we sat together. My grandmother's compliments surprised us.

"You've got a fine cook in your boy there," said Domingo.

After dinner, Grandmother Hingler rushed in to tell us Juan wanted to see us. "Everyone, around his bed. He wants you to hold hands. He has something to say." We followed each other down the hall, through the courtyard, and into the room where Juan had taken to bed several months before. We circled him: my father and mother and me; Domingo, Marta, and daughters. My grandmother joined us, between my father and me, taking our hands.

Juan, who had simply been staring at some point far above the ceiling, flickered his eyes. His lips opened. His tongue wetted them. He cleared his throat. His eyes went from person to person. His neck stiffened, as though he wanted to raise his head to speak. But he did not move. He closed his eyes. He drew a deep breath, and exhaled a sigh. We waited. His next breath was a snore.

Grandmother Hingler dropped my hand, then my father's. "Let's go back to the living room," she ordered. I went to finish the dishes. Domingo and my father began a game of gin, with the same deck of cards they'd used as boys.

Domingo's children turned on the television, a Spanish channel. A musical group wailed about love being *más fácil que beber un vaso de agua*—as easy as pie, as easy as falling off a log. My grandmother sang along, which surprised me. Love had surely been hard for her, but learning Spanish must have been even more difficult, at her age. Unless she knew it all along, and my father hadn't told me.

Grandmother Hingler disappeared again, and returned soon. "He wants you all," she said. We trooped to Juan's bedside, held hands, and waited. Again, he seemed present for a moment. He cleared his throat. One of his fingers moved. Then his eyes closed. We waited five minutes for them to open. "Juan," whispered Grandmother Hingler.

He smiled but did not open his eyes.

We dispersed again, back to rest, to cards, to television. Two hours passed. My mother wanted to go to bed.

"Just one more moment, honey," said Grandmother Hingler. She disappeared to Juan's bedside.

"I'm so tired," said my mother.

"We'll be in bed soon," my father assured her.

We circled up one last time. Juan was ready. He opened his eyes, smiled, licked his lips, raised his hands, cleared his throat. He struggled to speak. We heard a single choked word, "Child." Then he took a deep breath, let it out, and breathed no more.

He was dead. Together, holding hands, we wept. I wondered about this man, who, having no children of his own, would end his life by saying *child*, and in English instead of Spanish.

All that night I tossed and turned, wondering if anyone else thought what I did: maybe Juan was my father's father. My grandfather. Perhaps Juan had been with my grandmother Hingler. After all, my grandfather Hingler was Domingo's father through Conseca. Only Grandmother Hingler could tell us.

"We were all his children," my father said the next day at dinner, after the undertakers had visited, after the arrangements had been made, but before the mourners from Juan's community of friends arrived to keep vigil, as they had over Conseca. He looked at his mother. She showed no emotion but the grief we expected.

I hoped my father would continue his probe, then realized he wasn't probing.

"He nurtured everyone," said Grandmother Hingler. She had made dinner for us, including something she'd created for Juan, a jícama salad. My father, mother, and I—even Domingo—pestered her for the recipe.

"Juan taught me new ingredients," she said. "We both missed Conseca's cooking."

JÍCAMA SALAD

*1 large jícama**
Marigold leaves
1 small can mild green chiles, undrained
Fresh, frozen, or canned corn, 1½ cups
2 medium tomatoes, seeded and chopped

Juice of 1 lime
1–2 tablespoons mayonnaise
1 bunch cilantro

Peel jícama and slice into very thin sticks. Boil for about 10 minutes, until sticks are just about to lose their crispness. Soak in cold water until jícama sticks are cool.

Add remaining ingredients and mix well. Cool in refrigerator for best results.

*Jícama (a legume): *Native to Central America, popular in the Philippines, jícama is a tuber that can be eaten raw for its almost sweet crunch, or cooked like a potato. When boiled or steamed, it retains some crunch, much like a water chestnut. It looks like a turnip with thin brown skin.*

On the way home from New Mexico, my father rested in the backseat. I drove, my mother beside me. "So." My father sat up from his nap. "You want the restaurant? You ready?"

"I want *a* restaurant," I said. "Not the Tsil Café."

He said no more. In fact, for several months we continued as before—the Tsil menu with an occasional Wes Hingler special that cheated his kitchen of its authenticity.

Then, one night, he said, "I have a favor. And only you can do it right." He was separating turkey meat from the bones, making the broth he needed for soups and stews, for tamal dough, for cooking beans and wild rice, sometimes for his polenta.

I slipped a piece of dark meat into my mouth. "Sure," I said.

"I want you to write an obituary," he said. "For the Tsil. You and Carson. I'm going to join your mother. Cater *with* her, if not *to* her. Carson doesn't want to do a final review. And he doesn't want the new reviewer to do it. If *you* ask him to help you, though, he'll do it."

"What if *I* don't want to do it?" I asked.

"You want your restaurant, don't you?" He wiped his hands and dialed the number.

"Your father told me he'd get you to call," said Carson.

"Should we do it?" I asked.

"Ask him when," said Carson. "I'll be there." He hung up.

"Two nights from now. Friday," said my father.

"That's too soon," I said.

"Everyone's been invited, and accepted. I just needed you and Carson on board." He began skimming fat from his turkey broth.

Misty came, and Cocoa, and Pablito and Teresita, and Carson Flinn with Ann, the young reporter he was training to take his place, and Penelope, home for a vacation from school, and a bunch of shorter-time employees, some of whom I knew and some who had worked when I was away. And, of course, the regular customers.

We served a last supper, all the tried and true: chips with habanero salsa and cactus tamal for the appetizer; the turkey liver, potato, and green chile soup; the watercress salad; Carson's favorite main dish, the vanilla buffalo fillet with cran-berry chile pesto; sides of pumpkin fritter and green beans; with the palta pudding that had seduced my mother all those years before. In honor of their future catering together, they also served a side dish of quinoa and kidney beans, with an oil and vinegar dressing.

BUEN APPETITO/TSIL SALAD

1 cup kidney beans

1 cup quinoa*

2 tablespoons chopped fresh basil

1 red onion, sliced thin

4 cloves garlic

½ cup green olives

½ cup black olives

¼ cup capers

½ cup sun-dried tomatoes

⅓ cup basalmic vinegar

⅓ cup olive oil

1 teaspoon sesame oil

1 teaspoon Chimayo chile powder (medium)

½ teaspoon salt

¼ teaspoon black pepper

Cook beans and quinoa separately, as some things must remain separate. Then add everything together, making a dressing of the last 6 ingredients. Stir well.

This will improve in flavor the longer the ingredients stay together.

*Quinoa (also quinua): *First culitvated in the Andes, quinoa has the highest protein content of any grain in the world. The plant, chenopodium quinoa, is an herb that grows to one or two meters high. Flower clusters turn to seeds, very small, cream-colored, with a tough outer wall. When cooked, the seed turns translucent, and the germ ring becomes visible. If cooked for a long time, the germ separates from the grain and appears like a little worm to squeamish eaters. The taste is mild, with a hint of celery, and so the grain takes spice well.*

We ate the best of the Tsil, and the best of both worlds: quinoa and beans from the New, olives and onion from the Old; chile and tomatoes from the New, garlic and capers from the Old. After eating their salad, I knew my parents could navigate the globe. After dinner, Carson and I sat together with Ann, who demonstrated the impressive appetite Carson had told me about. Late into the night, we talked, we wrote, we reminisced, we ate more and more, we drank mescal, and we said good-bye to the Tsil Café. The review/obituary appeared in the Kansas City paper the following week.

Tsil on Ice

For over twenty years, Robert Hingler has been pushing Kansas City's food tastes, educating Kansas City's palate. He has been burning our tongues and laughing about it, stretching our minds and laughing about it. He has been giving us what we didn't need, and making us ask for it again. He has been surprising us and influencing us and making those of us in the restaurant business imitate him. And all the time he's remained eclectic, small in scale, large in quantity, high in quality.

And all the time, he's lied to us. His original menu said he was simply a cook, when all along he's been a chef. His creed said he didn't care if we liked his food or not, but he has cared enough to make his food likable. He told us that, as an experienced cook, he knew his foodstuffs, but he not only knows them but has added to his knowledge for many years. He promised us enjoyable meals, but has given us exquisite meals, occasionally Kansas City's finest dining, for years.

We lied, as well. In our first review we called his experiment "worthy." We must retract and substitute the word "amazing." In our first review we predicted that he would have trouble attracting a regular clientele. We must retract and admit that good food will always find its diners. We were overwhelmed at times by the spicy pungency of Robert Hingler's food, and our tongues were smoking after our first encounter. Now, food all over this town has become stronger, and good cooks have followed the Tsil's lead.

In every single way we doubted, we have been proven wrong. We are tempted to doubt once more, and write that Robert Hingler will not retire from the kitchen of the Tsil, and close it down at the New Year. Would that our doubt would change his mind. But it will not. He will be joining his wife, Kansas City's premier caterer, in creating dishes for *Buen AppeTito*.

We were treated to a last meal at the Tsil Café. The food reminded us of our first meal there, when, disguised, we initially encountered "New World food cooked New Mexico style." From then on, through countless meals, we have become familiars, both with the food and with the fine people associated with the Tsil Café. Perhaps the culmination came in Robert Hingler's 50th birthday meal, when the oldest foods of the New World again taught us tastes we thought we would never encounter in our lifetime. Although we weren't quite willing to approve everything served that night, the meal stands as the most memorable we've ever consumed. As a final word, we are left with two great wishes: May our memories always keep alive this unique experiment in Kansas City restaurant history; may Wes Hingler soon decide to cook for Kansas City, if not in the footsteps of his father's New World restaurant, then on his own two feet, with whatever ingredients he chooses.

"He didn't talk about the meal we served him," my father groused at the breakfast table. He turned to my mother. "And of course he had to mention Buen AppeTito."

"Carson is Carson," said my mother.

"Ann gave him some ideas," I said. "She was incredible, as though she'd eaten your food for years."

"So you like her as much as Carson does?" asked my mother.

I changed the subject. "And remember, Dad, I wrote it along with Carson."

"What parts did you write?" my father asked.

"What parts do you like?" I asked.

"Okay, okay," he said.

"Did you like the very last part?" I asked.

"You want the space? If it's not the Tsil Café, but whatever you make it? I'll move my stuff to your mother's kitchen."

I talked to my mother about the restaurant business the next morning, before my father was up. "You think I'm ready?" I asked.

She licked sugar off fingers sticky with pastry. She set down a cup of coffee for me. "Your father says so."

"What do you think?"

"You've cooked until your food is you and you are your food."

She was right. Food had been everything in my family: from seduction, to individuality, to anger, to love. Now it was *me.*

For a while, I used the Tsil kitchen to test recipes, dishes, combinations. My parents, two very critical cooks, helped me. Pablito and Teresita, and Carson and Ann—sometimes Ann by herself, with her sharpened taste and subtle tongue— became regulars for trial runs. In a year, I opened my restaurant. The menu should be easy enough to guess. The signature recipes were my life: my mother's Pasta *Puttanesca;* my father's Nopal Tamales; my grandmother Hingler's Jícama Salad; my god-grandfather Juan's Corn Bread–Stuffed Peppers; my friend Pablito's Turkey Mole; my mother's small strips of beef steak covered in a rich sauce of gin, juniper berries, allspice, and serrano chiles, from her first New Mexico recipe, cooked on the day she met my father; my father's

Black Bean and Gooseberry Enchiladas; my god-grand-mother Conseca's Posole Stew; my mother's Prunes Stuffed with Macadamia Nuts and Shrimp. And my own Green Sauce, my Roasted Corn Salsa, my Sweet Potato Tortillas, and my Yucca Soup, when in season.

My menu changed whenever I wanted it to, and my father and mother cooked specials for me. Together, we were Weston's One-World Café, Weston Tito Hingler, proprietor and cook.

My father once said he cooked to create a singular experience that needed perfecting. He created and perfected his world and he lived in it. I took a different approach: I wanted to keep creating myself so I could live in any world.

Weston's One-World Café on 39th Street in Kansas City was a place open to everything vegetable, animal, and mineral—New World, Old World, your world, my world. Carson Flinn visited, though he didn't write reviews. He left that to Ann, that refreshing woman hired by the paper to learn from him and then take over his job. But she refused to review the One-World Café. "Conflict of interest," she called it. After all, she had been married there, and to the owner and cook. My mother threw Old World white rice, my father New World rice* at the wedding.

*Rice (wild): *The long black seed that Americans call wild rice is not truly rice, but a grass that grows in the marshy areas in the cool climate of the upper Midwest. This exclusively North American grain was polished almost to white by the Ojibwas, who danced on it in moccasins. With a nutty flavor, crunchy texture, and interesting brown-black color, wild rice contrasts nicely with the white of fish and turkey.*

As the years passed, I knew how lucky I was. My food was my own. I cooked with hands scarred in the Tsil Café. I served with the warmth of my mother's kitchen. I was a man with three Hopi corn kernels for birthmarks, a man who had accepted his face. Like my father, I didn't call myself a chef. Like my mother, I stayed behind the scenes. I served with honesty, experience, and love: the best things that can be learned from a life full of spice, and handed down, generation by generation, as I hope to hand them to my children.

"Someday," I tell them, "you'll understand what I mean."

I remember when my parents retired from the catering business. We celebrated their new ending with a trip to the New Mexico mountains, where we rented a cabin in the Pecos Wilderness Area just north of where Juan took me to visit the Pecos Pueblo, now a national monument. My father regaled his grandchildren with stories of his New Mexico boyhood, all the things he told me when I was little. I didn't interrupt to say I'd already told them all his stories.

Because it was her first trip to New Mexico, Ann kept remarking on the color of the sky, a blue like no other she'd ever seen. As a writer, she was used to finding the right word: "Turquoise, cerulean, azure, robin's egg."

"Quit it," I said, "you sound like a paint chart."

"I don't care," she said. "There is a correct word for everything, and I'll find it."

I didn't agree with her. What is the correct word for how you feel when you are with your parents, at the end of their lives, and you and your wife and your children follow them, not wanting to run ahead, up a steep mountain path, and you rest on some rocks that seem to have appeared just for you, and the gentle breeze in that whatever-color sky is clattering aspen leaves, and you hear the gurgle of a mountain spring, and your father says, "There will be watercress," and you take your children by the hand—your son in your father's too-big hat and your daughter with the thick braid your mother has woven into her hair—and sure enough, the small green stalks, the thick leaves, are there, and you pick your hands full.

And later, for lunch, you wash the watercress while your parents prepare the family dressing and you sit down, each of you thankful for what you have and what you have found:

WATERCRESS AND BLACK BEAN SALAD WITH SUNFLOWER-TOMATO DRESSING

½ cup dried black beans, cooked
Large bundle watercress* (as much in volume as the beans)

Wash beans thoroughly. Break up watercress and add to beans. Dress salad to taste with Sunflower-Tomato Dressing and eat.

Serves 4. Hint: If you want this more like a cold soup, you can chop watercress more finely and add an extra tomato to the dressing.

SUNFLOWER-TOMATO DRESSING

4–6 roma tomatoes, roasted

¼ cup raw sunflower seeds, toasted

1 teaspoon mild chile powder

¼ cup peanut or corn oil

Pineapple vinegar to taste

Salt to taste

Roast tomatoes under broiler until blackened in spots. In a skillet, heat sunflower seeds over medium heat until they are dark brown, but not black. In a blender, add tomatoes, chile powder, sunflower seeds, and oil, vinegar, and salt and mix thoroughly.

*Watercress: Peppery stems add crunch to the milder leaves in this versatile green—can be used as garnish, or eaten like lettuce for a salad. Mixes well, because it is hearty, with other vegetables.

There is no single word for such an experience. There may be words, but you have to line them up correctly, one after the other. If you're lucky, you can do that. But you're even luckier if you can experience a life rich in the warmth of family, the heat of kitchens.

RECIPE: AN EPILOGUE

BOILED ZUCCHINI

4 small zucchini* (6 inches maximum)
Water
Salt

Bay leaf
Romano and Parmesan cheese, grated
1 clove garlic, minced
Onion powder
Basil to taste
Oregano to taste
Olive oil
Pepper

1 tomato
Mild chile powder to taste
Sage to taste
Allspice to taste
1 teaspoon pumpkin seed paste
Salt to taste
Peanut oil

2 spoons

2 small containers

*Zucchini (calabacita): *Soft-shelled summer squash, best eaten when 6 to 9 inches long (will grow to huge proportions when neglected). Anyone who gardens zucchini grows tired of its eager proliferation. Bland in taste, zucchini mixes well with other foods, particularly the tomato, and it takes on the flavor of any spice added to it. When tired of the squash, cooks pick the blossoms* (flores de calabaza) *and serve them as a delicacy. Or, if neglected long enough, the huge number of mature seeds (high in oil and protein) can be toasted or ground into a paste and used in sauces.*

Go to your garden and find the zucchini, the ones just ripened into the perfection your parents will expect (no longer than 6 inches, undeveloped in the seed). Put scant amount of water, with a shake of salt, in two saucepans. Add bay leaf to one pan. Cut two zucchini into cubes and add to bay leaf water when it comes to a boil. Cut other two zucchini and the tomato into pieces and add to other water. Cook both pots until quite mushy. Pour off any extra liquid.

Remove bay leaf from pan, and to that mushed zucchini add the cheeses, garlic, scant amount of onion powder, basil, and oregano. Mix in the olive oil, about 2 teaspoons, and pepper, and mash until the mixture is almost paste.

To the other pan, add chile powder, sage, allspice, pumpkin seed paste, and salt. Mix in the peanut oil,

about 2 teaspoons, and mash until the mixture is almost mush.

Put the two kinds of zucchini in separate containers. Put two spoons in your coat pocket. Put zucchini containers in a small bag. Accept your children's
decision not to come along on your errand. Drive to
Hearthstone Retirement Apartments. Arrive around
9 P.M. Proceed to your parents' apartment, left from
entryway, down the hall past the television set where
people are parked in wheelchairs watching reruns,
and, finally, to room 123.

Enter quietly: If they are asleep you want them to
stay that way. Put containers of zucchini on their
bedside tables, the cheesy Old World recipe next to
your mother, the spicy New World recipe beside
your father. Open the lids and sit in a chair.

Soon, they will awaken. "Wes," your mother will
say. "Chile," your father will say. You will say, "Your
midnight snack," even though neither of them has
been awake at midnight for several years. "Spoons,"
they will say, almost in unison. And they will eat.

One will be in her airy kitchen above the Tsil
Café, cooking for Buen AppeTito, surrounded by
light, by the shadows of leaves mottling the floor, by
the richness of possibility. The other will be in the
earthy kitchen of the Tsil Café, surrounded by
orange and deep red, by the richness of possibility.

For a moment, neither will be surrounded by old

age. You will be the only one thinking of finality: You, who were nourished by each and both. You have sampled both zucchinis before delivery and found them each satisfactory. You sit in the dark room while they eat their way into the pleasure of memory.